Normal Deviation

A Weird Fiction Anthology

Edited by
Lyle Skains
DeAnn Bell

WB

Wonderbox Publishing

Published by Wonderbox Publishing
http://wonderboxpublishing.com

Edited by Lyle Skains & DeAnn Bell
Cover photograph "Suitcase" by Valery Sidelnykov (Shutterstock)
Cover design by Lyle Skains
Interior design by Lyle Skains
Title font "Broken 15" by Misprinted Type (dafont)
Subtitle font "Normograf" by Samy Halim (dafont)
Text font "Linux Libertine" by Philipp H. Poll (dafont)

ISBN (paperback): 978-1-912110-67-4
ISBN (ebook): 978-1-912110-66-7

Visit http://normaldeviation.wonderboxpublishing.com for more about how this book came to be.

Contents

Normal Deviation

On Location

Jonathan Howard

"Say cheese!"

Ungh, why did I open with that? Not only is it from the first page of *The Clichéd Photographer Guide* (no longer in print, though I hear the e-book is doing great), but both my subjects are wearing masks.

ffwp—click

The sound of the mechanical shutter splits the silence and slaps back at us from across the sandy plateau. Means to an end, I tell myself. Again. I try not to pick favourites; a job is a job is a job. These little gigs are the only things keeping my artistic butt afloat as I watch the ebb and flow of my bank balance on a nifty mobile app. Perpetually scanning the horizon to avoid cruising face first into an iceberg of unpaid invoices.

"Shall I do another one for safety?"

The two plastic faces turn to stare at me without expression, as is their wont—or should I say mould? After an unsociably prolonged bout of eye contact they reset to their former position: each rigidly sat six feet apart in deep-red revolving lounge chairs, an unmarked rope-bound suitcase between them, engaged in a wordless conversation and dressed as if Yin & Yang joined the Ku Klux Klan. Note to self—great album title. Perhaps this is a band photo shoot? The brief itself had been pretty vague: Turn up, take the picture, paid in advance. Came through just after midnight via an instant message and not long after I accepted the job, the money was received via bank transfer. Social media is a great platform for small businesses but sometimes it feels like I've placed a soapbox outside my door and accidentally informed the world of its presence.

I look through the viewfinder, just in case I need to

reframe, but they haven't moved a millimetre. I buy some time fondling the focus ring. Got to make it worth my while, was no short trip after all. How did they even get the chairs here? The car park was at least two miles walk and I saw no other signs of life here or en route to this wacky charade.

ffwp—click

Once more, the phantom photographer sent a sonic reflection right back at us from afar. I wonder if that shoot is just as awkward?

"Lovely. Cut and pr—" How on earth did I get motion blur with these guys? Exposure and shutter speed checked and tripod secured. That's like getting red-eye when snapping a statue or, to spank the analogy on the nose, motion blur when snapping a statue! They couldn't have moved—they didn't even stand up to greet me. The only reason I know they're alive is on the rare occasion they slowly turn to look at me. Always admired method actors and their dedication to performance and commitment to character. There's a reason I'm stood this side of the camera. That and having a face better suited for podcasts.

"I must apologise, but it looks like I've got some movement here on the right. Sorry, I didn't catch your name?" Nope. Doesn't look like I ever will. "Well, I'm sure you didn't. Must be some obscure artefact from the sun reflecting off the black gown." Yin's white face made a slight tilt. Was that a nod? "We've got the first picture in the can; it's just always handy to have a backup."

There's only so much prima donna a human can handle and I'm starting to get hungry. I should have brought a snack. Last thing I want is hypoglycaemic rage featuring as feedback on my business page. The sooner I take the picture, the sooner I can leave. "This'll just take a sec." I've been on long weird-ass shoots before. Artists, those creative types, their gigs are always crazy and worth a laugh or two upon reflection. Gallons of Vaseline spewing from the heads of a plaster cast choir or a crowdfunding video for a dictionary containing 3,000 definitions of the word "dictionary". Something in my stomach lining, besides the hunger, is telling me this isn't one of those jobs, though. Three anecdotes at best, there's not much mileage in a memory you don't want to relive.

"Okay you're all in focus." Wish I could do the same. Come on, concentrate. Mind over matter; you're a professional and in it for the long haul. Perhaps if I fudge this one up I can ask if they have a spare costume in the suitcase and join their madcap cult.

ffwp—click

"Aha..." I don't believe it. I wonder if those cone hats are one-size-fits-all? "Really sorry about this but it looks like—" Not that I distrust the viewfinder, but I glare at them with my eyes and they haven't moved. "It kind of looks like you're getting out of the chair." Nothing.

I quickly flick back through the last three stills forming a crude animation. This is where I'd normally scream at the TV, fingers forming blinkers from my temples, "Run... Run... No, don't take another picture. Nope. RUN!"

I didn't know fingertips could sweat. It must be a prank, I'm not in the zone, my mind is elsewhere and they're playing a trick on me. Two can play at that game. "Okay, well it's looking good my end just—"

ffwp—ffwp—ffwp—ffwp—ffwp—click

"Whoops, my bad. Finger slipped in this heat, was just the burst mode." The ghostly ricochet almost sounds as if it's closer. "No need to worry."

I watched them as the camera took the pictures; with God as my witness they did. Not. Move.

The new five frames show Yin rising and releasing the rope around the suitcase and Yang leaning forwards expectantly. I peer up from my camera to see they're now both looking at me. The void beyond the eyeholes appears as eternal as the expressions on the mask. How I wish I were at home screaming at the TV.

The sun beats down around us, throwing up a haze that causes the clouds to vibrate along the horizon. The lens cap is still in my pocket; I can feel it next to my keys. Just need to pop that back on and be on my merry way. "So, you've got my email. I'll do a quick pass in Photoshop when I get home, send it over and see what you think!"

Probably the heat stroke talking but I do want to know what's in that suitcase. Curiosity kills cats, not humans. I'll take the picture, say goodbye and review it at home.

They're still facing me. Besides, it's ultimately why they hired me: Turn up and take the picture.

ffwp—click

"Perfect. That's a wrap." The picture was taken just as it always should have been; only now I have a Niagara Falls of sweat flowing freely from my cervical to sacral curve. "It's been a pleasure." I keep my head bowed, avoiding their gaze and looking at the camera. I select the playback mode and flick back through the session. Eight identical perfect photos. Agh, salt in the eye. It's hard to find the talent these days. Really hard. Ironically, the dead ones are least likely to corpse in front of the camera. I really think humour is the key to getting through this life; too many people have lost sight of that and take it all too seriously. "No need to get up."

∞

Jonathan's First Two Options

1. A pseudo-intellectual dialogue between Yin & Yang while on holiday.
2. A cult ritual where the followers must show they're worthy of a face (which are in the suitcase).

Blind Date

DeAnn Bell

Memory Mark 102

The photograph was imported to The Messier81 observation gallery by mistake. Nina had hung it up because space on a space station was severely limited despite this being a luxury observation station. So far, the only luxury that could be found here was the errant photograph scheduled to be shipped back to the Talitha14 observation station in 56 Talitha-solar rotations. Like most stations, Messier81 had colour-changing walls that could project art in an optical quality far greater than could actually be appreciated, but something about having this framed static image on the wall stopped people in their tracks. They gazed at it instead of across it with their brows knit into a frown of concentration. One was forced to actively ignore the photograph rather than to merely look over it.

Images selected for space transmission went through rigorous psychological screenings. The purpose of the art was to create visual pleasure without creating longing for any ground-based activities that could not be replicated in space. The images tended to be of nature, but not climbing mountains or diving in oceans. All observation stations knew these experiences existed, and some could be replicated up to a point, but because they were difficult to come by, all but the most restricted art forms portrayed them as unpleasant. So Nina and her colleagues assumed that this image was a representation of some kind of pleasant natural event that could be replicated on a space station. Unfortunately, what that event could possibly be was the cause of the many frowns.

Memory Mark 111

“I’ve seen an image of a box like that in a history class; it’s baggage,” Moore said, leaning forward and indicating the box sitting in between the two figures in the photograph.

“Its shadowing does indicate that it is soft, but it doesn’t look baggy to me,” Nina replied, squinting at the object even though medical tests indicated her eyesight was exceptional.

Moore frowned. “My ancient history isn’t great. Is ‘baggy’ a verbal mutation of ‘baggage’? Because I actually thought ‘baggage’ was an old turn of phrase meaning something emotional that you weren’t dealing with.”

“I don’t know. That looks solid rather than metaphorical to me. It has a handle on the top.”

“Maybe people really carried a baggage around to indicate to others they were emotionally blocked.”

They both bent close enough to the picture to set off the proximity alarm.

To Nina the picture looked neither natural nor pleasant, but a lot of what she’d observed on Messier81 was strange to her. She took the last of her allotted coffee to the front table. Since returning from her last mission she spent some of her pleasure time every 168 hours standing in front of the photograph with her first and only bond mate, Haven. Long-term bonding was particularly difficult on this observation station because of the time-slips around the supermassive black hole (SMBH) in the midst of Bode’s Galaxy, which was unofficially called “Foreboding”.

Residents choosing this station understood the potential for time-slip was enormous on missions around Foreboding and tended to bond one mission at a time because of it. Time itself was difficult to measure on observation stations because most had neither a consistent central star nor a planetary rotation to measure by. Messier81 claimed to measure time by the Proxima Century Time scale, which was said to be based on an Earth hour, but there was a lot of debate amongst scientists and crew about whether time on a station could be measured equally across galaxies, not to mention whether the original concept of Earth hour was appropriate in a galaxy that was 12 million light years away from the time source. This station only had PCT hours and years. There had once been months and days but this created longing for light changes and seasons that could not be consistently replicated for all species here and so had been done away with. That was why Memory Marks were so important. They were a way to physically mark time on the body and carry it anywhere you went.

Memory Mark 118

Haven's silver eyes had become cloudy. Where once she had been able to talk to Nina from the back of the gallery about the texture of the horizon in the photograph, she now often set the proximity alarms off with her wondering hands. Haven's time at Messier81 was coming to a close but rather than to wish for more time or volunteer for more missions as some did, she'd taken a double allotment of pleasure products and cashed in all of her remaining pleasure time. Nina sat down beside Haven, tucking a straggly strand of white hair behind her ear. "What do you want to see today?"

Haven handed her the glasses and then put on the gloves. She looked toward the photograph with a smile. "Block 6, Level C."

Nina's eyes went directly to the grid position point. "Textured box divided into three panels by grey lines resembling cords. Light simulation moving across textured box from upper left hand corner. Shadows on the box are not reflected elsewhere in the picture. Dappling of colour to denote changes of shape by light are on all three panels. Two elliptical circles on the furthest left—"

"August chose her first Memory Mark," Haven interrupted. "The ceremony starts in 36 hours. Will you come with me?"

Nina's hand went involuntarily to her own first Memory Mark. On Ursa Major the first Memory Mark was called a Regret Mark because most people regretted their decisions on what mark to take by the time their second Memory Mark was decided on. "What did she choose?"

"An Earth flower." Haven reached down and traced the familiar pattern of a poppy with her finger on Nina's skin.

Nina squeezed her eyes shut.

"Her mother, Poppy, and I tried to talk her out of it, but she's young and just as stubborn as I am," Haven continued, her voice achieving an emotional distance her actions didn't reflect. "August wants it to cover most of her shoulder and be orange and red, but her mother is still trying to convince her that less is more."

"What are you advising?"

Haven reached a gloved hand out toward the photograph to continue the viewing but Nina gently captured it and brought it to her own face. She closed her eyes, laying her cheek into Haven's open palm. The rough-fingered gloves skimmed over the familiar smooth surfaces of Nina's face, only briefly making contact. "I told her to record her own memories."

Memory Mark 103

Bonding night was awkward and Nina didn't want to go, but she'd been told by the station psychiatrist that bonding was necessary for mental health and that the partner who had committed to meeting Nina tonight was unlikely to be put off by her Memory Marks. Children of Ursa Major were known for two things: the first was their tenacity in accomplishing their missions and the second was their range of emotionally evocative Memory Marks. Ursa Major had been part of the Great Territory Wars and most of the 7th generation had Memory Marks related to losses of the type that other observation stations couldn't imagine and didn't want to face. The 7th generation had refused to cover their marks but the 8th generation had split into two core groups: people who made their Memory Marks larger, more colourful and emotionally provocative, and people that had made covering Memory Marks an act of modesty, privacy and respect. As successive generations moved on, tension and fighting between the two groups had turned into a long history of intolerance and violence distasteful, but not unusual, for the rest of the universe.

Members of the first group all took as their first Memory Mark an Earth flower that had once been a symbol for remembrance and regret of another war. Each flower after that was a marker for family members lost in the Great Territory

War and the fighting that followed. Nina's marks cascaded from just under her right ear down her throat and across both of her shoulders in as many colours as there were names of the fallen. In her own territory it marked her as the sole surviving member of her family, but in Messier81 it marked her as a political zealot. She'd grown her hair long and worn it down at first in order to be judged for her own actions rather than those of her culture, but all that had accomplished was to make her angry and embarrassed about being ashamed. In the end, she'd cut her hair off just below her earlobes and accepted the prejudices that came her way. She'd added more types of Memory Marks and colours, some so important that she didn't need any kind of symbol to remind her that they happened, and some so vague that the marks themselves now only reminded Nina of forgetting. After cutting her hair she would have happily talked about any of her Memory Marks but as is often the case, uncovering them turned out to be the best way to render them unnoticeable.

*

"Nina? My name is Haven."

Haven offered Nina a hand that had no marks on it whatsoever. Not even freckles. In fact, nothing but smooth unmarked dark skin. Nina's jaw dropped, her eyes wandering up Haven's blank arms, higher and higher until she reached the reflective surface of small round glasses that were almost as unusual as the blankness of her skin. Most genetic codes that required long-term medical assistive care were corrected before birth, meaning that Haven either came from a species that had extreme light sensitivity or her damage came from an observation mission after she was an adult and could not be corrected.

Haven's smile faltered. "You are Nina, right?"

Nina shook the outstretched hand, noting that Haven was wearing clear gloves that were rough and abrasive like tree bark. "Yes. Hello. I'm sorry, you caught me by surprise."

"That's odd considering you agreed to meet me here at this time." Haven took a seat without picking up the menu. Nina watched, fascinated, as her hands quickly wandered the contents of the table. "I'm damaged but not broken. I assume you are too, judging by the way the station psychiatrist paired us."

Nina felt the tension in her shoulders relax. "She told me you wouldn't judge me by my Memory Marks; she didn't mention you couldn't see at all."

Haven reached toward the drinking bottle in the middle of the table and poured exactly half a glass of the purple liquid. "That's because I can see. Not in continuous images as you do, but I can see. For instance, I can see that you have a very attractive shape but I can't see any of your Memory Marks. Are they ugly enough for you to be considered damaged?"

Nina laughed. "Not to me, but they make some people uncomfortable."

"I understand that." She touched the glasses. "They see in the direction I'm pointed at and transmit those signals to the gloves. The gloves give me a series of pressures and temperatures that I am able to make into my own version of what you call an image. When I combine my images with the scents and sounds around me, I can see just as well as everyone else, better in some places." She waited for Nina to say something. "If it bothers you, I'd rather you say so now."

Nina poured her own drink. "I'm not sure I understand the question. Why would it bother me that you can see?"

Haven smiled and held both her hands toward Nina. "Can I take a closer look at you?"

For the first time in her life, Nina laid her face in the palms of Haven's hands.

Memory Mark 104

They didn't allow Haven to travel on the missions to the outskirts of Foreboding. Although she had adapted without incident to her quarters and the observation station, the main function of the missions were to observe natural phenomena and there was a lot of doubt among the crews about how much Haven could comprehend and communicate. Each time she joined a new team she had to spend days, sometimes months, proving to them that she was capable of doing her job.

Missions further into Foreboding needed a crew that

trusted one another, but it wasn't just Haven's eyes they didn't trust; it was also her skin. She had no Memory Marks at all, no history or images that could help the people around her read and identify with her. Nina fought against the judgements that came from having the wrong marks but it was nothing compared to the judgements that came from having none. Nina had asked Haven about it but her answer was like an ouroboros.

"I can't see marks myself, why would I show them to others? If people want to get to know me, they are just going to have to talk to me."

Nina sat behind Haven and gently pulled a comb through her hair. "The marks are normally the way people open conversations with one another. Your lack of marks means that some people avoid you."

She pressed a kiss to the blank skin of Nina's wrist. "The important ones don't."

Memory Mark 187

After some time Nina got good at letting other observers hazard the first guess as to what was happening in the picture. A young lady she didn't recognize covered in the newest kinds of Memory Marks, the kinds that twisted and changed by mood and desire, the ones that transformed the skin into an endless diary of experiences, sat with a sketching pen attempting to draw a portion of the photograph on the tabletop. The table would clear itself as soon as she stood up and the impermanence of the artistic act struck Nina as beautiful. She sat down and watched the sketch take shape.

"They're not identical, you know. Their heads are different. The black one is smooth and the white one isn't. Like one is wearing a costume but showing its face and the other is dressed normally but wearing a mask. Aren't the Methuselahs supposed to have conical heads?"

The girl hadn't looked at Nina when she asked the question. "Yes, but they also have conical faces."

The girl looked at the picture again, grimacing. "A missing face is a good reason for a mask but I doubt there is any observation station in the galaxies that would allow that kind of depravity to be passed around. It's hardly pleasant."

"Some civilizations believe that shocking art is pleasurable."

The girl shrugged, adding the unmistakable conical faces of the Methuselahs to her picture. "I feel very sorry for those people." She glanced up to smile and was captured by the vivacity of Nina's Memory Marks. She reached out and touched the one blank spot on Nina's wrist. "Your Memory Marks are beautiful. What are you saving this space for?"

"Nothing. That space is already taken."

Memory Mark 110

Nina held Haven's reading device in her hand. Haven's device had been adapted to work with her gloves but Haven's face gave the message on the device away more clearly than any words could.

"They have to let you come with me."

Haven stood and retrieved the device from Nina's hands before the sensory inputs could be destroyed by her grip on it. "You and I both know they're not going to waste money on an extra berth that could be assigned to an additional data collector or artist."

Haven's acceptance of the station's judgement that she was unfit for missions was ridiculous to Nina. "You are an artist."

"I make food, that's hardly an art."

Nina threw herself down on their bed. "Believe me, I was here before you got transferred to this station. You are an artist. Besides, you have done data processing for hundreds of missions."

Haven threw herself beside Nina and sighed. "And I transferred to this station so I didn't have to do that anymore."

They were quiet. Haven removed one of her gloves to thread her fingers through Nina's. "How long have you been at this station?"

It was a question that had come up a lot recently. It was less a question about how long Nina had been here and more a question about how long she intended to stay. "Long enough that I am going to have to really start thinking about the size of Memory Marks or I will have to start covering Memory Marks with other Memory Marks."

"That's not an answer." Haven rolled over on her stomach with her face turned away from Nina

"I could make one for you." Slowly she drew her fingertips across Haven's shoulder, replicating the flower shape of her own first Memory Mark. "It would mean something to you if I made it."

"You know I'm not going to do that."

Nina leaned forward to rest her chin between Haven's shoulder blades. "Please. We are bonded. What if I slip while I'm out there? I could come back and you'll have been dead for a hundred years. Don't make me go without you."

"No one is making you go."

*

Moore was waiting for Nina in the observation gallery in front of the photograph with his reader held up in front of his face so that he could look at both at the same time.

"What are you doing?" Nina asked, trying to get close enough to see.

"Getting a second opinion." He captured an image of the photograph. "Did a little research. Thuri thinks that this is an image of a date."

"What's a date and who is Thuri?"

"Thuri is none of your business. A date is a slang term for a fixed point in time and location where a potential bond meeting takes place."

"Why is it called a date?"

Moore shrugged. "Thuri says bonding used to be arranged by people through computers on some worlds."

Nina grimaced. "That is really weird. How could they tell that they were chemically coordinated and mentally compatible if they didn't go through a bonding screening?"

"Apparently they just kept showing up to dates until they found the right match."

"That must have taken forever."

Moore frowned for a moment, looking at the picture. "Can you imagine what it would be like to have to choose your bond mate from an entire planet full of unknowns?" He shivered.

Nina took Moore's reader. "What is a baggage for on a bonding date?" Moore pressed his lips together without making eye contact. Nina rolled her eyes. "There is no baggage on Thuri's bonding date is there?"

Moore snatched his reader back. "That's why I sent the image to Thuri, to make sure."

"How long will it take her to get back to us?"

Moore thumped his reader against his thigh. "Should be back by the time we return from our next observation mission, but she's far enough away that one of those time-slips would be helpful."

Nina crossed her arms staring at the photograph. "Who would sit through a bonding meeting with someone that had an obvious emotional block?"

Moore grinned. "Haven, obviously, hopefully maybe Thuri."

Nina didn't return his smile.

Memory Mark 100

Most residents of Messier81 were temporary, and eventually came to an age where the mission time-slippage there became a nuisance. As a galaxy that produced stars ten times faster than any other galaxy, the one thing Messier81 always had was plenty of opportunities for ground-breaking research. Researchers made their mark and then headed back to parts of the universe where time behaved semi-regularly. Time was always slipping forward on mission, sometimes in little skips, sometimes in great leaps. Researchers naturally frowned on making a breakthrough only to return to the rest of the time-abiding galaxy to discover their methods were a hundred solar rotations out of date.

Haven had met Nina before, when she'd first arrived at this observation station. Neither of them had taken much notice of the other at the time but Haven remembered someone saying that Nina was a long-termer. Haven had handed a package containing the photograph to Nina as she'd come through the gallery. Partly because she didn't know where else to put it and partly because she wanted someone to acknowledge she was there. "Can you put this somewhere?"

Nina unwrapped the package, expecting it to contain a different type of viewing screen. The picture didn't strike her as much at first. She turned the frame over and ran her fingers around the entire surface. "There's no power switch."

"Maybe it has a voice command."

Haven's observation was uttered as she unpacked a crate full of small plants meant for the food nursery. Nina turned the frame back around and held it out in front of her. "Power location." A series of green and yellow lights jumped and glided over the item.

"Item does not require a power source," the station's computer responded, managing to sound both placating and superior.

"Do you mean it has an unknown power source?"

"Negative. Item does not require a power source."

Nina ran her fingers over the surface and gasped when she came into contact with the static image rather than any kind of protective field. To this day, she was only one of two people on Messier81 who had touched the photograph.

Haven paused her unloading when she heard the gasp. "What is it?"

"I think it's a static photograph."

*

A message was sent around Messier81 station first asking if there were any artists among them who knew anything about photographs, and next asking that artist to report to head office. The first so-called specialist had a background in historic Memory Marks, which was as close to a photograph as anyone could understand. By the time he'd shown up, Nina had already hung the photograph in the observation gallery and installed a coded proximity alarm and shield around it. Even if it was a copy of a static photograph, it was worth more pleasure time than anyone at the station could afford. At the time, Nina had thought of the photograph in terms of monetary worth. It was only after meeting Haven the second time that Nina really appreciated all there was to see in the photograph.

Memory Mark 112

"Show me again," Haven said, leaning against Nina with her arms extended. She was taller than Nina when they stood side by side, but with Nina sitting on the table, Haven could lean back into her and wedge her body inside of Nina's arms.

Nina hugged her first and then grasped each of Haven's wrists from the outside. She brought their hands to the middle of the horizon line and then gently pulled them apart until they extended to the same width of the photograph. "There are two horizon lines in the photograph, the first is here and indicates a long flat expanse of earth. The second is just above it and is so pale it is almost invisible. It follows the bottom horizon line almost exactly but it staggers in the left corner where another darker line appears, here." Nina didn't have to look at the photograph anymore. She'd shown it to Haven so many times she could trace it in the air with her eyes shut, but each time they viewed it, something new appeared.

"What do you think the dark horizon break is?"

"I think it's an island in a vast body of water. I saw a large body of water when I was a little girl. It had no colour of its own; it could only fill the shape of the pool that held it and could only reflect what was around it." She continued to pull Haven's hands to trace the perimeter of the picture.

"It must be hard for something to want to fit in so badly it will take any shape."

Nina didn't answer.

Memory Mark 115

In the first few days of the first mission without Haven, Nina had spent each morning tracing the phantom photo against the wall of her cabin. She waited for the routine of the mission to become the new normal for her like she'd done on every mission before this one, but it never happened.

After a week or so, Nina came into the cabin to take her station for her allotted time. Moore was taking information from two screens at the same time.

"Take a look at this," he said, sitting back in his seat to display side-by-side number sequences.

Nina looked hard at both sets of numbers, noting a skip in

the second set. "What happened there?"

"I think it's a time-slip. Not only that, I think it's a stable time slip. Check this out."

He pulled up seven more screens of numbers and then gave a command to the computer. "Map this information minus skipped data sequence." A 3-D map appeared in front of them with a hole just a couple of parsecs left of the outer rim of Foreboding. Moore turned the map with his hands to distinguish the regularity of the hole from the fringes of Foreboding. The hole in the map distorted the spherical shape that Foreboding was supposed to have.

"Do you think I could use this software to make a map of the photograph in the observation gallery for Haven?" Nina asked, running her fingers along the projected rim of the hole.

Moore snapped his fingers in front of her face. "Who cares about a photograph. Listen to what I just said. I think we've just discovered a stable time-slip. Each ship that has touched this data hole has slipped forward in time."

Nina blinked. "How far?"

"It's not consistent. I think it matters what part of the time-slip you touch. Maybe it depends on how long it takes you to travel through the time-slip. There are countless observation hours available for this." He patted Nina on the back. "We are going to be rolling in pleasure time when we get done here."

*

The crew got a choice about whether or not they wanted to continue the mission. Time-slips were unobserved territory and there was expected time loss, but how much couldn't be estimated. The opportunity for discovery was a bigger draw than the potential loss of time. Nina was the only crew member who hesitated to take the mission.

The captain had requested permission to record the first round of observations without returning to the station but she needed the entire crew to agree before they could leave. She'd asked Nina to join her for dinner. "If we don't take this opportunity now, we might never get another chance. The next crew will launch the second we turn back toward the station."

"My bond mate isn't here. When we slip—"

The captain cleared her throat. "You don't have a bond mate any longer. When our ship left the station, your bond was dissolved."

"Haven—"

The captain leaned forward and put her hand on Nina's brightly coloured shoulder. "I'm sorry to be the one to tell you. I thought you knew. Haven is the one that dissolved it."

*

Nina sat in front of the mapping computer Moore used, drawing the photograph. Although she'd brought an actual image on her reading device, the mapping computer needed her physical manipulation of items in the mapping space to correctly recreate the image. It also required that she divide the picture into a flat grid. She translated each box by movement and then coordinated it by sight to make sure Haven's image was perfect. The file was huge, so big that both the captain and Moore had to spend an hour of pleasure time each to figure out how to send it. When it was gone, Nina turned the lights out in her berth and traced the pattern on the wall for the last time she would ever do it.

The orders from the observation station had instructed them to take two passes. The first around the outer rim of the time-slip hole, and the second straight through the middle of it. The observations would be split into two missions depending on how much time loss there was.

Memory Mark 118

Nina knocked on the door that had once been her own. It slid open to reveal a teenage girl with hair as black as the spaces between stars and eyes a familiar silvery colour.

"Mom! I think it's for you."

A tall woman with a very prominent blue Memory Mark of a planet surrounded by flowers on her bicep came to the door. "August, what did I tell you about shouting with people standing in the doorway?" She looked at Nina for a long moment. Her smile wasn't familiar but there was no mistaking the way she tilted her head. "You must be Nina. I've heard so much about you. Welcome home." There was kindness in her gaze but on the edges of that kindness was pity.

"Haven?"

"Mom's in the observation gallery."

Memory Mark 120

Haven was sipping her second allotted coffee in their designated spot. Nina was carrying her personal reading device but nothing else. The captain had told them to bring only the essentials for the second mission. Haven was sitting cross-legged on the top of a table right in front of the photograph. When the photograph had first arrived, this would have caused grumbling, but no one felt the need to disturb an old woman while she still had time to look. That was the nice part about growing old in a space where both time and residents were temporary. Nina walked up to the table and leaned back against it. Silence settled between them in layers so impenetrable that Nina decided that this must be what it felt like to drown. Haven moved forward on the table to drop her legs over the side and to pull Nina into her arms. Where before there had been passion in this position, now there was only love. Nina leaned back and tucked herself into Haven's embrace.

"Look what I found in your photograph," Haven whispered and pushed Nina's arms forward in the position they used to use to trace the edges of the flat image. "We always thought that there were only two people in this story, but there are five faces in the photograph. Two are hidden by masks," She traced the familiar conical shapes with Nina's fingers, "and two are hidden by expectation." She pulled Nina's hands to the left side of the traveling case. "Both black and white faces are looking at the top middle of the box. That's why they can't see the other two faces." She brought Nina's hands to the left panel of the divided box. "This face looks out at us in anger. Two connected spots of light shine over its shoulder. The right side of its face is obscured by the dividing line." She moved Nina's hands to the furthest right panel. "This face is turning away from the dividing line. The left side of its face is touching the dividing line, but is not defined by it."

Nina wasn't looking at faces; she was looking at the thin hands that held her wrists. "Where is the fifth face?"

Haven's trembling hands cupped both sides of Nina's chin turning her head first one way and then the other. "It's the only face that has the sense to make sense of the whole picture."

Nina dashed away the moisture in her eyes, then coaxed Haven from the table and led her toward the photograph. She keyed in the code for the proximity alarm and then the code for the proximity shield. She placed Haven's hand on the cool, smooth, featureless surface of the photograph. "This is what I see when I look at it without you."

The launch alarm on Nina's reading device sounded.

Haven pulled their hands away from the photograph and kissed the blank skin on Nina's wrist. Her voice wavered. "When you come back next time, we'll talk about what happened."

Nina reset the proximity alarms and then hugged Haven close. "It's a date."

∞

DeAnn's First Two Options

1. A conversation between traveling aliens about the adventures of Earth travel. (What we view as a traveling pain in the ass interruption, they view as a pleasurable opportunity for experience.)
2. An intergalactic photographer specializing in iconic photographs only. (I was thinking along the lines of the Abbey Road/Beetles photograph taken by Iain Macmillian and how the meaning of that photograph is not connected to what is happening in it.)

Where Angels Fear to Tread

Jetse de Vries

In the early 2020s, over a period of several weeks, Miskatonic University's Shenzhen research station, part of China's hotbed of the rapidly developing electronics and synthetic biology sector, a fierce focal point of both piracy and innovation, *shifted.* Its accelerated technological development became a blur and Miskatonic University's Shenzhen campus shifted into what is now referred to as SIS, an acronym whose meaning remained elusive.

As such, it became a higher dimensional space within a space, an ineffable knowledge state within a state, a hyper-culture within a culture. A veritable fountainhead of innovation where raw materials entered and futuristic gadgets—years ahead of their time—exited.

While this made MU's Shenzhen campus both the most advanced and the weirdest in the world, and increasingly high in demand, its application process was not for the faint of heart. Below is just one example of such an application.

*

Aiguo Zhang is at the forefront of China's young scientific talents, with a PhD in computer science and a BA in applied molecular biology already on his CV. He stands at the very edge of the SIS zone, where a local recruiter will pick him up, as he fondles his wooden Yin Yang amulet. From out of nowhere, an entity appears: a white-masked person in a black robe with a tall, pointy hat. Then, Zhang needs all his restraint not to run away in terror, as the entity that suddenly emerges from under the black robe resembles a Feng creature with the jaws of a dragon. “Don’t fear, good applicant,” the abomination says, “we just needed to clean up a synthetic biology experiment that had gotten a little bit out of hand.”

Frozen in a mix of fear and indecision, Zhang can only manage: “A *little* bit out of hand?”

“Don’t pay attention to my external appearance, as it’s merely ephemeral,” the hump of unidentified flesh says through its dragon mouth. “Let’s go in and join the fun.” The left-hand-side-extruding piece of meat moves with a “come-with-me motion”, the right-hand-side-extruding piece of meat appendage holds, for whatever reason, a whip. Zhang has no choice but to follow. Through a twilight zone they enter a blurry world where everything just moves and happens faster.

“We’re in the zone now, so we can choose decent transportation,” the creature, who’s shape-shifting into a kind of insect heap, says. “Anyway, welcome to Über-Shanzhai.”

“Über-Shanzhai?” Zhang says, as contraptions that defy description pass by at speeds varying from stupidly fast to utterly insane. “And what do I call you?”

“I’m Positive Feedback Loop Entity Alpha Pi Tango 888-bis,” the entity says, “but my friends call me FleaPit.”

“Okay, well, FleaPit, I’m Aiguo Zhang.” Zhang tries to concentrate. “Is there something like a bus or a train here? Maybe even a metro?”

“Are you crazy?” The laugh coming from the dragon mouth belches fire. “We’ve grown way beyond those authoritarian means of transport. No, we make it up on the fly. Feel free to go ahead.”

Zhang is at a loss. “How?”

“We brainstorm the design of your über-transportation. What would you prefer: a swarm of drones? A constantly shape-shifting blip in turbulent joyride mode? A slithering ground-snake with an ever-changing, interestingly-smelling lubricant? A thunderbolt-driven porcupined hedgehodgepodge that glows in the dark?” FleaPit gloats as it lists alternatives. “But don’t let my humble hints limit your imagination.”

“You mean that we order a complete new means of transportation just like that?” Zhang says in utter disbelief. “Like a self-levitating pod with a continuous track of superconducting coils?"

"Consider it done," FleaPit says. "Our mega-flexible and ultrafast production lines will have it delivered in no time." FleaPit unleashes its whip, which hits Zhang on the shoulder. "*Pull über push!*"

Zhang is too stunned to react.

"BTW, are you still a man?" FleaPit asks as they wait for their transport. "Did you have your hourly sex-change yet? The possibilities are endless, and the first six are on the house. It'll loosen you up."

"I'm not sure if I really—" Zhang is interrupted by the arrival of a pod levitating atop a continuous track that alternately pulls and pushes with a vehement force on his smartphone, smartwatch and smartearrings.

"I took the liberty of implementing your bio-adaptation," FleaPit says. "It's the least I could do for an honourable guest with such an exquisite taste in transportation."

Zhang wants to protest but screams in pain as his smartphone, smartwatch and smartearrings heat up and eventually melt in the onslaught of the rapidly pulsating electromagnetic fields of the superconducting continuous track. Thank dog his Yin Yang amulet remains intact. FleaPit, who now metamorphoses from flesh hump to insect swarm devouring the flesh hump, laughs it off.

"They forgot to implement a Faraday Cage in the pod housing," FleaPit guffaws as Zhang's gadgets melt away from him, "but you know how it is"—FleaPit lashes his whip against the pod's roof—"*practice über theory!*"

"But it hurts," Zhang says, his voice rising at least an octave. His head of hair grows out, his breasts expand, his waist narrows and his reproductive organs reform as muscle, fat and other flesh is re-arranged throughout his body. "And I'm becoming a woman," she says with a mix of disbelief and terror.

"A charming one, at that," FleaPit, who now resembles a colony of insects crawling over rotting flesh, says.

"But my phone, my watch, my smart jewellery," the female Zhang says, "they're toast."

"Your pre-historical gadgets are damaged beyond repair," it says through snorting giggles, "but they were useless here, anyway, and slumbering clumps of metal and plastic most of the time you weren't using them. Allow me to introduce you to our cloud-based interfaces. Fear not, they will adapt and improve as they absorb your quirky personal preferences. Our cloud won't remain static, but is already evolving beyond something like mere cloudiness. Forget about MicroGoogøl-Book and SoftFaceFruit; welcome to the era of the continuously improving Mythosweb, which cannot be named as its name changes faster than it can be pronounced. The IT, the id, the bit-to-byte, the sod-it-unmentionable." With a quick flick of the wrist, FleaPit lashes its whip at an ever-moving sky. "*Systems über objects!*"

"First you were a Feng with dragon jaws, now you look like an insect-infested carcass." Zhang struggles to keep up. "How do I know you are still the same... well, entity that picked me up at the edge?"

"Does it matter? My external form is still comprised of mostly the same atoms, while my mind constantly evolves. I suppose my spirit is more-or-less the same, but who can tell? The Elder Gods? Who cares?" FleaPit cracks the whip and it lashes around Zhang's now hairless wrist, surprisingly gently. "*Compasses über maps!*"

They arrive at some place that might somewhat resemble a plaza or a food court, if most of it would just stay in focus. "Time for a tea," Fleapit says, "as we outsource your amusement."

"Yes, FleaPit." Zhang nods in agreement. "I could use a simple tea."

"I'm not FleaPit anymore," the entity previously known as FleaPit says. "I've moved to FlyLord."

Zhang has to admit that many of post-FleaPit's characteristics have metamorphosed into the Diptera realm. "Okay, I suppose," Zhang says. "And the tea?"

"Indeed," FlyLord says, "how about a fresh yellow? Junshan Yinzhen?"

"Actually, if you could be so kind," Zhang says, "I'd rather prefer a soothing green, like a West Lake Dragon Well?"

"Fine," FlyLord says as it signals for the waiter. With a flash and a bang, a robotic contraption somewhere between The Shrike and a Battlemech explodes right next to Zhang's table.

"You wished to order?" it voices in a hyperfast, mechanical shriek.

"Indeed," FlyLord says, as flies of its colony gobble up flies, becoming bigger. "A fine white one, say a Silver Needle?"

"Two White Peonies coming up," the waiter, who now evokes shadows of Darth Vader, says before it leaves the scene with an asthmatic growl.

Before Zhang can protest, the mecha-waiter is gone. Within seconds it's back with the order. "Here's your Keemun Experimental House Reserve," as it places the black tea in front of FlyLord. "And here's your Wenshan Baozhong Special Batch," as it places the Oolong tea in front of Zhang.

Zhang wants to roll her eyes, but fondles her Yin Yang amulet and just gives up.

"Excellent," FlyLord says while two of its six legs groom its transparent wings. "*Disobedience über compliance!*"

Reluctantly, Zhang tastes her tea. Contrary to her worst fears, it's quite good. "It's got all the hallmarks of a classic Wenshan Baozhong," she says, "with some unexpected depth and exciting extras. Quite interesting."

"It took some convincing," FlyLord says, "but finally teahouses are willing to experiment with our synthetic biology recipes."

"That tea was quite good," Zhang says, "but now I feel like I have a double need to pee."

"Which you indeed might." FlyLord flashes a sardonic, insectoid smile.

Zhang looks at FlyLord in disbelief, then carefully touches her—correct that, ber—nether regions. Yes, both male and female reproduction organs. "What the hell, I'm a hermaphrodite!"

"Well, that took long enough," FlyLord says, "but it'll speed up your unproductive waste release by a factor of two."

Zhang asks for directions to the toilet and goes there, before thoughts of how to pee from two organs at once and the idea of what toilets might actually look like in this indefinable campus might stop ber.

*

Be comes back, mission accomplished—don't ask—and faces an entity like a swarm of beetles crawling over something pungent that's better not described. Still, Zhang is fairly sure this is where be came from.

"It's okay," the entity says, "it's me, BeetleDung."

"I thought you were FlyLord?"

"FlyLord is so last minute." The entity stretches its half-domed wings. "BeetleDung is where it's at." From somewhere inside the myriad of creepy-crawlies, a whip lashes around the insect mound. "*Diversity über ability!*"

Zhang wants to say something, but is distracted by the constant "Zzzzip-Dong/Zzzzip-Dong/Zzzzip-Dong" sound that seems to come from somewhere close by. "What's that irritating sound?"

"That's just your sex becoming volatile," BeetleDung says. "While you were enjoying your tea, our cloud-but-not-quite-cloud estimated your taste, preference and sense of humour. Experience your personalized performance."

While fe didn't pay attention, a whole mini-cinema-cum-street-theatre was erected behind Zhang. A mix of actual actors and projected entities perform a play/sitcom/vignette/newscast whose topic, tone and subject change just as quick as the actors—virtual, real or augmented—change appearance. It's fast, furious and almost over before it begins.

"This doesn't work," Zhang says, needing no hormones to express fis utter disagreement. "The narrative is a jumbles, the tone is inconsistent, the theme so thoroughly unthematic it gives Dadaists migraine."

"It didn't work for you?" The disappointment is unmistakable in BeetleDung's voice. "Too bad."

"Bad's the word," flashing Zhang says, "godawfully bad."

"They win now, a Pyrrhic victory," BeetleDung says, "but we will bounce back, Yog-Sothoth willing, like the ever-improving army of phoenixes that we are." It lashes its whip at a giant sign that flashes from Hollywood to Bollywood to Shollywood. "*Resilience über strength!*"

"I feel strange, BeetleDung," Zhang says, "as if I'm locked in."

"BeetleDung is last minute's news," an entity so overwhelmed with insect-like appendages it resembles an insect god, says. "InsectIDecide feels much better. Shift for the moment."

"I'm sweating like a pig," Zhang says. "I never do. What gives?"

"Because you're a neuter now," InsectIDecide says. "To get rid of your excess liquids you need to sweat."

"I need to perspire my superfluous fluids?" Zhang says in despair. "So that's why they smell so funny. Now I'm afraid to eat."

"No problem," InsectIDecide says, "we can design food whose waste will crawl back from whence it cameth. Our marketing cloud suggests 'Vomitorium Automaticum'."

"I think I'll eat tomorrow," Zhang says, "after I've acclimatized a little."

"You sure?" InsectIDecide says. "Our cuisine is so much more interesting than the dull stuff they serve on the mainland. On your plate as soon as it's made."

"There's no authority testing your food?" Zhang says, fearing the answer. "Food safety is important."

"Of course not," InsectIDecide says, "that would only hold back innovation. It's never the same, like your thoughts, your whims, your sex." Seemingly out of nowhere, its whip lashes dangerously close to Zhang's nether regions. "*Risk über safety!*"

Utterly overwhelmed, Zhang doesn't even bother to check what the hell is happening between nis legs. "I'm tired, I need a place to sleep," ne says, fearing the answer. "Do you have anything resembling a dorm here?"

"Not really," InsectIDecide says, "but we can manufacture one for you on the fly."

"Okay," Zhang says, accepting the inevitable, "but make sure it has a decent bed."

"No problem," InsectIDecide says. "It'll be the most innovative bed you've ever slept in."

"I'm pwned and tired beyond my wits," Zhang says. "I need a good night's rest."

"Of course, the bed you'll wake up in will be different from the bed in which you went to sleep," InsectIDecide says. "If you're lucky it'll have remained mostly a bed in between. It'll have to do until you learn to ignore sleep."

"Ignore sleep?" Zhang asks, against ner better judgement.

"And similar minor distractions like sex, drugs, alcohol and other earthly diversions," InsectIDecide says, unleashing its whip at a structure behind Zhang. "*Emergence über authority!*"

Zhang turns around, and isn't even surprised to see that a one-bedroom dorm has arisen while ne talked with InsectIDecide who increasingly morphs into a giant moth. "See you later," ne says, strokes ner Yin Yang amulet for luck and gets into nis personal dormitory.

Inside, the bed is surprisingly good. Zhang undresses, decides not to check what's happening between ner legs and almost immediately falls in a deep sleep. But not quite dreamless.

*

Zhang's in a realm where angels fear to tread, where bleeding edge, constantly modifying production lines, effervescent synthetic biology labs and berserk coding parlours are but the baseline of the madness arising from their mouths. A veritable transformocracy where flash-adaptation reigns supreme. A parade of paradigm shifts conceptually breaking through boundaries like tachyons through time. A software nirvana where code transcends context, consistency and conditions. The place where change goes to change. The realm where reality surpasses the real. The commonality that condemns common sense. The things that should not be.

Zhang gives up trying to cope with it. *Let it be,* ne thinks, *go with the flow.* As ne lets go, nis vision enhances and ner sense of time speeds up. Slowly—no, scratch that—quickly the pieces fall into place, and a vision surfaces.

InsectIDecide's whip is key, Zhang now sees. The beautiful, Art Nouveau-styled reverse ellipses as it travels through the air. The short, sharp crack of pain and revelation as it hits. This is how the truly innovative hits the unsuspecting newcomer—unexpected, painful at first but with a sense of wonder and sheer efficiency as its meaning slams home. Why invent so painstakingly slow when you can unleash the new with a snap? Whiplash is the true way forward!

Innovation. Embrace-the-new. Novophilia Supreme. The whiplashtic fantastic.

- Of course using latent resources is better than producing dead stock—*Pull über push!*
- Creativity must not be constrained, but rather encouraged, nay, spread like a benevolent and contagious virus—*Disobedience über compliance!*
- Why spend years in education if you can fiddle, tweak and improvise until it works? *Practice über theory!*
- Don't get stuck in a rut of compliance, but innovate or die—*Risk über safety!*
- Use everything, and that means literally absolutely everything you've got and can get your hands on—*Diversity über ability!*
- Never give up, never give in, never say never again—*Resilience über strength!*
- Don't try to draw the path you'll be taking beforehand, as it limits the real paths you can take—*Compasses über maps!*
- The polyphonic subject: all feelings are mixed, all thoughts are shared, all deeds are collective—*Emergence über authority!*
- Our brains and the world at large are loci of overlapping systems, not singular objects in themselves—*Systems über objects!*

The dorm around nim has disappeared. Zhang nerself has become a motørcyborg on two wheels, with miniature exhaust pipes emerging through its sideburns. "Hello MothRa," Novo-Zhang says, polishing its exhaust pipes, "I feel much better now. Better, tauter, faster than before."

"You know my new name. You're finally getting the hang of it," the giant moth with the aura of a Sun God says.

"It was written all over you. Now we must hurry up," Novo-Zhang says, "so much to invent, so little time."

"Speed is of the essence," MothRa says. "*Über über essence!*"

Their words and actions become entangled in one big

razzamatazz of innovation mumbo jumbo, hypertechno patois and *shanzhai* jargon that changes as fast as they can pronounce it.

*

Carrie-Anne Piscatore is a young talent at the forefront of American research. Her CV already features a PhD in synthetic biology and a BA in applied mechatronics. She stands at the very edge of the SIS zone, where a local recruiter will pick her up. She fondles her wedding ring. From out of nowhere, an entity appears. Piscatore needs all her reserves of willpower not to scream in terror, as the entity resembles a walking atomic bomb with the head of Peter Sellers whose mouth has the shape of a rocket launcher. The whole contraption is enveloped with a radioactive sheen, glowing menacingly. "Don't be afraid, good applicant," the monstrosity says. "We needed to clean up after we somewhat overestimated the critical mass of a nuclear-charged widget."

Biting through a stupor of pure fear and sick fascination, Piscatore says, "Only *somewhat*?"

"Please ignore my outer shell, it's only temporary," the radioactive nightmare from Hell says through its rocket-launcher mouth. "Come in and join the fun." Atomic Sellers' left hand gestures to follow it, while its right hand holds, for whatever reason, a whip. A wooden Yin Yang amulet hangs from a chord around its neck. Piscatore has no choice but to follow.

∞

Jetse's First Two Options

1. Ku Klux Klan hires mime artist to assassinate the government's figurehead.
2. Waiting for Godot (d)evolves into a rain dance as the mysterious suitcase is unpacked.

Three and a Half Thoughts

Olivia Berrier

The test began, and the choice was simple: Fight. Or Don't. But there was a correct answer, and choosing wrongly resulted in death. Seph was content with this. He would pass the final test—never once in these six weeks of training had he doubted this. He would be inducted as a new assassin for the Muuaji Shadows. One day, he would become the greatest among them.

As soon as his blindfold was yanked off, his four minutes of contemplation began. Seph had to use this time to decide if the cloaked figure sitting across from him was one of the current Shadows who had been training him, or a fellow initiate. The psychological intricacy of the game had intrigued him from the start, as did the likelihood of death. If you were paired with an instructor and attacked—you died. If you were paired with another initiate and neither of you attacked—you died. If you were paired with an initiate and they were a better fighter—you died. But if you were smart enough to know that your partner was an instructor, or strong enough to slay the other initiate, then you earned your place among the most elite group of assassins in the world.

The Shadows were named after the Muuaji viper—a creature brought into existence thousands of years ago, in the age of black magic. The snake had a slender body, sapphire-blue scales, and a poison so powerful a drop of it could melt through plate armour. Muuaji Shadows caught these snakes by the dozen, but not to use them as weapons. In fact, there had never been an assassination that could be traced back to Muuaji poison. Instead, the Shadows killed one snake for each target, and left the two corpses to be discovered together. It was both their signature and a reminder that these assassins possessed the most lethal poison known to man and did not need to use it.

The mystique surrounding the Muuaji Shadows extended from the most desolate village to the King's own castle. Seph could attest to this, having been born in one and employed by the other. It was only because of the Shadows that people of Seph's unscrupulous background were allowed to serve on the First Guard. Four generations ago, one of the Shadows had assassinated the Crown Prince, proving beyond doubt that no one was beyond their reach. Since then, the Guard turned a blind eye to past crimes while recruiting. All the King cared about was whether they could protect him against an assassin.

The King had been smart to recruit Seph. In his years of service, he single-handedly thwarted three separate plots against the King. The Muuaji Shadows had likewise been smart to make Seph one of their initiates, even though they probably didn't realize it at the time. In addition to being on the First Guard, Seph's true career (known only to himself and the Crown) was that of a spy and a silencer. This test would finally allow him to prove what he'd always known.

He peered through the inadequate holes of his mask at the figure in the other chair. Initiate? Or assassin? Peripherally, he could see four figures in blue robes silently observing his test. Two of them were his instructors. He was sure of this because he had been paying close attention to their footfalls during the two-hour march through the desert. His testing partner, of course, had been escorted to the site by a different route.

And now they were all silently watching him, waiting to see if he'd been paying attention to the right details.

Seph had studied the other seven recruits extensively during training. Ever since the first day when they learned the rules of the final test, they had all worked on memorizing each other's body language. A true assassin, they were told, should be able to deduce a target's identity just by the sound of his breathing. But the game wasn't so simple, because the other initiates knew they were being evaluated.

Some whispered that they would set up your test depending on what they perceived to be your greatest weakness. If your observational skills were in question, you would get an instructor. If they had doubts about your fighting skills, you would get an initiate. If they doubted both, the weapons provided in the suitcase would be inadequate for the task, which would ensure your defeat. Seph had his own theory about the test, but he'd never shared it. He was excited to see if it was correct.

From under the black robe, Seph saw his partner tense his left shoulder. It was Tyril, then... or was it? Seph smiled because this really was a worthy game. After all, everyone had probably noticed Tyril's shoulder—it could be an instructor trying to trick Seph into fighting. Seph needed to prove he was observant enough to know the difference. And he was. The sunlight struck his partner's mask just right, revealing pale skin. Tyril's was dark—almost as inky as Seph's own. It wasn't Tyril under the robes.

The moderator announced that they had two minutes left. Seph leaned forward, not caring if the other person could identify him or not. If it was another initiate, Seph would win in the fight. The other leaned forward as well, mirroring Seph's posture.

Seph decided to use this to his advantage. He tipped his head from side to side—watching the other do the same. He crossed his arms, then spread them wide. He took a deep breath through the mouth, hoping that the dry and dusty air would make his partner cough. When that didn't work, he tapped one foot on the ground. He scraped a fingernail along armrest of the chair. He clicked his teeth together.

He smiled.

He could hear that his partner was missing one of his teeth. He doubted an instructor would go so far as to yank out a tooth just to impersonate an initiate. He knew exactly who was under the robes. It was Arden, which confirmed everything Seph had suspected.

Arden had always been an oddly talkative initiate. He was constantly asking questions of the other initiates. As if they were friends. As if they wouldn't murder each other in the final test if they were paired. At first, Seph thought this was just his personal strategy for the final test—to talk all the time so that it would be harder to recognize him in silence—but then the questions became more detailed, more personal. It took five nights of trailing Arden before Seph caught him whispering with the Shadows. Arden spoke to them not as an initiate, but as an equal.

Of course, once Seph knew Arden's questions would be carried directly back to the Shadows, his answers became frequent and honest. He told Arden about every secret mission he'd completed for the royal family, as well as the few he'd done as a freelancer. He emphasized the assassination of Sir Olwin, which was the greatest unsolved murder in the Kingdom. At first, Arden didn't believe Seph could have orchestrated the great knight's death, but once Seph laid out the specifics of his plan, right down to where he stowed the knight's severed head, Arden's attitude changed. They probably checked, and when they found the rotting trophy under the fourth step of the temple, they would know he belonged with them.

It was perfect, and Seph had to admire the Shadows' plan, even if it hadn't worked on him. So many initiates would recognize Arden's body language during the test and attack, and then die. But those who recognized Arden for what he truly was—those were the only initiates who had earned their place.

"Ten seconds."

Time was nearly up, but Seph wasn't worried. He'd figured it out. All that remained was to hold his stillness, and he would be welcomed as a full member of the Muuaji Shadows.

The moderator stepped away from the other observers and approached the suitcase between the two chairs. Part of Seph was curious about which weapons had been chosen, but he resolved not to look down. He wanted to keep his eyes forward, wanted to impress the Shadows with how sure he was.

He would have done just that, except that when the suitcase opened, it really was the last weapon Seph had expected—no weapons at all. The surprise caused him to divert his attention down to the empty suitcase, perhaps for a second.

If he hadn't been looking down, he might have seen Arden preparing to attack, and that extra moment of preparation might have given him time to put up a more substantial defence before Arden tackled him to the ground. They grappled in the rocky soil, and the fight might have been equally matched if Seph had made an attempt to fend off his attacker. But he didn't, because Seph's first thought was that this was all an extension of the test. Perhaps they wanted to see if he could hold true to his intuition. He held still, not fighting back, showing that even under stress such as this, he wasn't going to change his mind about Arden. The other took advantage of his pacifism to break his arm—twisting it backwards at the elbow until the bones creaked, groaned, and finally tore apart. The sound of his unmaking was chased across the barren landscape by a scream.

With the elbow shattered, the upper and lower halves of Seph's arm were connected only by their shared pocket of skin, like two tallow candles stored in an old sock. It flopped around obscenely as he tried to get into a more defensible position, but he wasn't truly thinking about defence.

Seph's second thought was doubt. Maybe he was wrong. Maybe it was just another initiate. With his functional arm, he ripped the mask from his opponent's face. It was Arden. The man smiled, revealing his missing tooth, before dropping a lightning-fast punch into the centre of Seph's breastbone. The pain was blinding, and when Seph was once again aware of reality, he was lying on his stomach, face crushed against the unforgiving soil. His mouth was filled with blood and broken teeth, though he couldn't remember receiving that particular blow.

Arden was on top of him, with one knee digging into his back. Arden's arm, still swaddled in the heavy initiation robe, was wrapped tightly around Seph's neck.

Seph was sure he was about to die, but his third thought was that he needed to understand how he could have been wrong. "You..." It took all his strength to grind the words past the muscles Arden was squeezing against his windpipe. "You're... not... a Shadow?"

Arden laughed quietly behind him and eased up on the pressure just enough that Seph no longer saw the grey specks dancing behind his eyelids.

"Oh, I'm a Shadow," he said. "Clever of you to figure it out. Most don't. But here's your mistake..." He leaned close to Seph's ear. "You aren't an initiate. Never were. You're nothing but a target."

The arm around Seph's throat constricted again, this time to the point where no amount of effort would have enabled him to speak. As he thrashed uselessly, Arden added in a conversational tone, "We thank you for your cooperation. Sir Olwin's widow will be happy to lay her husband's remains to rest properly."

As his lungs burned and his eyes swelled against their sockets, Seph almost had a fourth thought. He never quite formed it, but it was something about death—Not wanting it. Hating it. Fearing it.

It was only a half-thought, at best.

∞

Olivia's First Two Options

1. You are presented with two robed figures and you get to question them to determine which one is you from the future. The twist: the "you from the future" is actually inside the suitcase.
2. The suitcase contains forbidden power. Heaven and Hell have both agreed not to use it. It must be guarded at all times by a representative from both Heaven and Hell.

A Suitcase of Small Stories

Arathi Menon

A Stamp

The stamp remembers how he looked at it. With envy. Deep, uncontrollable jealousy. As soon as he found the stamp at a bus stop, he picked it up and saw it wasn't from where he was. The stamp still gets flustered at the memory of pure hate that flooded through the man. He crushed the stamp, closing down his fist on it, and put it in his pocket.

That night, when he was ironing the stamp, he spoke to it with a piercing unhappiness. He was quite drunk and he yelled at the stamp loudly. He showed the stamp the empty pages of his passport and cried, huge, gigantic sobs, which swayed his body and left him trembling. He kept muttering, "Even you are better travelled than me." The stamp thanked its stars it wasn't born a human and was just a normal well-adjusted stamp.

The stamp didn't understand this angst. It was a born traveller. It couldn't comprehend why some human beings had feet of cement and were forced to stay where they were. All it had to do was find an envelope and it was off. The man would often run his fingers over the stamp and mutter "One day" with a ferocity that scared the poor thing.

All stamps knew they get to undertake one journey in their life. That's all they wanted from this world. This stamp was lucky. It had taken a very long journey and had travelled by all sorts of transport: plane, ship, bus, car, on foot in a bag, and finally it was dropped from a backpack to be found by the man.

One evening, he looked at the stamp. He wasn't drunk and he quietly said, "I'm off." That's when the stamp came into the suitcase and made friends with the safety pin, which held in its steel case a love story.

The Safety Pin

This was before he met the stamp. The pin was one of those large pins with a giant head and a long, firm body that could keep things in place forever.

It remembered its history well. It was strung around a girl's neck on a black cord. They couldn't afford gold. The pin was her multi-purpose fix kit. It remembered being used for a number of things. For taking away the dirt from under her nails. For holding together her blouse so her bra wouldn't show through. For putting a string through her salwar. This was fun, going through a long, dark tunnel with a trailing worm and finally arriving on the other side into the light. It would then be taken off the salwar string and strung back on her black cord. Once she lent it to her friend whose skirt hook had come off. That night, she walked a full ten minutes to the girl's house to get it back. No wonder the pin felt important.

It was a Tuesday and she was holding the pin in her mouth when her mother fainted. The pin remembered her lips parting and an endless drop to the floor. *He* picked it up and slid it into his pocket. That night, when she sobbed into her pillow he slid the pin in and out of his mouth, remembering her, her ways and how she filled him with life by being alive.

All his unspoken love was lavished on cold steel. Every night he'd kiss the metal and let his tongue play with it gently. The pin wished this strange man would use it for its created purpose. He always had a missing shirt button or two and the pin knew it could help. But no, not even once did the man use the pin to hold things together.

His tongue worship stopped the day she got married in a hurry to someone who could buy her that gold chain on which she could string more pins. He never showed his pain for he loved her enough to want her to be comfortable in the arms of money. That night he kissed the pin tenderly and kept it in the suitcase. It was the first object to enter this cave of memories.

The Black Crayon

It seemed to have been overused. Just a tiny stub was left, one end of which was eroded to a fine slope. A baby beetle could slide on it. Wheee. The man had used it to colour the sunshine away. He first drew a bright, orange, yellow sun, so fiery and happy you needed sunglasses to look at it. Now that he had caught all the happiness in him, he started to work on it with a black crayon.

Carefully, he first shaded the ends so the blackness trapped everything. Then, he began working his way inwards. Soon every bit of the yellow was black. Satisfied, he paused. The darkness was all over the paper and spread itself deep within him. He caught the sheet in his hand and told himself sunshine was overrated.

Bits of his sunshine-ness attempted a weak escape, but the black crayon was a thick sludge pressing it all down. He stayed quiet, without moving, accepting the blackness.

Then over time, he learnt to peel away the layers little by little and let the multi-coloured sunlight peep out again. It did so without complaint. It was beautiful in that way. Whatever happiness he wanted, it gave. Black wasn't the only colour of his world.

As yellows, reds, oranges and greens exploded into his life on invitation, the black slowly began to disappear. He was a clever man; he didn't throw away the black crayon. He never knew when he might need it again. Gloom was a good antidote to destruction.

The Twig

They had gone for a walk, for the weather was a pleasant grey. That says something, doesn't it? To be married for fifty years and still be able to walk out of the door together, without a purpose other than that of spending time together. He didn't think about whether he had a good marriage; he just knew he had a marriage, and in his time that was more than enough.

She was as usual filling him in on all the details of the lives of the relatives he didn't care about. He didn't mind. He liked the sound of her voice and her wickedness. Talking about someone's annoying habit of advising her husband in his business, she remarked, "Thank god the man wasn't in the army. Or we would have definitely lost the war."

He laughed; he could do this with her. He realised, suddenly but with absolute clarity, none of his friends did that. Or had that.

She smiled at him, knowing he would not contaminate her delightful malice with morality.

As she rambled on he saw the twig. It was interesting, for it had colours on it other than brown. Yellow, green, blue and some bits of white. Together they admired the fungus and then walked on. He held on to the twig, to mark the day when he knew what a lucky man he was to be able to share laughter.

When they got home she cleaned the fungi off it, claiming it would make him sick. He felt sad. The colours dissolved away but the twig still looked beautiful. He used to keep it on his office desk. Occasionally during the day he would pick it up and then he would have an urge to go home to her, quickly, now. Once, a new office boy threw it into a dustbin full of lunch leftovers. He didn't hesitate. After threatening to fire the bewildered boy if he dared to do such a thing again, he picked up the twig, once again coated with colours. This time they were of gravy and spices. Just as his wife had done, he washed away those bright, dripping, smelly liquids. He decided he had to keep it somewhere safe. After spraying some eau de cologne on it, for it still smelt faintly of a green peas curry, he put it in the suitcase, along with the rest of the objects.

His cave of memories was slowly getting filled.

The Panty

Neatly ironed, crisply folded, tenderly preserved, it was hers when she was alive. No frills, simple, white, washed-out cotton with faded blue flowers and a roughness in the centre where the stains had been stubbornly scrubbed out of existence. The panty didn't know its continued existence was an act of love. All it remembered was that it had a full, happy life, where it was worn, washed, aired, ironed, worn—and then suddenly, the circle stopped.

Another set of hands held it close and then abandoned it in this darkness. It wasn't the complaining sort, but some kind of warning would have been nice. It missed the smells that came from her. Spicy, pungent, vinegary and sometimes, it had to admit, a little stinky.

It wasn't one of the panties that she had stained with her blood; those days were long over. It was a panty of comfort, a condom of dead sexuality, a stroker of wrinkled skin that nobody saw. Till she died, nobody gave it a thought, including her. It was just another ritual of living like making tea or wearing a bra.

When she said goodbye to the world, he didn't know what to do, how to express what he felt in an age of senility. Quietly, when the kids and kids' kids were asleep, he took a set of her clothes. He chose the saree with care. He remembered her in it. The rest, he only had a vague idea. A blouse, a bra, an underskirt and this panty, all randomly picked but carefully folded. He preserved them in the suitcase with infinite care. He never looked at them again, but he knew they were there, hidden from his eyes, like her.

The Sandalwood Box

A box within a box within a box.

The sandalwood box was beautifully carved. He couldn't recognise all the figurines on the outside but some of them did bear a resemblance to the mythical stories his grandmother had told him. He would hold the end of her saree and pretend-cycle in the air, while her raspy voice would fill his head with images. Of a child stealing butter; an elephant being slayed to replace a decapitated head; a woman crying alone under a tree; a dark, ash-covered man with a flowing river enslaved in his hairdo; a monkey holding a mountain. He would look at the box and remember her smell. Powder mixed with sweat and a faint trace of the green soap he couldn't find anymore.

He had never opened his grandmother's box till her death. After her cremation his mother gave it to him and said she had asked her to give him this. He was surprised. He had never shown interest in the box.

He opened it and saw a note on a small card, written in blue-black ink. The writing looked like calligraphy: long, elegant strokes. On it were these words: *To my daughter, from your father.* Somehow, it moved him, this lack of hyperbole, the quiet assurance it carried, the omission of the word *love* or *dear.* He had never met his great grandfather but he kept the card simply because he couldn't throw away a history he knew nothing about.

To the right side of the box was a pair of dentures. He didn't know if his grandmother wore them. This was a particularly dirty set. The left side of the tooth still had something stuck to it. A slight blackish greenish discolouration over time. Why hadn't his normally neat and tidy grandmother washed the filthy dentures? Was what was stuck significant in any way? What if he was washing away something that was a part of him, a part of his lineage? Maybe his very existence had something to do with this piece of unidentifiable matter stuck in that antique denture.

There was also a little box within the box. It contained a marble. He looked at it in disbelief. Why would an eighty-year-old woman save one marble? He held it in his hand and rolled it around his palm. He felt nothing. No enlightenment raced across the barriers of time and told him the importance of the green globe with a lighter green leaf pattern embedded in it. Normally he would have taken it out to play, but somehow her death held his use of her things hostage.

He preserved her box as she had: not moving it much and opening it rarely. When he put the suitcase in the attic he added this box of unclaimed hereditary memories. Perhaps the next generation would have the courage to throw it away.

The Transistor Radio

It was as old as he and was put into the suitcase two years before his death. This was the only thing placed to trigger someone else's memory and not his own. It was a small black box, with a cross section of a hive single speaker, insect antennae, and a broken volume knob.

He had taken his daughter to a shop in a bustling commercial area. She had never been there but she was used to being taken to queer places by her strange father. He was eighty years old and still walking miles to get what he wanted.

The man who owned the shop was as old as he. It was

perhaps the only shop in the world that still serviced transistor radios. In a world of smart phones and tablets, only the very quirky and those who refused to adapt to newer technology listened to the news on these outdated contraptions. If she thought about it hard enough, her father was a hipster.

He had brought it here to get the audio knob fixed. The man in the shop said he had got the spare part around thirty years ago from Singapore. He just had to find it. Shuffling on his old feet, his shaking fingers started searching the hundreds of shelved boxes with small parts in them.

While waiting he told his daughter about his death, in a very matter-of-fact way. He said all people will die; so will he. He ignored the surprise in her eyes and continued telling her what she already knew. He didn't believe in rituals. When he died, he wanted her to cremate him and throw the ashes into a flowing river. She asked whether he wanted any specific river. She thought he might say the Ganges. His long-forsaken Hinduism would finally raise itself when the end was so near. He impatiently replied, "It doesn't matter." It chilled her more than when he used the *death* word.

Then he turned his attention back to the radio man, who was still looking for the spare part. It couldn't be located. The radio man had the confusion of the very old, swearing he had kept it in a red box on the fourth shelf, ashamed of a memory that was failing him so deeply. Her father pacified him and told him he would be back. Both of them knew this was a lie to assuage the humiliation age subjected them to.

This man who hadn't spoken to his daughter about life, boys, careers and saving money had warned her about his death. Perhaps it was the only warning he needed to give her, for the rest he was confident she could handle.

The day he died the suitcase was thrown away by an aunt who wanted to clean the house. It squatted on the floor of the dustbin where, much to its alarm, it slowly began to disappear in parts till it completely faded away. When its molecules re-assembled it found itself between two chairs. There it stood for an eternity, as a decision couldn't be made. No matter how much they glared at each other or thought through their thinking caps, they just couldn't decide whether a memory goes to heaven or to hell.

∞

Arathi's First Two Options

1. The first idea was about a brain-washing worm inside one of the caps talking to a brain-erasing worm under the other cap.
2. The second idea was about how they were holding all the money of the world as ransom and what humanity would have to give up to get it, individually, collectively, horribly.

Prophecy

Jesse Rodriguez

In the vast, empty land where nothing grows, the suitcase stands between Black and White. While sitting in plush, green chairs across from each other, Black and White lock eyes. For now, they must wait, fighting the temptation to open the suitcase prematurely. The suitcase stands upright, on the ground and untouchable, as if mocking them. Black and White know the rules. For weeks, the suitcase was not to be opened, but now the time has almost arrived. The time is almost upon them to finally open the suitcase. The time is nigh to finally unearth and read the Third Option Short Story Submissions.

Black's wristwatch reads sixty seconds until the deadline, and White's cell phone confirms it. Impatiently, they sit and wait. Both Black and White fidget with their masks: black mask for Black and white mask for White. Then, they each tug on the cuffs of their respective robes, white robes for Black and black robes for White, draped over their arms. White's finger taps anxiously before finally saying, "So, it's kinda hot out here."

The sun looms large overhead, beating down on them. "I agree," Black says while adjusting the elongated, cone hat worn by all Masters of the Black. "I know we needed a secure place to review these submissions, but I think we could have just gone into my basement."

"Nonsense. You know how important these submissions are," White says. "We can't risk anyone stealing them. One of these submissions could be the key to glory. One of these submissions could be the one the Prophecy has foreseen. One of these submissions could be the one to free all Writers from the tyranny of unliveable wages."

"You're right, of course," Black says underneath the black

mask and thinks back to the words of the Prophecy:

To whom that submits the best of thee
Authored among the options of three
Submitted for all Masters to see
Leads all the dreamers from poverty.

White's cell phone chimes. The time to review has arrived.

Black unlocks each latch of the suitcase and opens it. Black pulls out the first submission and starts reading. It's an easy, predictable read. After a few moments, Black scoffs. "Eh, this one's okay. The two light and dark wizards are portrayed as metaphors for good versus evil. It's a decent read but too cliché. Not enough deviation. It's pretty well written, though."

White pulls out another manuscript and begins reading. White's head shakes disappointedly. "Here's another. Too obvious of an ending. Again, too symbolic with the black and white robed figures. The white wizard is, of course, symbolic for one faction; the black wizard is symbolic of another. Blah blah. I'm looking for something truly weird and unique."

"Agreed," Black says.

One by one, Black and White pull out submissions to read and review, each one more cliché than the last. Black reads another submission about good versus evil involving two warring wizards. White reads another obvious submission involving symbolism and allegory. After an hour of reading submissions, Black pulls out yet another manuscript with tiresome interest and reads it.

Black suddenly pauses. Black straightens up, looks over to White and utters, "What the..."

White looks at Black. "What is it?"

Black jumps out of the velvet chair and looks down at the hardcopy submission after dropping it to the dirt. Black stares at the manuscript like it's a jinx. Black finds the nerve to pick up the submission and then walks over to White. Black holds it in front of White and says, "Read this."

White takes it and reads word for word of the submission, "'Black suddenly pauses. Black straightens up, looks over to White and utters, "What the..."'" White looks up from the manuscript at Black and says, "Okay, that's a little weird."

White's black hat slopes to the side. "Who sent this and how did they know you were going to say that?"

"Oh my god, that's the next line right here in the submission," Black says wildly. "'Who sent this and how did they know you were going to say that?' It's all right here in the text. It knows what we are going to do and say. I know this is impossible, but do you know what this means? We're the submission!"

"How is that possible?" White says, a little bit terrified.

"I don't know," Black says.

"Well, how does it end?"

"It says this is the submission that we have been searching for," says Black. "This is the one the Prophecy has foreseen! According to the submission itself, this submission is the Chosen One!"

"Well, then it must be!" White says with arms raised.

Black stands up and says, "I declare, we have found the Chosen One hidden among the Third Option Deviation submissions!"

Black and White shake hands and nod at each other in agreement. Then, Black and White both embrace. Both grin ear to ear under their masks and chuckle. "This is great," Black says.

"It sure is," White says while looking at the endless desert surrounding them.

"Yep," Black agrees while kicking a clod of dirt. "Ahem, so, what happens now?" Black says, looking at White with uncertainty. "Did it work? Did the Prophecy come true? Are we rich?"

"I don't know," White says. "I don't feel any different."

"Yeah, me neither. What the heck?" Black and White look around for a sign of what to do next. White looks to the heavens to find answers. Black turns to the infinite desert and sees nothing at first. Then, Black notices something in the distance.

On the horizon, a figure walks towards them. White notices Black motionless and fixated. White stops to focus and sees it too. Just barely visible to the naked eye, the dark silhouette of a person walks closer to Black and White. Neither Black nor White is expecting anyone. The figure's appearance clears as it gets closer. The figure is a man wearing khaki shorts and a *Lord of the Rings* t-shirt. Eyeglasses rest on the man's nose, shaded under his hand held to his brow. He stops just short of Black and White, in front of the opened suitcase.

Under the white mask, White stares at the man. Black stares silently as well, under the black mask. The man stares back at them with his eyes squinting from the sun. After seconds of a silent stare off, the man finally says, "Hi."

Black glances at White. White shoots a look back at Black, then both Black and White look back at the man. "Hello?" White replies, puzzled.

"Hi," the man repeats once more. Beads of sweat form on his forehead.

"And you are?" Black asks.

"Oh, I'm the guy that submitted Third Option Submission," the man says. "The one that you picked as the Chosen One."

"Wait, so this is your writing?" White asks, holding up the manuscript.

"Yes, it is," the man says with pride. "I'm really glad you enjoyed it."

"Wait," White says. "How did you even know we picked yours?"

"Well, you did just declare it, didn't you?"

White nods but remains confused. "Right..."

"So, are you like a god or something, because this submission is kinda weird," Black says. "You know, knowing what we were going to do and say."

"Yeah, no. I'm just a normal guy," the man says. "I kinda just let the story take me to where it needed to go and cut out as many tropes as I could. You said you wanted weird, right?"

"Right... So, what about the Prophecy?" White asks hopefully. "It predicted the end of poverty for all Writers. So, is this true?"

"Oh, it's true," the man says. "This submission will free writers from poverty—poverty of the soul and mind."

White looks at Black and says, "We were kind of hoping for the poverty, you know, of the economical kind."

"Oh, bummer," the man says, pushing up his glasses. "Yeah, sorry. Wasn't going there. I took the Prophecy in a whole different way. I really do hope I freed your soul with my submission though. But, like I said, just a normal guy over here."

Black and White both sigh and groan. Black whispers into White's ear, "We really should kill him right here. No one would know."

"Shh," White says to Black. "Calm down. It's okay." White pauses and looks around at the emptiness around them. However, White realizes Black is accurate. There isn't a creature alive for miles. No one would know.

"Ya know," the man says, interrupting their thoughts. "I really don't put much stock into prophecies, but I do put a lot on karma and faith. I'm not sure if any submission or writing or work of art can take us all to the Promised Land or do anything for the good of all Writers. I do know that eventually everyone gets what they deserve in the end. When my success comes, I won't forget what happened here today. I won't forget you. I will pay it forward. And maybe that's how, in the end, the Prophecy comes true after all."

White and Black ponder at the man's words, but White is the first to brush it off. "Okay, okay," White says at last, "now you're just getting sentimental. Congrats, you wrote the 'Chosen One.' We're all very enlightened now. Cheque's in the mail. Now hit the road."

"Thank you for your time," the man quickly says, bowing out. The man then turns and walks toward the horizon from whence he came.

Black sighs, "Ugh, so much for that."

"Eh, at least it wasn't a total loss," White says. "We got a few clicks on the website."

"Touché."

"And, hey," White says, "you never know. Maybe the Prophecy, you know, the one we want, will come true one of these days. Or even better maybe that mysterious stranger will pay it forward like he said. I mean, we can all dream right?"

"I guess we'll just have to see," Black says. "I'm still not sure what just happened. Did the Prophecy come true or not? Did we find the Chosen One?"

"Good questions," White says. "Well, we could always ask our readers."

"Great idea!" Black says. "I guess it's time we create

another weird poll!"

"Hell, yeah! Those are always fun," White says.

"Awesome, let's get out of here," Black says and picks up the suitcase.

White gestures Black to lead the way out. White follows Black in one direction through the desert until Black abruptly stops in place to think. Black points in the other direction and turns to walk the other way instead. Again, White follows Black before both stop once more in their tracks. White looks around while Black's hat slopes to the left. Once more, they are alone in the vast desert, standing before the wasteland around them. Both Black and White look straight at the split between lifeless dirt and limitless sky when Black says, "Now, where the hell did we park?"

∞

Jesse's First Two Options

1. White-robed figure represents good, Black-robed figure represents evil. Inside the suitcase is Power given to a man. With this limitless Power, the man must choose good versus evil. Both White and Black make their case.
2. White and Black have been warring. After a century of peace, they were promised a powerful gift given by the gods. After arguing you should open it and have whatever is inside, they finally open it together, revealing grey robes to their dismay. After more arguing and cursing of the "cruel" gods, they realize that only their offspring can wear "the grey."

Lumière, Noir, et la Valise

Sam Hirte-Runtsch

In a crowded Paris café, a man and a woman sat at a small table, gazing at each other across the rims of half-lifted cups. A leather valise sat on the bench along the wall behind the table, its buckles cinched tight around the wrinkled, time-softened body of the case.

The woman drank first, though her steel-blue eyes never left the young man opposite her. As soon as the cup touched her lips, he followed suit. They simultaneously set their cups down on porcelain saucers with a clink that permeated the chatter and rattling of the café, almost creating a pause in the bustle.

He folded his hands in his lap and she reached for a cigarette case on the table at her left elbow. She took one from the case and raised her eyebrow at the man.

"Trying to poison me?" he asked. He managed to affect a Boston Brahmin accent, despite speaking in French. It went with his carefully-parted hair and sharp-edged pencil moustache.

"Isn't that more in your purview than mine?"

He shrugged and smiled like a child caught reaching for a cookie before they were cool. "Are they decent?"

"They're Gitanes, not the *tabac de troupe* people are selling, if that's your question."

He shrugged again and put one hand on the table, two fingers out as if he already held a cigarette.

She withdrew a second cigarette, as well as a slim lighter, put both cigarettes between scarlet-painted lips, and lit them. She took one with fingertips and deftly flipped it over to hand it butt-end to the man, a trick that belied the age of her bone-slim hands. He took it and leaned back, resting one ankle on his knee as he took a drag and exhaled a cloud of the sharp smoke. His tailored suit was sharply pressed. She crossed her legs, one hand held fashionably by her shoulder, the other fiddling with the cigarette case on the table. Her dress was just as carefully tailored as his suit, and the height of fashion. Steel grey hair shot through with streaks of dark blonde was curled to bob around and frame her face. Despite the difference in their age, they looked very much like a couple sharing a smoke and a cup of coffee.

"This brought you here?" she asked, gesturing at the case between them.

"It's powerful enough I can feel the energy rolling off of it. Even in the chaos surrounding us, it rings clear as a bell."

"And you intend to bring it back to your masters?" She took a drag on her cigarette, tossed her head a bit to clear a stray lock of silver back into its place, returned to her statuesque pose.

"Of course I do. What do you think I'd do, hand it over to your straight-laced clique?" He picked up his coffee and drank the rest of it, grimacing slightly as he set the cup down.

"And to what purpose would the Black Society put such power?"

"Take care of this, for one." He gestured around him. "Drive *les boches* out of the city."

Her eyes went wide at his use of such a pejorative in a crowded public place. Her fingers flowed in a seemingly impossible pattern and she quietly uttered a single syllable. The entire café went silent for a moment, and then those who were looking at the couple's table returned to their coffee, cigarettes, and conversations, as if they hadn't noticed such a dangerous comment.

"Hypocrites. You pretend that you only use your power for benevolent purposes, but have no problem with twisting the minds of others."

She waved the accusation away like a fly in her face. "Would you be so kind as to not antagonize them? We have more important things to do than kill countless people while we are trying to both survive and escape."

"Like decide who's leaving with the case?"

"Precisely."

He idly fiddled with a cufflink. "And you don't think that process will result in at least one of us having to kill countless people while trying to both survive and escape?"

"It's a possibility."

He took another drag on his cigarette. Picked up his cup and looked at it, remembering that he'd emptied it. He gestured for the waitress and tapped his cup. "So why bring the case here at all?" he asked the woman.

"Why indeed?" She held her hand over her half-full cup as the waitress reached for it questioningly.

His eyes widened and he leaned forward, his elbows on the table. "Just a moment. You truly don't know what the case holds, do you?"

"Of course I don't. I'm not the one who brought it here."

"Then presume for a moment that I didn't, either." He held up a hand. "Just play along. If you mislike my reasoning, you can always ignore it and we can get on with duelling in public."

He glanced up at the waitress as she brought him a fresh cup. He held the cup below his nose and inhaled, making a noise of appreciation before continuing. "So presume that I didn't bring the valise. And you didn't bring it. Yet it is here, radiating power that anybody with half a measure of talent would notice. Why is it here?"

"All right. Going with your presumption for the moment, an old leather valise appears in a Paris café—"

"Appears? You don't think someone left it here?"

"Perhaps. Or perhaps not. Perhaps it appeared here when a teleport went awry. Or someone enchanted it to appear here on this day. Or it may be a fragment of power that coalesced here."

His only reply was a nod acknowledging the possibilities.

"Or, you might be lying, and you left it here as a trap for me."

"Possibly. I must admit that, with your faculty at deceit, I have similar concerns."

She opened her mouth to argue, then made a little circular motion with her cigarette hand. "A fair notion, though that is more the hallmark of your camp."

"Quite. Though at least we are more honest in our lies.

Either we tell falsehoods, or we speak truth. The Light prefers to tell just enough of the truth to obscure the lie they commit through omission."

The woman took a sip of her coffee. "While I am happy to philosophically argue the varying forms taken by our indiscretions, perhaps we could focus on the matter at hand?" She set the cup down and gestured at the valise.

"Very well, though I feel that such an argument can be directly tied to discussion of the case, as a lie, or omission, on your part could conceal the nature of its contents. If we are acting on the presumption that neither of us brought the case here, then how shall we proceed?"

"You did suggest duelling over it." She took a slow draw from her cigarette, staring at a point over his left shoulder.

"I did. But in deference to your wish for subtlety, I am willing to examine other options."

She chuckled. "Perhaps we should simply open the case."

"Oh? And which of us would you suggest be the one to open it?" The waitress stepped up to the table. He nodded at her and waved with his hand. She took the cups.

"I thought perhaps you would have an opinion."

"So we remain at this impasse. Coin flip?" He reached into his pocket.

"Not your coin."

"But I should be expected to trust yours?"

"As a compromise. My coin. You may toss it."

He looked like he would argue, then returned his coin to his pocket and held out his hand to accept the large gold disc she handed over. "*Liberté, égalité, fraternité.* Do you have a problem with work, family, and the fatherland?"

She glanced around the café, but nobody seemed to have noticed his outburst. "I find the traditional motto to be more inspiring."

"A fair point." He stared at the coin for a moment.

"You don't trust me?"

"No more than you trusted me."

He perched the coin between his forefinger and the tip of his thumb. "Call it in the air." The coin sailed. A few heads turned to watch, eyes drawn by the glitter of moving gold.

"Heads."

The coin fell to the floor. They glanced down at it. "You win." He reached down and picked it up, then handed it to her. "Do you wish to open it, or shall I?"

By way of answer, she lifted the valise onto the table, its clasps facing her. He leaned back again and watched with feigned disinterest. She worked the clasps simultaneously and gently pushed the soft leather top up.

Her face twisted in confusion for a second, then her eyes widened in fear as tendrils of black energy reached out for her. Patrons began shouting and screaming in fear and confusion even as she tumbled backward from her chair. Tables were overturned. Porcelain cups and plates shattered on the floor in a cacophony. She held out her hands, a partial dome of white mist flowing from them. The blackness ate quickly at its edges.

The man stood. Whether to help his rival, hasten her end, or some other purpose wasn't clear. I chose the moment to act. I honestly hadn't expected both of them to be alive when the case was opened, but no matter. Standing, I drew the Mauser C96 from its holster at my side and pointed it at the man. I pulled the trigger twice. I shifted my aim to the woman who was beginning to push the black tendrils back, attempting to seal them into the case or simply destroy them with light. She probably would have succeeded had I not put two bullets into her.

My targets slumped to the ground, blood spreading in pools around them as I holstered the Mauser. I was unconcerned about being identified. Nobody had paid attention to the *gendarme* sitting in a corner of the busy café. Most of the patrons were fleeing for their lives. Few noticed the four barks of the Mauser over the commotion. Anybody who looked would not see past the uniform of the *gendarmerie*. Nobody would want to see past the uniform. They would not be able to provide any reliable details of the attacker.

The blackness snaked from valise to the ground, feeding on the woman's blood. I took a small brass tube from my pocket, striking it against the back of a chair and tossing it into the suitcase. That accomplished, I strode toward the door. As I stepped onto the sidewalk, light flared behind me, the incendiary tube setting the valise on fire, consuming both evidence and black entity.

An alarm rang out as I stepped into an alley and divested myself of jacket, hat, and holster belt. I produced a folding knife from my pocket and sliced the binder from my chest and the tie from my neck. It all went into a bag waiting between a pair of crates, to be picked up later by another agent.

I stepped out the other end of the alley, a woman heading home from some factory or another at the end of the day, the wrinkles and sweat from binder and jacket further lending to the illusion of a day of labour. I kept from my face the smile of satisfaction I felt, and studiously avoided meeting the gaze of a group of soldiers rushing toward the alarm.

I would have no need to report my success. By evening, knowledge of the assassinations would be spread throughout Paris. My superiors would know that we had successfully struck a blow against the societies of both Light and Dark sorcerers, and thus, against the cloud of prejudice and superstition that obscured the world.

∞

Sam's First Two Options

1. Light and Dark discuss the fate of the suitcased soul.
2. A wizard of the White asks a favor of her colleague, who is of the Black. The contents of the suitcase are payment for the favor.

No More Clouds

Dan Cox

It began with the photograph you pulled out of your purse like a bribe. It was a picture of a dog wearing a neckerchief, or was it a ruff? It intrigued me, I'll admit, and of course I wanted to know more. Knowing me as you do, it was inevitable I would begin to probe. You had banked on that. And so it began, the questioning. The dog. What was its name? Badge? Something like that. It was an elderly dog, statesmanlike. What was it trying to tell me? Its eyes implored me to act, to go chasing the ball across the sand. The dog was familiar, but where did it come from? And why was it dressed in that ridiculous fashion? This was all your doing, I was sure of it. It bore your trademark stamp. I slowly admitted to myself that I was harbouring doubts about your sanity and I fired off salvo after salvo trying to get to the bottom of your state of mind. What did you want from me? What was this image? It was imperative that I found out.

In the station waiting room I asked you about the connection times and I knew instinctively from your vagueness there and then that you were making everything up. As you stared at me quizzically, chewing on that banana, I saw through your disguise. The penny dropped. You had an agenda and you were trying to hoodwink me. You had dragged me to the station under false pretences. A day trip, you finally said. But this was unusual. Was this a dirty weekend away? We had never been on a day trip in all our life together. I was suspicious and I told you so.

Emotionally, I left you behind on the platform as I lugged the heavy bag onto the train. Even though your physical presence was beside me in the carriage I no longer cared about anything you were talking about. I could see your lips moving but your explanations meant nothing. You were a shadow to me, muttering shadowy things. I found myself beside a strange woman, so much like you but clearly not you.

Eventually I broke the awkward silence. "Who are you?"

The result? She looked upset. And was that a tear running down her cheek? I became conscious of some sort of flapping about in my vicinity, but I couldn't quite focus. I was unable to concentrate; the shadow woman in my mind had evaporated, and now it really was you sitting there looking a bit crestfallen and still holding on to a picture of our dog. That dog picture seemed to symbolise everything that was wrong with our relationship. Why would anyone dress up a dog? Dogs are not meant to be used in puppet shows. I hated you for it.

And then I began to delve deeper—it wasn't just the dog. There were other things too. Incidents that grated and invaded my consciousness like a swarm of angry bees. Like the time you fell out of that window and blamed it on me. How could that have been my fault? Why would you lay that one at my door when I was on the beach eating an ice cream at the time? Yes, I was dressed in that clown costume, terrorising the beach children. Yes, I had left you there knowing full well that you had a propensity towards self-defenestration. Perhaps I secretly hoped you would do yourself in, but I have no intention of exploring that thought any longer.

You are still flapping around. What's that in your hand? Is that a passport? Hold still. I'm trying to focus on what you're saying... something about moving on and taking things one day at a time, standing by one another. What's the point of offering me all that when I've left you behind on the platform and you don't really count anymore?

As my mind wanders, I remember other times... Yes, other times I thought you were off your trolley. Like that time we went swimming and you tried to drown yourself to see what it would feel like. You imagined you were a mermaid or a platypus or something but I thought it was silly, got out of the water and went for a beer on my own. You would pull yourself together when you were ready, I thought. Or else, you wouldn't. Either way, that was your choice. You were always in up to your neck, drowning in something.

Do you remember that time we went to the theatre to see

that Strindberg play? You know, when you screamed hysterically because you spilt your wine all over the programme. The actors had to pause to give you time to shut up, and to allow the stewards to wag their admonishing fingers. Good god, that was embarrassing. I was mortified. I swore to myself that I would never be seen in public with you again after that. We both knew this was a lie. Still I played along with the charade.

At first, I thought you were quirky, that these little tricks you pulled were playful and flirtatious, part of your need for attention. Gradually alarm bells began to ring and build up into a cacophony. Now I am here on this train, speeding into the unknown with this strange woman, almost your double, stroking a picture of that faithful dog. It was a loyal old friend, unlike you. But why are you getting angry with me?

My memory retrieves piece after piece of you. I am formulating a hideous jigsaw from the fragments. Fragments of fragments. If I zoom in on the particulars I am lost.

From now on I want only certainty and clarity. No more clouds.

But we speed on through the countryside and my mind is distant, far away. Things are happening, but they don't feel connected to reality. I am away with the fairies, as they used to say, hellbent on my future without you. Yet, somehow, I feel you're still there in the background, influencing my movements, the things I say and do. The more I dwell on it, the more I feel as if I'm caught in some sinister web with your shadow as the spider. You flicker on and off in the varying light of the tunnels, one moment you appear malevolent, the next you are quiet and calm.

Refreshments come and go but are neither here nor there. Announcements are announced but are gone without my registering any information. What are these sounds buzzing around me that have no connection to me? I believe I understand the language but it is just noise and does not connect to any real meaning. I think I can hear distant music, the echoes of a Wurlitzer organ seeping through the abandoned music hall of my consciousness. Somewhere there is a waltz playing, but I am indifferent to this as I am indifferent to you.

"Do you remember?"

I hear you, or I think I do, but does it matter? I am

selective about what I hear when it comes to you. Often, you're irrelevant, but I caught these words, like birds hopping along the wires of my brain.

"Yes, I suppose I do remember."

Was that my voice penetrating the darkness? You look at me like I am deceiving you. Am I in the midst of some sinister dialogue, like a tennis match, batting meaningless words back and forth until one of us scores? But what is the game?

The coast. We are heading towards the coast. Towards the beach where the endgame will play out. I know this intuitively but I don't know where this instinct comes from.

"I still love you," you say. A point well scored. I have no answer to that.

"Where are we going?" is all I can muster, like a simpleton.

Your lips compress into lines of disappointment and you appear to be weighing me up. You go to speak then stop yourself. "To the end of the line," comes the eventual muted response, whatever that means. You look vaguely out of the window.

I drift off to sleep and when I wake I have the impression of the same skies and rolling green hills slipping past, broken sporadically with gorse and scrub like a serrated panorama. To the end of the line. Not a holiday then? Slipping away. Opened up and opened out. Singled out like a fly at the end of the lizard's tongue. But hold on, *I am* in control. This is me running away, not you. You twist everything in the end to confuse me, even my escape. Why is it that my bag is at my feet while yours is nowhere in sight?

I am on my own again. So, no change there, like the time I brought home the foreign delegation from that trade mission to the East and you nearly poisoned the ambassador with those stale profiteroles. That incident set back my career for nearly a year, and if it hadn't been for those favours I did for the governor, I may never have got back my high office at all. So what if I stitched up my political rivals in decades of legal quagmires? So what if I was embroiled in so many accusations of corruption and nepotism? Yes, I may have squirrelled away some cash for a rainy day and helped fund one or two dubious regimes to make sure of a safe bolt-hole if I needed it. Of course! You would have done the same in my place. So I feathered a few nests and got rich along the way. What of it? Did you back me up? No, you made out that it was my fault by claiming I had a fling with the *au pair* and by going to the press with your grubby sob story. Nothing really matters because I can always blot you out. You are like the iron filings in a child's toy. I simply turn off the magnet and you disperse. You are a butterfly in a Rorschach test that I smudge when I fold the paper.

And now you are wearing a hat. Not just any old hat, but that famous hat. The one you married me in. The one that got all the attention in the society pages. A spectacle, they called it, a dash of colour drawing attention to you like a tropical fish or a bird showboating around, strutting for a mate. Well, you got your mate, but he is flying the nest. He has had enough of the humiliation.

"I still love you."

Did I say that, or was that an echo of your own lost words? Somehow it feels as if the words are emanating from me but I can't be sure. Am I a loudspeaker broadcasting to the rest of the carriage or am I receiving transmissions like an antenna, sensitised to every vibration you make?

My nerves are stretched taut as I anticipate your words and the vagueness of the demands you make upon me. I imagine you as you were in the beginning at that formal dinner where I found you crying in the arms of the waiter. You left him and draped your drunken arms around me. You divulged some private information about your ex-husband that helped me greatly with a business deal I was working on at the time, and I was flattered to be the one to reassemble you from the broken pieces.

I responded to your call like a circling seabird. I guided your vessel away from the rocks. I welcomed your charms, your excitement, your body. And I responded. Oh god, how I responded. We were in tune then, but now you are out of step. One of us is sinking as the rhythm of the waves laps against the rickrack. Or is that the gentle rocking of the train? Perhaps, yes. We are in thrall to a powerful movement, insistent and relentless. I could get off I suppose, but my body still responds to yours.

My body is a drum. My skin picks up your transmissions and your nervous twitches. There are things you are not telling me, but I pick up the quivering arrows of your thoughts. What is happening? Perhaps something frightful, perhaps something wonderful. In any case, the train is still moving. That alone should reassure me but somehow it doesn't. I push you away growling incoherently, rambling perhaps.

"Quiet, quiet. It's all right. Stop shouting, calm down," you say.

But I'm not shouting. Or at least I don't think I am. But I have the unmistakeable sense that something in me is running out, that I am emptying faster and faster as this game draws to an end. As the train speeds on towards that full stop where judgement waits, black clad, white clad, in contrasting robes. My fate hangs in the balance.

And the other travellers are beginning to look now too. Not the awkward glances of embarrassed passengers but the sinister look of vultures. They've spotted this old grandee in the corner babbling away and struggling with a domestic incident. They'll harry me like a pack of dogs, if they get the slightest whiff of how important I am. Give them any hint of scandal or my ministerial portfolio, and they'll be sniffing around me like a swarm of wasps around a ripe fruit.

And again, strangely, I think of the portrait of the dog in pantomime clothes, the unlikely starting point of this ridiculous chain of events. The dog was called Badger I think, but even that is uncertain. First black, then white, yin and then yang, the drama plays out. Badger the dog in an Elizabethan ruff, dressed for the stage, the son we never had. The loyal dog of our middle years when there was still hope or at least the excuse for pretence.

He was a fabulous dog, that animal. He held us together in many ways as we competed for his attention. As he woofed around with his stick I used to wish I was a dog myself. What a life! An escape from the cut and the thrust and the machinations, the who's-in and who's-out of favour. No, to be a dog, that was the thing. The easy life, a simple existence. Just loyalty, and honesty. No deception. No scapegoating or backbiting, no deals done behind closed doors. A dog's life is the life for me; I am chasing after a dream.

Other memories drift over me. They spill across my sky like cumulus clouds in a brisk wind. I watch them into the middle distance, but then they pass on. I am back at the theatre again, with someone else now at my side. I will take care not to spill wine over her, whoever she is. My mistress, your sister? I struggle to remember. During the interval, we skip through the auditorium under the bright chandeliers. She holds out her hand and I kiss her, but rush off to the bathroom, leaving her standing in the foyer uncertain. When I re-emerge, she is being escorted hurriedly to the door by another man, her flaxen braids jumping behind her like a hangman's ropes.

And I am crying now, slow hot salty tears. It is as if I am dissolving away into nothing.

"It's okay, it's okay," you susurrate in my ear like a friendly, bumbling bee. I turn to you but you have no face. I recoil. Pain and self-pity alternate like traffic lights. Then, the whole gamut of feelings: an exhausting rollercoaster of extremes. A mistress? It sounds so dismissive I suppose, but what a woman she was, so different from you. And she is lost to me forever now... forever... such an impossible idea, but there is no going back... Ha! Going back, yes...

I am jolted to my senses by a screeching of brakes as the train pulls into a dark station stretched tautly along a single track. It's hard to see out, as the windows of the carriage are grimy with experience and mud picked up along the journey. Is it morning or night? It is hard to tell. I cup my hands to my face to try to see, but only catch my own grizzled reflection. Disembodied voices are shouting on the platform, porters ordering baggage trolleys this way and that.

You whisper, "We're here," and you hold the arm of my tweed jacket the way you used to when you would escort me to a press conference, with that little pinch under the elbow which let me know that you were on my side no matter what. Your hands, I notice, are smaller than I remember, and your nails are chipped. Why are you trembling? I look into your face.

"Do you love me?" I ask. "Where's your bag?"

Your answer is instinctive, like a soft pat on the head, a soothing fillip to a child who has fallen, but is reassured by the comfort of the familiar, by the smell of perfume and the soft brush of silk across the knee.

"Come on," you gesture and we are off. One step at a time. Down the steps and out onto the platform where the smell of soot and seaside air hits my nostrils, along with a humidity I remember from a childhood holiday. Is this Italy? Have we arrived?

This could be the start of an adventure rather than the beginning of a nightmare. I increase my pace and take your hand. You're leading me like you know where we're going, leading me forward to do my duty, to face up to my enemies with one last characteristic flourish. It's brighter now, but day and night appear to alternate more quickly here. The clouds are reeling drunkenly above, but you keep me rooted with love, guiding me into the milky light ahead.

The other passengers from the train have dispersed like so many scattering ants and we find ourselves alone. We walk along the sepia streets of a coastal town smelling of ozone. The light comes and goes, occasionally illuminating the shop fronts that are all boarded up as if closed for the season. There is no sign of life in the abandoned pharmacies, the endless junk shops and chip shops with their antiquated signs and their picture postcard vitrines. A seagull squawks our arrival, an unseen sentinel. And I imagine gentlemen putting down their long drinks and dusting themselves off one last time as they stand to attention, preparing to see off an old chum.

At the end of the road, we reach the beach, where a snaking path of boards and broken sleepers leads towards the sea... discarded plinths to keep the soles of the feet from burning on the hot sand. But the sand is cold. The dunes are windswept after a storm and an insistent salt breeze stings and sharpens the senses. I shiver and you rub my sleeve.

I am alert now, and necessarily so, because I have been lured into a trap. Two figures come at me from nowhere, with outstretched arms. I yelp. I hear you mutter the word "convalescence" but I'm not sure what this means. Get away from me! Why are you taking the bag? No, you've got it wrong! It's the other way round. You're the one who's sick. It's you that needs treatment for your manias and delusions, your constant death wish and your unhealthy obsession with appearances.

Ah, god, am I that naïve?

Terror clutches me like a vice as I anticipate the touch of these apparitions. And now? Who are these robed priests who lead me out across the beach? Towards what? A pier? And is that a boat beyond? The wind whips the sand up into my straining face as I squint and stare, trying to make out the faces of my puppet captors. But they are masked and expressionless, anonymous shepherds escorting me across some unforgiving River Styx. Is this really happening, this beach, this journey, these accusers? You?

You've been plotting against me all these years, have you? You've been storing up years of hatred to entrap me when I'm at my most vulnerable. Plotters everywhere. Conspirators! I knew it! When all I can think of is that missing dog and the woman I lost my heart over... back in the ball room, that state banquet, when there were no people, only personages, and they wheeled like dervishes and were whisked away. Premonitions, luxurious phantoms from another time, so elegant, and projected onto the circling skies.

Are these enemies from my youth, are these people I have wronged, or are they the interpreters of my future? Show your faces, damn you! What have I done that I should be delivered thus? Yes, I did leak information about that promising civil servant with his unusual proclivities, I cannot deny it. When I sold old whatshisname down the river, I had no choice. It was him or me.

I turn to you, imploring you for help. For forgiveness. Your hat is missing, and your bag, and your picture of the dog, but I know it is still you. "Don't walk away! Don't walk away!" I call out in desperation. I am on my knees. I have nothing left to lose. I'm not sure if this is some macabre hallucination. If it is, it is vividly real. I flap around like a felled bird. I scream, louder and louder, for you to redeem me. "Come back, come back, don't leave me with these... ANIMALS!"

But you glide across the sand, back towards the empty road, floating as if you're electrified like a tram. You don't turn. You cannot hear me. You are gone.

One of the robed figures gestures for me to be quiet, then tugs at me to move on. Its hands are smothered in dark silken sleeves embroidered with a gold script that I am unable to decipher. The being stands there, impassive and horrifying, with the vacant stare of an automaton. It is silent. And it points forward, out across the flat sands, where other figures hover like chess pieces waiting to be manipulated by an unseen hand.

I remain on my knees, shouting, looking up and waving my hands like an obstinate child.

I'm not going anywhere.

I'm digging my heels in. I'm not prepared to budge. I have reached the end of the line. There are no more clouds now.

∞

Dan's First Two Options

1. Inspector Malbec is investigating the disappearance of an office worker and, while looking for clues, finds the competition image amongst his personal effects, plastered on the walls of his flat, on his laptop, as his office screensaver etc. Is the image in any way connected to the missing person's whereabouts? Has he joined a strange cult?
2. A series of art galleries holding photographic exhibitions are targeted by an unusual hoax. Photographs are being stolen at random and replaced by the competition image. Gallery owner S. Grundman is concerned about supernatural happenings and convenes a meeting of leading luminaries in the art world, however it turns out to have been a promotional stunt to advertise the new LP by Howlin' Stan and the Bad Neighbours who have "appropriated" the image as their album cover.

A Young Evil Departs

Chris Loud

Eight summers of evil. My life savings collected and allocated, but the allocation comes as a surprise to the hand that feeds. Payments for evil come in small bits, mostly ladder rungs escalating to a position of power, and a little bit of money. Therefore, you really have to want to be evil. Summer jobs are the pits, but it's what you have to do if you want to climb the ladder of evil, or, in my case... GET THE FUCK OUT.

Normally, a family of evil stays evil together. I am dressed out of respect for my elders, but this will be the last time. It's hard to see the emotions on the face of your father. Not because it's hard emotionally to witness it, but because the elders' faces are literally impossible to see because of the masks. I haven't earned my mask, and I don't plan on earning it. Still, what I imagined behind the mask was also hard to see. He is, after all, my mentoring kin. But today is different. I will have no mentoring kin anymore. I will have no mask.

These decisions do not come easy. This is generational. This goes further back than I care to fathom, but it's not unbreakable, as I had been told by the elders. He just sat there, barely a twitching muscle, barely an audible gruff. I hate when he does that. It's very hard to read someone when they're trained to not only never show emotion, but to never feel emotion. The mask is arguably redundant, because with no emotion what does it matter to hide an identification? You have no identification with no emotion. I just have to figure out how to end this conversation.

After several minutes of very little physical movement and virtually no verbal communication, I stood. I stood as tall as I could, next to the tattered old suitcase, passed down to me from my father. That probably didn't help at the moment. Every up and coming evil gets a suitcase. The lesson from the suitcase is simple. To spread evil, all you need to do is get around. Evil spreads easily, like wild fire or cancer. You just have to be there, and the evil takes on its own life, moves at will, and defeats the weak and ignorant.

The funny thing about evil is that it doesn't try; it just is. We exist in quantity, not quality. We can't be measured by less or more. We just are; evil just is. I don't try to be evil—I just learn what evil is, why evil exists; it becomes me, I become it, and I get around. It's the "why" part that brought me to this moment today, with my empty, symbolic suitcase. I guess I forgot to mention that I wasn't taking anything with me, but I hope to fill it as I travel.

I've been told that evil must exist because beings need to make their own decisions, and if evil is chosen, the being is marked and categorized as such. It there aren't categories, no one can identify their counterparts or comrades. Beings need, so I am told, classifications to assist in order. An order called society. I'm getting out of this, as I've said. The suitcase will be opened and filled with artefacts of declassification. If they even exist. I really hope they do, because I can't come back.

As I stood there, it became clear that if I wanted to leave, I'd better just do it. If he came after me physically, it would be to show emotion moreso than was practical; at least that's what I measured. Therefore, I thought if I just started to leave, there would be very little consequence from my mentoring kin. My father. I'd have to leave him, and expect consequences from others. I didn't say goodbye; I just said I'm sorry.

At the end of the path, mountains built like piles of broken glass lined the horizon. A jolting contrast to the furry card stock that is the landscape of evil grounds. Two cloaked evils stood at the end, maskless but stoic. They'd earn their masks soon; maybe this was their last go-round at the exit. I stopped, anticipating perhaps that this might be as far as I could go. I asked if Father sent them; I heard nothing. I asked if they were there to make sure I could not leave. One spoke, quietly with grit, just as we were taught. "We are here to make sure you don't come back."

I headed towards the shards of mountain peaks ahead,

feeling a light burn in the thighs as the elevation slowly increased. There was no pattern to the range, no discernible grouping, as if no peak belonged with another—but they could not be more interconnected. I knew I was heading in the right direction.

∞

Chris's First Two Options

1. *Only One Evil Can Stay on Earth*: The last evils on earth strike a deal to see who stays, and who needs to go.
2. *The Secret Job is Done, Payment is Made*: Two secret societies, normally rivals, work together for the first time to defeat a shared rival.

Conjuring Tricks

Cath Barton

They have been waiting since first light. It seems a strange place to wait, this expanse of parched grassland. Even more surprising when they arrived was the absence of a queue. Usually, applicants had been told, the queues stretch into the distance. But today there are just these two individuals, wearing the costumes issued to them on arrival. They have been given chairs, plush high-backed chairs more suited to a casting studio than the outdoors. They sit, they watch one another and they wait. Until, at last, one of them can no longer contain his curiosity.

"Come far, have you?" he asks the other, adding, without giving a chance to reply, "I'm Jan by the way. Old Dutch name—my mother dug it up from somewhere. It's taken me three weeks to get here, would you believe that? Three whole weeks. Ridiculous—it had better be worth it. Look how battered this suitcase is. Bloody baggage handlers. I'm not letting it out of my sight now."

The other appears to have brought nothing with him, unless he has a retinue around the corner. But on this featureless plain there is no corner around which anyone else could come into view. They are here, the one called Jan and the other who has not yet given his name, to audition for roles in a new painting by the Master for which the working title is *The Conjuror*. It is a site-specific piece, as is the fashion of the day.

"Weird there's only the two of us, I thought there'd be loads of people, didn't you, usually are for anything like this where I come from," says Jan. "How did you hear about it anyway? Me, I read it in *The Star*. Strange but true."

"In the stars?" says the other, finally getting a word in.

"Ha, ha, like your sense of humour! Nah, *The Star*,

newspaper, well, not much of a newspaper, more of a rag, but I like reading the small ads. You know, stuff like 'Rabbit hutch, £5, rabbit not included.' Ha, ha, bit of a laugh. And then there was this one. 'Artist seeks participants for new work. Excellent rates of pay.' And a phone number. Got me thinking. Make a change, I thought. Get me out of the house. Do something different. So I rang and got the info. Nice lady. Sounded foreign but good English, not like those call centre people. Sorry, I can see that you're foreign, no offence meant. Anyway, she was very pleasant. Not that she told me how long it would take to get here. Or about the camels."

"Camels?" The other looks alarmed. "We were supposed to bring our camels?"

"Nah, that was just to get the case here. My valise, as the camel boys called it. Very posh, they were. Long story, tell you another time. You're sensible, travelling light. Hang on though, what about your costume, er, what did you say your name was? Shocking memory I've got. Ever since the accident, long story, you'll have to excuse me."

"I go by the name of Melchior," says the other.

"Nice one," says Jan. "Stage name, is it? If I'm going to do any more of this kind of work I'll have to think about getting one of those. But, look here, I hope these auditions start soon. I'm bloody roasting in this outfit."

Applicants had been asked to attend on this day, in this place, and to dress as they would imagine those in a magician's audience. There would be in such a crowd, most probably (said the guidelines) those robed in carmine and the deep green of frogs, men with the extravagantly coiled silken headwear of the Orient and women with neat velvet caps topped off with lustrous feathers from the tails of male pheasants. Yet these two are wearing enveloping robes of cheap satin, dunces' caps and neutralising masks. The one wears light robes and a black mask; the other the inverse. The difference between them is nothing more or less than that between day and night.

It was advertised that the Master would arrive and the selection process commence when the sky was empty of cloud.

"Never seen so many clouds and it still be this hot," says Jan, pulling out a large handkerchief from a pocket and going to mop his brow, but finding that his mask gets in the way. "We could be waiting all bloody day."

Melchior nods. He knows only too well that clouds take time to travel and to disperse. He falls to thinking of clouds he has seen on his travels. Those summer scuddings across the vast skies of continental Europe after the hay has been cut. The hay which is built into high stacks, places where owls—creatures beloved of the Master, if he mentions this during the selection process, it will surely aid his chances, he thinks—pause on their daytime flights. And three continents away, the vast rising cumuli that presage the daily drenchings suffered across the archipelago by tuk-tuk drivers who must continue to work no matter what. He, Melchior, had sat in comfort in a small restaurant watching one such, in a distant time and place. Yet the tastes of that meal, its strange and subtle spicing, are in his mouth now as if he had eaten it only last night.

When Melchior returns to himself from his cloud-dreaming he sees that Jan is walking up and down and round about impatiently, as people often do when they are waiting, be it for transportation, to see a doctor or, as in this case, for the sky to clear. Melchior's gaze falls upon Jan's case, left there unattended, and he considers whether he might stand, walk towards it, lift it and feel its weight. This would, after all, be something to do, and could even offer him a kind of reassurance. He goes to stand, but something stops him. He does not feel fear. Yet the uncertainty about what will come next pins him down. He finds, though, that there are words demanding to be spoken.

"Your valise," he calls out to Jan. "You have left it unattended." The words leap from his mouth like sudden frogs.

"Leave it alone!" yells Jan as he hurries back, nearly tripping over his robe on the way. "Don't touch!"

If Melchior feels the rebuke in this response, if it stings him, Jan cannot tell, for his mask is without expression. Behind the masks, the black and the white, they must, these two, have their own distinct features. Jan may be swarthy, Melchior of a smooth and pale complexion. Or the other way round. Either way, their faces will surely be capable of expressing a variety of emotions—surprise, pain, anguish or even, though it is rarely required by the Master in his works, a sense of joy.

The pair fall silent once more, and the burden of things long carried hangs between them.

Far from clearing, the clouds now gather and darken. As the first pregnant drops of rain fall the applicants are beckoned forward and into a large tent that has appeared, or perhaps was there all the time, just out of sight. When Jan and Melchior emerge at length, it is late afternoon and the clouds have, finally, disappeared, as have the chairs.

"Well, that was something else, wasn't it?" says Jan. "That woman on the phone talked about jumping through hoops, but I didn't think she meant literally. I mean, you don't, do you? But I just went for it. I mean, you don't come all this way and refuse like a horse at the first fence, do you? Though the tantric contortions and lying on the sharp edge of a knife were a bit strong, didn't you think?"

"Excuse me, I am not understanding," says Melchior. "What is horse refusing?"

"Sorry, mate," says Jan. "Horse racing. Long story. Some other time. Got to be off now. Get to the place where they want us. Could take a while. See you there." And he leaves before Melchior can ask him to explain what "tantric" means.

Then a change of scene occurs, done with the conjuror's slight of hand, so that the shift is achieved as it is in the modern cinema, imperceptibly.

The new scene is set, some hundreds of years back, in a place as full as the grassy plain for the auditions was empty. From near and far come sounds soft and shrill, musical and harsh. There are noisome vapours from the ordure of animals upon the ground and from open sewers. A group of gypsies has arrived in this town and the call has gone out to locals to come and see a show, a performance of magic and mystery by a conjuror. Here is the tableau for which the Master has auditioned Jan, Melchior and others who must have arrived at the tent at the last minute and from another direction. Here is a motley crowd of men and women dressed in garments of rich stuffs and vibrant colours. They are all watching a man clad in red, at his feet a small hooded dog that has pricked up its ears at the distant baaing of sheep. The man in red has attached to his belt a wicker basket from which peeks the head of a little owl. The bird is a warning to the unwary, for there are rogues in the crowd, people who would pick pockets for the smallest prize. Or rather people playing that role.

"Here, get off me—stop pushing," says a man in the crowd, wrinkling his nose at the rank breath of the character pressing up against his back. This could be Jan. He would say something like that.

"Let us talk, afterwards," says another to his neighbour as they are called to silence and stillness so that the Master can do his work. This could be Melchior. The voice has his inflection.

The two of them are surely amongst the crowd, but altered. Identifying them now is nigh on impossible. The nearest match to their previous apparel is that of an androgynous nun, but of course they will both have put on a new disguise. Perhaps that is Melchior spitting a frog from his mouth, and that one further back, gazing lustfully upon a lady, could be Jan.

The sharp-nosed man in red holds aloft a small ball, which he would cause to disappear were he given the opportunity. But now his is a more difficult task, to hold that pose while the Master records the scene, however long that may take.

And here is the proof that the pair from the grassy plain are indeed in this scene. To the side of the group, out of the picture composed by the Master, lies the heavy suitcase belonging to Jan. It is open and has clearly been cast aside in a hurry. Clothes spill from it, a rich array, too much to have ever fitted within. There is no sign of the black and white garb worn by Jan and Melchior earlier today, or possibly yesterday, for who can say how much time has elapsed. Those anonymising costumes may already have been passed on to others who are, even now, setting out from distant times and places. Those who will come in the hope that they too may be chosen, for the Master has many projects.

∞

Cath's First Two Options

1. Two people carrying round their ancestors' ashes in a devastated world.
2. Two people who are rejects from a painting by a famous painter.

Gemini

Charlie Wilson

Two dolls sit on my dresser. Every morning, they tell me who I'm going to be today. One is all black with a white face. The other is all white with a black face. They both have long pointy hats and long robes and long eyes that say nothing and everything all at once. They used to be my mother's until one day she gave them to me.

"Mara," she said to me, "Listen to them. Keep them close." She didn't tell me what they were going to become, but somehow I knew anyway. I was a little girl then. I still believed in the Tooth Fairy. My mother was tall and round and warm, except for when she was small and flat and cold. She took me to school every morning and left a sticky pink kiss on my cheek. Her kisses were always the same, even though everything else changed.

After she gave me the dolls, she went away.

*

I work in an office full of other twenty-somethings with nowhere else to be. Most of my job is paperwork—or, more accurately, passing paperwork from one department to another. It's an important job, I'm told. The company wouldn't function without us.

I don't say: *Why don't they send it straight to the other department.* I don't say: *I'm a waste of a pay-cheque.* I don't say: *I hate you and I hate this place and I hate this city and I hate myself for being here.*

On the days when I'm one person, I say, "It feels so good to be vital to the company! I'm so glad to help." On the days when I'm the other, I say, "Sure."

My contracted hours are 9am-5pm with an hour for lunch.

I turn up at 8:55 or 9:05, depending on the day. I always leave at 5pm. Mornings are for work. Lunch, either at my desk or at the café down the street—never in the break room with the other employees—is a tasteless salad, with pine nuts or avocado sprinkled liberally around as if I actually enjoy eating those things. They're often exclaimed over by the people I work with—Sasha, our supervisor, who's 32 but pretends she's 28 and dyes her hair blonde every month at a salon that she can't really afford; Benny (never Ben, nor Benjamin), who cycles to work every morning and ruffles his hair when he takes off his helmet, leaving it flat at the back and messy at the front; and Cara, who laughed when she met me and declared us "twins" since our names rhyme. Sometimes, the office intern shows up—Vic, a kid whose hair changes as often as their pronouns. Sometime after they'd been there for three weeks, I gave up trying to remember. I should put more effort in. I don't.

Afternoons are spent anticipating the evenings, when we all grab our coats and saunter to the stairs, descending from the second floor in style. We wear high-heels and the type of office-wear more suited to a bar than to an office, our faces painted and nails buffed and hair coiffed. We split up for no longer than a couple of hours, always ending up at the same bar, *Gemini*, sitting together in a booth in the corner, laughing to ourselves as if this isn't sad and predictable.

It's funny because, no matter who I am, some things stay the same.

*

These days, bars aren't smoky. Dark, yeah, and loud—full of bad music and drunk people, the kind who've had two or three more than they should and somewhere along the line forgot that yelling isn't the only form of communicating. Tonight, I'm one of those people.

I could claim that it's all Benny's fault—he was the first one who screamed, "Shots!" as if it weren't a Wednesday night—but really, I have no one to blame but myself. Today's a black-dress-white-face-doll day. It means that I'm leaning against the bar with an ache in my side that's half from dancing and half from laughing. The warm-queasy feeling in my stomach, the one that's neither entirely pleasant nor unpleasant, is at the forefront of my mind, making me think that maybe I should order water next. Cara leans against me, giggling into my shoulder, her mouth wet against my skin. I wonder if her lipstick will leave a mark, but then I catch sight of myself in the mirror behind the bar—black dress, hair half fallen out of its bun, pink lipstick all but rubbed off—and realise that it doesn't matter either way.

That's when the bartender turns to me. She looks harried, stressed that this place is so packed with people when she was expecting a quiet mid-week night, but I don't spare her much more than a glance. I'm staring at my own reflection when I tell her we want two vodka shots. After I pay, I slide one in front of Cara. She blinks at it blearily and giggles again, wobbling on her stilettos.

"No," she moans, the protest more for show than anything else. "I can't! No more!"

I raise an eyebrow at her and down mine in one motion. I'm long past feeling the burn by now. She follows suit a minute later and bangs the glass back on the bar, coughing as she does so.

"Ooh, I hate you!" she exclaims. Drunk Cara never *says* anything. "Why do I let you do this to me?"

I shrug and pull her away from the bar. I don't feel like talking tonight, instead leading her straight onto the dance floor, or what passes for a dance floor in a place like this, where the light-effects focus on the wooden floor as if that changes anything about it, and we lose ourselves against each other in a rhythm born from years of familiarity. It's comfortable and blurry and it lets me float for a while. I wish I could be grateful.

*

On Monday, after five days of black-dress-white-face, the white-dress-black-face looks at me and tilts its head. I feel my heart clench.

I go for a jog, ignoring the pounding in my head and the aches in my body after last night's excesses. I don't go far—the same route every time, the one that takes 32 minutes—and when I get back, I drink a half-pint of water and make myself a smoothie. I leave that on the side as I shower then drink it while I get dressed, smoothing my outfit into place with steady hands.

Before I leave the house, I stare at my reflection. I look good. More than that, though, I look like a *good girl.* My hair is in a neat chiffon. My make-up is light, natural, the pale pink lipstick the only splash of extravagance. I'm wearing a blouse that buttons to my neck and a knee-length skirt, with mid-heeled shoes. From head to toe, I'm the image of *nice.* I bare my teeth in the mirror. It's the last bit of truth I'll show until I get ready for bed tonight.

Today's salad—avocado and kale—goes down like cement. I sit all afternoon with it in my stomach, all my focus on the way it just *sits* there, the bitter taste in the back of my mouth never going away. When Benny stops by my desk to complain about his hangover, I smile sweetly and hand him a bottle of water from the bottom of my desk, cooing over him and telling him to find me if he needs painkillers. I take a sip of my own drink—chamomile tea, unsweetened and unsatisfying—and I'm filled with the overwhelming urge to throw it across the room, just to watch the carnage it would cause. The urge doesn't pass, but I don't act on it. I can't.

At the bar that night, I smile demurely at the bartender and ask for an orange juice. I sit in the corner and cross my legs at the ankle. I tell jokes and my colleagues smile back at me. I don't dance. I don't take a shot.

Sasha sips her rum-and-coke and watches me with frown lines etched into her forehead. I want to tell her that she's showing her age tonight, that she looks closer to forty than thirty. I want to tell her that pink is *not* her colour and that, if she had any sense of propriety at all, she wouldn't go drinking with her subordinates every night of the week. I want to snarl and spit at her.

I ask, "Are you okay?"

She smiles. "I was going to ask you the same question." I don't know how to respond. I think it's clear on my face, because she smiles again, a smaller, bitter smile that makes me uncomfortable. She shrugs and adds, "There are days when...

you're so different, you know? The others call them your good days and your bad days."

Curious, I ask, "What was today?"

She raises her eyebrows and glances at the bar, where Benny is trying desperately to convince Cara he's straight by ogling her breasts. "They'd say it's one of your good days."

"And what would you say?" I push, tightening my grip on my orange juice. It's gone warm in my hands, a puddle of condensation making a ring on the table beneath it.

She looks at me. It's uncomfortable and leaves me feeling vulnerable, as if she'd peeled back my skin to take a peek at what's underneath.

"What?" I demand, nerves prickling at the back of my neck.

She shrugs and leans back in the booth. "If I were going to call it anything, I'd call it one of your lying days."

I stare at her. My heart stutters in my chest, a fluttering sensation that makes me want to throw up. "I don't understand," I tell her. I lie to her.

She nods, as if that's what she expected to hear. She takes a sip of her drink and I watch the cool, casual motion as if she hadn't split me in two with one sentence. I hate her.

"I don't understand either," she tells me. "But Mara, if you ever need anything... You know we're your friends, right?" She stares at me, brown eyes to grey ones, and I think she can see how much I hate her. I think she can see everything. I don't know how I never saw it before. "Whatever you need, we'll help you."

She's lying, too.

*

The night my mother leaves, she acts completely normal. It's one of her lying days. She's been kind and sweet all day, going out of her way to cook my father's favourite meal, to clean and iron his shirts for the next week. At 8:30pm she takes me upstairs to read me a story, and I get a kiss on the cheek from my father, a grinning man who never stopped grinning, even after she was long gone. He calls me his "muffin" and I loved him for it until I hated him for it.

In my bedroom, wearing my Pooh Bear pyjamas with the taste of mint fresh in my mouth, my mother sits beside me. I am eight years old. There's no book in her hands. There's a lie on her lips, stretched into a smile, but there's truth in her eyes.

"Mara," she says, "I love you."

I don't know if that's a truth or a lie.

She sets the dolls on my bedside table and she tells me to listen to them. She tells them they were hers, and her mother's, and her grandmother's. She tells them that one day, I'll give them to my daughter. She looks sad when she says that.

Next to the dolls, she puts a small tube of lipstick. She doesn't explain that, but I understand anyway. It's her shade. It's my shade, now. She kisses my forehead and leaves a sticky mark there, one that she doesn't bother rubbing away.

"Sleep well, my love," she says. I am eight years old. She calls me "my love" and I think I can see the truth of it on her lips, even though they should be forming a lie. She's whole, for once, telling truths with her mind and body.

I am eight years old when she splits me in half. I never see her again, but the dolls stay.

∞

Charlie's First Two Options

1. A conversation between Life and Death.
2. The people setting up the scene in the photo.

The Fly Catchers

Nicola Thompson

Of course you don't run out into the desert. That's stupid. If someone wants to kill you, and you run into the desert, all you're doing is your enemy a favour. Stupid. Stupid. Stupid.

But that's me. I'm the moron who thought that I could lose them under the heat of the Nevada sun, that the blanket of empty sapphire sky against the red of the sands would cloak me into the safety of nothingness. I suppose that's exactly what it did, though.

I disappeared. Perhaps not the way I would have liked to, but I did it. Actually, I did it a little too well. I think I must have been drugged by the idiotic decisions I had made. I wasn't thinking. My brains were sizzling and I kept moving away from the city, away from what I thought was the real danger. But what is more dangerous? Guns? Or *maybe* roasting alive in the desert? I thought it was the men carrying the guns, personally, but it was May, and extra hot. Like, a hundred degrees hot. Like people in the Sahara Desert at high noon would be complaining kind of hot.

It didn't matter. They were after me, had my details—my purse, in fact. They had my money, my phone, my ID, and my damn cigarettes. I had to keep going.

You know, Las Vegas isn't that big once you're in it. I hear a lot of tourists marvel at its size, its colour and flashing lights. But once you consider that's just the Strip, there's not much more to it. And when you consider how many people live there, make their money there illegally, the town is pretty small. There's no way to hide in a place like that. And where else do you go if you're running on a whim? All there is, is the desert.

I must have been dragging my feet along in the sand, kicking up stones, stumbling along for maybe 45 minutes, possibly an hour. In that heat, it felt like days, like that scene in *Beavis and Butthead Do America* when they're crawling through the desert. "The sun sucks." But I wasn't crawling yet. Just keeping a watchful eye out that I wasn't falling onto any scorpion nests when I stumbled.

A singular scorpion nest might be preferable, perhaps. I mean, after all, if the Charlie Brown gang—yeah, no joke, that's what they call themselves—found me, they might stick me in a pen full of scorpions. Even now, I couldn't be sure they weren't just toying with me, letting me get a head start so that I had the illusion of potential safety. Who knows, those guys are crazy.

What I did know was that my mouth was dry, my throat was sticking to itself, and I was losing clothing against the heat. As improper as it might be, I was down to my bra, my shirt wrapped around my head, and I was contemplating losing my jeans too, for whatever good it might do me. My fine, Irish skin that my Southern Baptist mother had been so proud of was already suffering. It would blister. No doubt about that. And worse of all, I was dying for a smoke, which was doing my stamina no favours.

Okay, I'm not entirely innocent in this. I slept with the wrong dude and happened to notice the rather large zip-lock of colourful pills in his possession... in his bedside drawer, that he kept locked... with a key around his neck. I might have ensured he continued drinking heavily enough to put him in a deep, passed-out state to procure said pills.

Hey, don't judge. I had student loans, and I was behind a payment or three. I could only do so much working as a waitress in Vegas. Part of me thought maybe if I got in with one of the gang, maybe he could help me out. But then again, maybe I could help myself out. Those pills would sell—

I stopped mid-thought. I had been mulling over my stupidity, trying to find a way of reasoning, bargaining with the gang if they caught up with me. All the while, I was running, tripping, crawling, jogging, hoping I never had to say a word to them.

However, with what I saw before me, my movement

slowed, nearing to a stop, though I was too afraid to stop. My legs were threatening me, warning that if they rested, it would be for hours. And with what I saw in front of me, I thought there might be a chance I would need to start hurrying again.

I must have been three miles out of the city, yet there before me were two figures in plush, expensive-looking computer chairs, leaned back, as though bored and waiting. Something was between the two of them, square. A table maybe? No, it was a suitcase.

They sat there, motionless. As I neared—because what else was I going to do?—they remained still. I could see them better now; one of them was in a black robe, with a long, thin, uppointed cap, almost like some KKK member, or goth wizard. The other, dressed in a matching robe, though stark white, angled toward the first. I wasn't even certain they were real. The one in the black robe had a plastic mask on—was it a mask? No, its entire face, neck, hands, all completely white, matching the whiteness of his companion's get-up, smooth, like a mannequin. The one in the white robe also matched, though was completely black, like onyx. They were like the embodiment of yin and yang.

The suitcase between them was old, beat-up. I think I had seen one in my professor's office, used as a book table. That's all it was good for.

My own movement was at a sluggish, falling step, my knees threatening to buckle with my weight. I had heard that the desert makes you see things, that it's not uncommon to hallucinate. I just thought it was urban bull. Yet here I was, seeing these statues, some weird ass art piece, in the middle of nowhere.

I approached the one in the black robe. It was just a statue. Nothing else. A dummy.

Weird prank, I thought.

I began patting at the thing, thinking maybe its owner, creator, artist—whatever—might have left a bottle of water or something behind. The body of the thing was plush, but crinkly, like a Halloween scarecrow stuffed with dry leaves.

"If it's water you want," a voice said. "You need only to look in the case."

I stumbled back, flinching at the clarity of the voice,

androgynous and familiar. I spun around—searching the horizon for anything else living. There was nothing but the grim ripples of the desert heat.

"Man," I said to myself. "My brains are scrambled."

"The water you seek is in the suitcase," the voice repeated. I jumped around again, looking for anything, anyone that might be playing this trick on me. I began shifting at the dummy closest to me, looking for a speaker before moving to the next one.

"We would appreciate it if you refrained from touching us," the voice requested. I recoiled from the one in the white robe. "Our invitation stands to drink from our case."

This time I listened, hard, trying to distinguish the direction the voice was coming from. I couldn't. It was as if it was already inside my head.

It probably was inside my head. I was going batty. Loop-de-loop.

Wacko or not, my throat was beginning to burn from the heat of my breath. I needed H_2O, and *now.* I crept toward the ancient thing between the two dummies. It was perched upright on its spine, cracked leather belt, buckled it at the top. I didn't realize that my fingers were suffering the same burn bubbling the skin on my shoulders until I bent them to undo the case. But the idea of water was worth my splitting knuckles.

I let the case fall apart, each of its sides going opposite, lying flat. And empty.

I leaned back and was on my butt, the dirt hot through my jeans, just staring at the thing.

Good move, Janelle, I scolded myself. *Listening to voices in your head.*

Sitting felt good. The sun did not. I needed to keep moving.

There was a gurgle sound before the susurration of the stream birthed from the middle of the suitcase. Some unseen spout was pushing water—*water!*—from the tiny gap between the two rusting hinges of the suitcase. My bewilderment didn't outmatch my thirst, which launched me forward, almost diving into the bag, sticking my whole head in one of its halves. I gulped at the refreshing liquid with my face submerged, suppressing a moan. My shirt, wrapped around my head like a scarf, grew heavy as it soaked up the liquid. I submerged it in the water, drenching it, before pulling it over my shoulders and bra. My skin drank in the cool and I plunged my head back into the seemingly endless depths of the suitcase half.

I didn't even notice that I could have gone for a swim in its depths. All I knew was that I needed the water like I needed air, and I swapped back and forth between the two until I had my fill.

My chestnut hair lapping over my face, my ponytail dripping pleasantly down my back, I sat back and stared at the stream burbling from the middle of the piece of luggage, which was slowing, slowing, stopped. The water settled, mirroring the sky, then began to lower until the suitcase was completely dry.

What the hell had I just seen? I was hydrated, I was wet, so it couldn't have been a hallucination.

A crack in the distance echoed. A gun.

My head whipped around, and, to my horror, a plume of dust rose from behind the black dot of a car, racing from where I had run from to my very spot. They were coming for me after all.

I'm not a fit girl. I smoke, I eat diner food at work, I melt in the heat. Running, exercise, even when I'm filled with adrenaline, is not my strong suit. I tried to stand, and my legs weakened at the knees, causing me to collapse. I tried again, trying to keep myself steady, to be slow, while inside my head I was screaming at myself—*Move! Move! Move!*

"Hide in our suitcase," the voice said.

"What?!" I demanded of the two mannequins.

"Do not hesitate to use it, if you wish," it replied, calm, as if it was explaining the history of cigars.

I could hear the engine of the car now, at full speed, hurtling my way, the cloud behind it growing as the tires kicked up the dust. There was no way I could outrun that. And where would I run to? It was flat in every direction I looked.

The suitcase had just created a spring out of nothing. Maybe this voice was on to something. After all, what were my options? I wasn't going to outrun the car. Die now, or die trying another idiotic decision.

"What the hell," I mumbled to myself, scrambling on all fours toward the open carrier. It wasn't endless. There was the royal purple lining, just like any other old suitcase. I put my butt in, tucked my knees up against my chest, reached for the corresponding side and pulled it up.

I was falling.

I didn't fall far. I mean, when I landed, I didn't break anything. It was dark, and it did feel like I was on shallow, long stairs, the kind you could draw a decent enough sized picture on if you had chalk. I couldn't see what I landed on though. It was completely black. And better yet—completely cool and out of the sun. I couldn't hear anything from the desert, no car, no guns, nothing. Somewhere, though, was a distant drip.

"You are safe from your danger," the voice said, echoless, separate of the drip. It had to be in my head. Maybe I was already dead, and this was the result of the DMT being released in my brain. Isn't that what's supposed to happen? My final trip before I fade into nothing.

There was a glow from somewhere. I can't even say where it came from, because I had no directional sense in the blackness. But it grew, and I was able to see the shape of the place I was in. It was definitely a cave. With the growing light, I looked up to see where I had come from. I only saw the glint of damp on the cave ceiling, which sloped low enough to hit my head on if I stood.

My jeans were wet in the butt area; my arms were too. Everything was wet. I felt the floor where I had been leaning back on my elbows to find an algae kind of slime carpeting it. Definitely underground. This wasn't something you really found in the desert.

The light came around a corner, dull brightness of blue tinged with white.

It was running along what looked like a stick, and compiling in a large bulb at the stick's head. The hand carrying it looked weak, twig-like, from what I could see of it, before it disappeared into a robe, a very similar design to the dummies in the computer chairs. The being was shorter though, and the hood neither as elongated nor erect. It just hung back, in a point off its head, which obscured the being's face. The light only served to demonstrate the absence of light, which was this being, a silhouette against the blue.

"It is required that you follow me," the voice said, without atmosphere, without reverberating within the cave, a communication from whatever its source into my mind.

Maybe I should have been scared, maybe I should have asked questions—whatever. I don't know. But I will tell you this. I'd been running in the hot, midday sun with no water, yet somehow had ended up in a damp, dark tunnel. At this point, I really was convinced I was dead, that the gnawing in my chest for a cig was just part of the experience. What did I have to lose? Maybe the initial gunshot I heard actually *had* killed me, and the rest was just my dying brain juices.

I moved myself into a crouched stance, being mindful of the low ceiling, though it sloped upward, eventually allowing my average height to be accommodated. As I caught up to the... whatever it was, I towered over it, by at least a foot and a half. I'm maybe five-foot-five? If that? I don't know, I always lied on my driver's license, and never paid attention when doctors corrected me. Either way, this thing was *bitty*.

It took me down a hall, and put its light-stick in a holster on the wall, and continued to walk. Darkness only closed in briefly before brilliance entrenched us. The entire hall began to glow—all its walls, the floor, the ceiling, all of it produced this blue-white light, sometimes transitioning to a green-white, but mostly sticking to the blue. The hue was magical, something doused in fairy magic lore and brought to life. The magnitude of it caught my breath, which rumbled slightly in my lungs (though that might have just been phlegm).

"It's called bioluminescence," the voice said. "Come with me."

I continued to follow it, breathing in the oddly fresh smell of the cave. It reminded me of camping on the Olympic Peninsula in Washington, where lakes reached their wetness into the branches of the trees. The air even tasted like water, cooling my lungs, my muscles, my skin.

The hallway opened into another room, a large room. I wondered if I had somehow found my way to the centre of the Earth, that maybe all those nerds in geology departments were wrong, that the Earth's core was slime and glowing plants, *Journey to the Centre of the Earth* style.

For the first time, there was enough light for me to fully see more than the shadowed outline of the guy leading me. The room gaped, revealing lofts of passageways clustered with beings moving, like a beehive. In the centre of the ceiling, one of those cave-spikes hung, almost directly to the ground, perhaps ending ten feet above it, and completely covered with the bio-light stuff.

The space was warmer, I assume from so many bodies moving. The goosebumps forming along my arms soothed, and I could feel the damp moving into my chest. While the movement never stilled, all the heads turned to stare at me, and I thought I heard some of them whispering "oxygen breather" to one another. They all wore the same long-hooded gear, though with the glow of the cave I could make out the shininess of their masks, much like the mannequins with the suitcase. They were either paper white or pitch black. There was no variation. Just smooth, plastic faces without movement or expression. Their garb differed slightly from the one leading me. They all wore long hooded cloaks; that was the same. But they were different shades of greens, and some even browns and oranges, like leaves turning in fall.

As I followed the initial itty-bitty into the crowd, I saw they weren't hoods at all, but actually *part* of these beings. They were *leaves*—massive singular leaves to act as one hood on each creature. Though some of them didn't have leaves, but rather straggly strands of brown grass, an overflow of padded moss, and one of them even just had a mushroom cap for a "hood".

The crowd did little to ease my passage, but as I pushed by, they were light yet solid, reminding me of thick bamboo poles, the thickness of your arm, but hollow. I could hear their whispers, without echo, without atmosphere, just the voiceless communion of overlapped "*oxygen breather.*"

It was more than just the echoless voices; a feeling came across with the noise. They weren't just using words, they were transferring emotions, like their voices, in a form of motionless emoting. I felt their curiosity, little twinges and pulls of nervousness, and a hunger, a *needing* hunger. It wasn't sexual, wasn't an appetite, but a bodily craving. Like a soulful wanting, needing to be touched. The need of connection, but to the depth of survival.

Oxygen breather.

"Why are they calling me that?" I found myself demanding over the voices reverberating in my brain. My voice echoed, sending the hisses to silence, and ceasing the emoting.

"You breathe oxygen," the singular voice replied, which I assumed belonged to the being I followed.

"Well, yeah. But would that imply that you don't?"

"Carbon, actually. Dioxide, to be more specific."

The room sloped to the next hall, and the leader plucked another bioluminescent torch from the wall as it passed. It lit the passage enough for me to see the glint of the dampness and the height of the ceiling, which was high enough for me this time. We plunged into darkness, guided only by the blue light outlining the itty-bitty.

"Where are we going?" It was the first time I thought to ask it. My curiosity, acting as adrenaline, was faltering, and fear started to course through me. I was fairly certain at this point that I wasn't dead, that this was something I was actually experiencing. Things began to click in my brain. I took biology in college, a couple classes, even. How had I not seen exactly what this all was?

The voice remained silent.

"You're a plant," I blurted, feeling stupid as the words left my face.

"You're an animal," the voice replied.

"No, I'm a person."

"Perhaps," the voice responded, the itty-bitty showing no sign of being a part of the interaction. "But you are an animal person. We could be put into the plant genre, but we are people too."

"Where are we going?" I repeated, trying to sift through the growing nervousness.

"I could answer that, but surely you would have to have a concept of where you are now in order for me to fully disclose our destination. Do you know where you are, currently?"

I didn't. The brisk, damp of the air filled my gaping mouth as I tried to produce a response. But I had none. The idea again posited in my brain that perhaps I was dead, and this was the dying brain chemicals, or that the afterlife was far more bizarre than theologians had surmised. If that was the case, then there wouldn't really be any harm that could be done, could there? Perhaps the suitcase had ported me to another dimension, another planet. I could be underground on Mars or Titan for all I knew. Or I could be in an alternate reality where plants had evolved to be the dominant species.

The last idea struck fear in me. I didn't know if that was because it seemed most ridiculous or most plausible. If I was somehow on a planet in the solar system, in this universe, then at least then there were certain laws of physics and reality that had to be adhered to. I felt quite clever at coming up with that last bit of logic.

However, if I had somehow stumbled into an alternative dimension, some other reality where plants had evolved into humanoid creatures, then what was the rest of the world like? Why were we underground, why did they seem to know what I was, and how on Earth (was it Earth?) did I get here?

"Are we still on Earth?" I ventured, terrified of the answer.

"We call her Gaia, but yes, we are."

The voice changed, not in tone, volume, or speech pattern, but in the emoting that seeped through it. That feeling of need accented it, like sun trying to break through a rain cloud. Except what was really prominent was the cloud, a foreboding darkness that surrounded the end of the sentence like a threatening piece of punctuation. I was being warned.

A chill settled through me, though not of the cold. It's one thing when you hear a tone in someone's voice and interpret it. It's an entirely different experience when a threat is projected into your cells, courses through your blood and infiltrates the creases of your being.

I struggled to keep each foot following one after the other. Left. Right. Repeat. But what were my options? Run back, into the mass of them? Knock the itty-bitty over and run forward, to whatever might lay ahead? The last time I acted irrationally, I ran into the desert and wound up in this situation. Where would it take me this time?

Be cool, Janelle, I told myself as the flesh along my arms rose. Meanwhile, the drive for some nicotine was edging me closer to something paranoid, my usual irritability transforming into anxiety.

As my mind caught itself in a loop of my options—stay calm and continue on, run back, or push and run—the hall began to widen again. This space, too, was lit in the blue and green white light of the algae. And through it, I could make out the many beings lining the floor, on multiple tiers. There must have been at least a hundred lumps of life, their chests rising and falling in their own rhythm. They were human! And some animals as well, but mostly, unequivocally, human.

They appeared to be sedated, with masks over their heads, like those creepy World War II masks with the hoses coming from them. The stench of the place was nauseating. It didn't take full lighting for me to realize they were all living in their own filth through their sedation.

As I was about to demand what the hell was going on, I stopped, as the bleak understanding settled over me: this was my fate.

"Nope," I said, reversing my step. "Nope, nope, nope, nope, nope, nope."

"There is nowhere for you to go," the voice said. There was a calmness snaking its way around me, a dangerous calmness. This was more than a soothing voice; it was trying to *lull* me into complacency. "Stay here."

But I was already scrambling backward, slipping on the damp of the floor in my Converse, falling to my knees on the rough, rock floor.

I picked myself back up, with the grace of a panicked, wet cat. I disappeared down the black tunnel.

Now, you need to hear me right: I *disappeared* in the black tunnel.

There was no light, nothing. It seemed as though there was no air, even. My breath caught in my chest as it squeezed everything out of me. I felt nothing outside my being: no temperature, no motion, no pressure, nothing. I was nothing.

My mouth opened and closed like a gold fish at a carnival, except they can at least breathe. There was nothing for me, and I was beginning to suffocate. My lungs were bursting for something to replace the expelled carbon dioxide, but even that didn't seem to be available. The blackness, the nothingness, was consuming me.

My vision began to fade.

It's silly, the notion of vision blanking into nothingness when we are talking about the darkest darkness that one can experience without being dead. But it was a mauve fuzziness that shined through the darkness to envelop my consciousness, nudging the nothingness along, taking hold to nuzzle me to sleep.

I've never been able to sleep through daylight. I've had to install black-out curtains in my bedroom just so I can sleep through the summer mornings. In high school, I had cool-blue Christmas lights in my bedroom to keep vigil during the night. But for all that they failed to provide enough light to see anything by, I couldn't nod off with them on. They were too bright.

It was the same cool-blue that woke me, confusing me, making me wonder if I had somehow been transported back to my parents' house five years ago.

But you know how this goes. You know full well that's not how this ends. It seems almost boring to fill you in on the glowing details that brought me back to life, that forced me to recall my far more sinister fate than death.

It wasn't the itty-bitty I had been following that was silhouetted against the bio-lights, looming over me, but rather the mushroom-head. I could feel its relief as I gasped for air, as the pain of emptiness burst through my lungs. It projected into me a sloppy, drunk tranquility, leaning further forward with each breath I struggled for.

"If you do not want your fate, then you shouldn't run from us. You only urge us further," it informed.

I began coughing, bringing up phlegm and spewing it from my chest at its feet. The urge for a smoke was almost pushing the fresh air from my body, while my lungs battled to keep it, devour it. I could feel the thing's repulsion at my act, and thought I saw its shadowed figure lean back.

"You're defective," it said.

"I need a smoke," I snapped.

The initial itty-bitty approached, emoting its pleasure at seeing me caught. There was communication between the two, the same whispered hiss I had heard as I walked through the forest of them in the dome room, yet too shallow for me to understand. The term *defective* rang through my mind, repeating in a loop, like a bad rap beat. Their projected emotion altered to concern, fear, repulsion, and the term slowly morphed to *tainted.*

I felt repugnant, disgusting. Yet the mucus in my lungs kept coming, no matter how much I tried to suppress it to make out what the two were communicating between them. Blobs of the stuff were coming up into my mouth, rolling over my tongue, and I expelled them, hacking the stuff at them.

Tainted. Defective.

The recognition hit me, the room brightening to me with my understanding. I remembered the sedated people, beings, lying in their own waste with the masks on, and knew: I was tainted. This would be my saving grace. They needed me to breathe, just like they needed the sedated people to breathe. Of course! I was a smoker, a pack-and-a-half-a-day girl. I would only pollute their own respiration.

I had no idea if that was true, if that was something that could actually be problematic. After all, they hadn't seemed to mind as I was being led to the room. If they hadn't known then, would they know now?

"You require medication," the mushroom-head said. Its voice was indistinguishable from the other; I could only separate them by its motion in my direction.

I could feel their annoyance through my silence, as I didn't click on to their meaning.

"Your sap," it urged, pushing forward its disgust. I spat more to the floor, and it shifted back, hastily. There were enough globs to form a gelatinous puddle. "It is a defect. You need medication, your *smoke.*" I felt its uncertainty at the word, unsure if that was really what it meant.

"Yes," I replied without hesitation. They resumed their whispering. I could feel the rattle in my chest from another bout of coughing trying to rupture, but kept it down. I could just about make out, "... may not last long...", "... tainted carbon...", "... But it demands...", before I gave up trying.

"Enough!" the initial itty-bitty emoted toward the mushroom-head. "It is defective, it will go to Rajah."

"But it would serve better—" mushroom-head protested.

"It would only go to Rajah before long without its *smoke.* It will only die, and must be dealt with. The live offering will please our Lord."

"It must be done," mushroom-head agreed.

I scrambled backward, frantically kicking them away as they reached for me. I was on my hands, crab-walk style, trying to move as fast as I could, until the side of my face met furiously with the solid, craggy wall. It was enough to speckle my vision with stars while they retrieved me. As they pulled at me, their hollowed bodies suddenly rigid and strong, I gave up.

I could feel the bloody trickle of warm transcend to chill down my face as I dragged my feet along the corridors of the cave. They had bound my wrists in twine, pulling me along. I hardly noticed the fetor of stagnant bodies as we made our way along the rows of them. Humans. Dogs. Rats. Armadillos. Hares. All sedated, with masks attached to their faces in a bed of faecal sludge.

I followed with the remainder of my energy as the room closed to another hallway. The place was a maze of tunnels dotted with rooms. I was going to die, I knew that much. Whoever this Rajah thing was seemed unlikely to keep me around, not if I was "defective."

I hacked again, my lungs aching from the residual sensation of suffocation, aching further for my nicotine fix. I spat, causing the itty-bitties to swerve slightly in avoidance, even though that thick splatter of it landed nowhere near them.

What did I have to live for anyway? The sake of living? If I got out of this mess, what would happen then? Who would I tell? Would I tell anyone? Would I suddenly summon bravery and destroy the mannequins? It was a nice thought, but I'm a runner, not a fighter. I felt deflated, defeated, defective.

A hum reverberated through the tunnel, faint at first, though growing as we marched closer to the next open cave chamber. The room glowed neon green, far brighter than the bioluminescent lighting I had seen before. I could taste the sweetness in the air, like nectar, reaching through my nasal passages and caressing the back of my tongue, soothing my craving body. *Blissful* would fall short of the euphoria wrapping petals around me, like a mythical siren urging me closer.

There was a giddiness to my captors, a buzz that seemed to lighten their steps, their hold on the twine binding me. I hardly noticed the slack. I was transfixed, spellbound by the tasteful energy pulsing from the room we were about to enter.

The floor of the cave slanted downward easily, finishing in a wide, gaping hole from which the lambent green was sourced. From the cavernous well breached a magnificent, fleshy, amaranth-collared petal, speckled slightly with dark red and black spots. Vines climbed the walls, meekly twinkling their own light, which paled to nothingness in the awesomeness of the ambient luminosity. Love coursed from my captors and from the thing in the hole. Their Lord. Rajah. If I knew no other thing, I knew that this being *was* Light, the Sun personified as a plant. No burning, no blinding brightness, but simply as something that primitive understandings of the sky might have called God.

I wanted to be in its presence... "Forever," I whispered absently.

"And you will be," the echoless voice replied.

"What?"

"You have a holy role, oxygen-breather," it continued. "You shall feed our Divine Lord, who in turn shares Its Light with us, providing us our food and warmth."

"Praise It," the other said.

"What?" I gawked, telling myself to pull away, to rip myself from the laxed grips of the plant people. But the Love and glow of this *thing* swaddled me in comfort, having a force of its own, and animated my steps forward.

Fight! I urged myself. There was nothing. My body was no longer my own. It belonged to Rajah. The ledge was leering nearer, and I had full view of the being below: the gaping gullet of some carnivorous plant I had seen in my biology class, its sweet digestive liquid pooled in its throat. As fear niggled at me, a wave of Love pulsed through me, with such veracity that my step faltered. I toppled forward, the neon green enveloping me into nothingness.

*

That isn't the end of my story. No, you have found me, after all. I, like you, found myself in the desert, in the middle of nowhere. I, too, came across the robed beings void of motion, ample in magic. And oh yes, there is a magic here.

In some sense, I have always been here, watching, waiting, assisting. I have been, and always will be a Charger of the Sun, the collector of nutrients for our Lord Rajah, and I, Its vessel. My counterpart in white brings down the energy of the Moon, while I, in my black robe, attract and absorb the energy of the Sun. Together, we are the Catchers, catchers of light, energy, sustenance for our people.

Janelle is still inside me, still part of me. It is she who remembers. I am just the vessel. Eventually Rajah will be done with her, will have digested her, and she will fade from me, just as the others have. I saw her approach, just as I saw your arrival, dust kicking up behind your tires, your guns exploding behind your triggers.

Unfortunately, she is gone, for your purposes, and, perhaps, to your satisfaction. However, I offer an alternative opportunity to you. I have told you the world inside our suitcase. I have provided a verbal map to a world you can overtake. If the plant people don't find you, if you're not accosted to be farmed, who knows the possibilities ahead of you.

Go on. Trust us, oxygen breathers. Step into our suitcase. After all, they're just plants.

What's the worst that can happen?

∞

Nicola's First Two Options

1. In the heat of the sun, two wizards sit, waiting impatiently. They have a package that is of the utmost importance, and they must be sure that the right individual collects it. However, they don't know who the being is, what is in the package (concealed in the suitcase), or when the collector is meant to arrive. So they wait, discussing their curiosity at the situation, which leads on to philosophical topics of debate. Before it goes too far into this, something arrives, a

bird, and they try a number of tests to see if this being is actually the collector. They decide it's not, and shoo it away. A knight arrives, and they attempt to produce the same tests, only for the knight to fend them off, and steal the package.

2. There's a convention in Phoenix, Arizona, and Phillis and Ester's car has broken down on the way. They wait for their lift in their costumes, with their make-up within the suitcase.

Becoming Death's Personal Assistant

L.G. Keltner

The heavy bass of generic dance music rattled Roxy's bones as she stumbled away from the undulating throng of people in pursuit of a restroom. Strobing multi-coloured lights swept across the room, befuddling her alcohol-fuzzed senses. An errant hand swept across her backside, but she didn't bother to identify it. Her goal had been to drink enough so nothing seemed bothersome and she'd accomplished that goal.

Becoming unbothered was almost worth the pain in her knees when she hit the tile floor and dunked her head into the toilet bowl. The retching, which painfully strained muscles Roxy hadn't previously known she possessed, resurrected a fraction of her ability to be irritated, but she couldn't focus on said irritation while vomiting her brains out. Once she'd rid her stomach of all its contents, her brain got back on track again. She took stock of the mess she'd made, and while the toilet itself had seen better days, she was pleased to see the floor had escaped mostly unscathed.

As Roxy wiped her mouth with the back of her hand, something written on the inside of the stall captured her attention. The words were large, red, and clearly not scrawled in pen like most bathroom stall messages. There was a drip effect, indicating it had taken a little while for the letters to dry. Nail polish, maybe. Or paint. Or blood, she thought with a grin. That would be an overly dramatic way to go about it. While she typically wouldn't take the time to read bathroom stall messages, she found herself leaning in close. The words appeared to be wobbling, but after a second, Roxy realized that she was the one doing the wobbling.

Do you want to see the world and meet interesting people?

Do you long for a career that accommodates your flexible sense of morality?

Are you tired of the ephemeral nature of human existence and long to find something more reliable?

If you answered yes to all these questions, you might have what it takes to be Death's Personal Assistant. Call 1-800-DEATHPA to apply.

Death is an Equal Opportunity Employer.

That last line earned a giggle from her. "Death really doesn't discriminate. That's good to know." Roxy grinned as she unzipped her purse and fished out her phone. "Drunk dialling Death from the bathroom floor. That's a new low for me. Monty would love this."

Monty. She knew she should visit him sometime. How long had it been? Three months? She considered texting him instead, but decided against it. That would only remind her how much she missed going on their crazy adventures and she didn't feel like being sad. She'd moved to Hollywood to have a good time and make a name for herself. Weeping to her best friend next to a toilet didn't fit into that picture.

It took several tries to get the number right. When the phone finally began to ring, she sank back on her heels and leaned against the door. A toilet flushed somewhere to her right, making her flinch.

"Hello."

The word sounded deep and rich. A man's voice. Not a bad voice for Death to have, she supposed. "Hello, there," Roxy slurred brightly. "I'm calling about the job ad."

There was a pause and shuffling of papers on the other end. "What Earthly ties do you have?" Death asked matter-of-factly.

She made a face. "Pardon?"

"What keeps you tethered to the world of the living?" The voice down the line sounded a mite impatient.

"Gravity." She giggled and silently congratulated herself on her witty response.

There was an irritated sigh from the other side of the line. "I can't employ you if you don't answer this question. You called me, didn't you?"

The guy was being more serious about this than Roxy had expected. "Fine. Earthly ties. I assume you mean family, friends, and crap like that, right?"

"Correct."

Roxy considered weaving an elaborate tale of intrigue and horror, but her drunk brain wasn't cooperating. Her normal social filter, minimal as it was, had been dissolved by the alcohol, resulting in more honesty than she'd intended. "Let's see. I have a best friend I never see anymore, so that sucks. I work in a customer service job I despise, I had to borrow money from my parents this week to pay rent, and they admitted they're ashamed of me. So yeah, my Earthly ties can bite me."

Death was silent for a moment. "Do your Earthly ties routinely bite you? I've heard of worse, but that does sound irksome."

Roxy leaned her flushed cheek against the cool metal door. It felt nice.

Death, apparently unperturbed by her lack of response, kept rattling on. "Stay where you are. I'll have you brought in for a meeting."

She frowned down at her phone, thinking she should just hang up. She had to wonder if this dude was serious. He probably intended to ask for her bank account number or something similar. She set the phone down. This, she felt, was an entirely reasonable reaction, but reason had little to do with her decisions in this poorly scrubbed toilet facility. She simply murmured, "You're weird, dude." Then she closed her eyes. Rest seemed like a far better idea than anything else.

*

Something felt distinctly off when Roxy's consciousness rose from the depths of the alcohol-related stupor she'd fallen into. She blinked several times, struggling to bring the world into sharp relief. She pushed herself up to a seated position and took in her dusty surroundings. Bare dirt speckled with random patches of gnarly grass stretched out for countless miles. Fluffy clouds hung heavily in the brilliant blue sky. Something felt strange about those clouds, but she couldn't put her finger on what it was. Two robed figures in pointed hats, one black and one white, sat in plush chairs with a suitcase bound in rope between them. She thought she must still be dreaming. She closed her eyes and tried opening them a second time, hopeful that the image would be different. Nope!

Regret bloomed in her chest as she wondered which of her poor life choices led her to this moment. She risked closing and opening her eyes a third time but the continued existence of two pointy-headed, robed figures confirmed that whatever brought her here qualified as one of her poorer decisions. The figure in the black robe stared back at her with an unblinking bone-white face. A shiver wracked Roxy's spine. "Who are you?" she asked.

"I am Death," he replied. "We spoke on the telephone."

The statement triggered a memory of a bathroom stall and bright red lettering. "Yes, we did." She cast a glance over at the figure dressed in white. A mask, dark as midnight, made it impossible to tell if this one's eyes were trained on her, or even if it had eyes at all. "Who's this?"

"One of the PAs currently under my employ," Death replied. "She's moving on to a management position in our Data Entry and Analytics Department."

The featureless masked face turned slightly and stared in Roxy's direction as well as anything that may or may not have eyes could manage. Thinking she should say something, anything, she spouted out the first thing that came to mind. "It's good to know there's room for career advancement."

Death gave a curt nod. "For now. We're recruiting extra help for the apocalypse since that's going to be our busiest time, so you may want to rein in your expectations in that regard. Once we run out of humans, we run out of work. A couple of us will remain in place if a handful of humans survive and try to rebuild society. Some personnel may be transferred over to the Flora and Fauna Department, but the apocalypse, depending on how it all goes down, could conceivably put a dent in their workload, too."

Roxy let that statement sink in for a moment. "The apocalypse? Is that coming up soon?"

"Soon enough from my perspective," Death amended. "You might've been able to live out a normal human life if you hadn't opted to offer your services."

Might've been able to. Those words rattled around inside her brain. "Am I dead?" She felt instantly that this was a silly question considering that she was talking to Death.

"Yes. Being deceased is a job requirement."

"But being dead will get in the way of my... life plans," Roxy muttered, realizing again how silly she sounded. Monty would have been the first to remind her that she'd never planned past what she would wear the next day. Life planning had not been one of her talents.

"All occupations have their requirements. I can't be making unreasonable exceptions for potential employees. I inquired about your Earthly ties for a reason. Perhaps you should have considered this." Death sounded mildly annoyed.

"Actually, I thought it was a joke." Roxy sighed. "You posted your job ad on a bathroom stall where most of the visitors are likely to be intoxicated. Didn't that kind of reasoning seem feasible?"

Death shrugged. "Two types of people are likely to respond to my ads. The first is those who believe in life after death and are somewhat prepared for the types of things they might see. The second are those who have so little to lose that they are willing to investigate the unknown. You fit within the bounds of that second category."

"You know, someone once told me that Death is simultaneously the most and least fair thing in the universe," Roxy said. "It comes too soon for some, but it ultimately comes for everyone."

"That also means you have no room to complain about me ending your life now. You had more agency in your own destruction than many people do." Death sounded smug.

"Touché," Roxy replied bitterly as she ran her fingers through fine grains of sand. Death tapped the gloved tips of his fingers together as he considered her. At least he seemed to be considering her. The mask left a lot to the imagination.

"Most employers would look at your recklessness as a bad

sign. Why should I hire you?"

She froze, the sand falling through her fingers. "What? I'm already dead and I'm not guaranteed the job? That doesn't seem fair."

Death chuckled, the sound deep and raspy. "Didn't you just say that unfairness was an undeniable aspect of who I am?"

"Yes, but what happens to me if I don't get the job? It's not like I can go back if I've already been autopsied."

"It'll be the same as all the others who failed the interview or decided not to take the position," Death said. "You would go on to the part of the afterlife you've probably pictured before. Heavenly music, beautiful scenery, relaxation and all that. One of the benefits of this job is that you'll get a better paradise when you retire than you would have otherwise, but it won't be too shabby if you move on now."

Roxy suddenly felt this was less a job interview than an existential conversation she could've expected to have with a bunch of friends while passing a joint. She paused and turned her eyes to the sky. The fluffy clouds continued to hang above her in an odd way. It only took a few more seconds for her to realize that the clouds hadn't budged at all. "How about this? I don't fancy the idea of disappointing Death, so I'll do my best not to screw this up?"

The silence that followed unnerved her, but she tried to keep her face impassive.

"That's good enough for me," Death said at last. "We'll see how you do with your first assignment."

She nearly deflated with relief. The idea of having a job to keep her occupied sounded more entertaining than hanging around with nothing to do in a subpar version of paradise. Roxy expected to be told where to go, or for Death to stand up, or something else of that nature to happen.

It didn't.

The three of them sat in stillness and after a few moments Roxy longed for anything that might cut through the awkwardness. She thought about how Monty might've told a joke or done a random dance number at a time like this. That brought a tightness to her chest that she recognized, even in her non-living state, as regret. The atmosphere grew heavier.

Roxy had to break the silence. "So, are we done here?"

"Not yet," Death replied. "We are waiting."

Another long pause followed. "What are we waiting for?"

"You will see."

Roxy shrugged. So, Death was going to be cryptic. Why wouldn't he be? She resigned herself to the unpleasantness and gazed off into the distance. An irregular lump caught her attention. She squinted, slowly realizing that this rather lumpy thing was making its way toward them. The progress was lethargic at best, but it moved nonetheless.

"Is anyone else concerned about this blob?" Roxy asked, hitching her thumb in the direction of the lurching blob in question.

Death glanced calmly in its direction. "I'm concerned that it's taking too long for him to get here. My time is valuable." He looked to Roxy and his silent PA. "Keep quiet and observe." With a snap of gloved fingers, the unidentified smudgy object disappeared.

This left Roxy stunned and wondering where the lump could have gone. Then she heard a muffled thump and a frantic voice uttering unintelligible grunts. She whipped her head around and realized the sounds were emanating from the suitcase, which was now rocking back and forth while something struggled inside.

Several moments passed while they all looked on.

Finally, with another snap from Death, the ropes binding the suitcase slithered away like serpents, and the ancient hinges popped open. A dishevelled young man rolled out, coming to a stop by Roxy's feet. He had brown hair, tanned skin, and was dressed entirely in black. His blue eyes looked stunned as they landed on her.

"Who are you?" he asked, his voice barely a whisper. "What happened?"

"You should be addressing me." Death's voice shook the ground beneath them.

Roxy wondered if perhaps the pop culture portrayals of Death weren't entirely wrong. The man's eyeballs nearly jumped straight out of his head. Trembling, he pushed himself up, listing slightly to one side. Whatever had happened to this guy, he'd seen better days.

"S-sorry," the man stammered.

"Are you Wolfe Anders?" Death asked.

This was clearly the man's name, strange as it sounded to Roxy's ears, because his jaw dropped.

"Y-y-yes."

"You're here because you've been unwise in your actions. Those actions have brought you to the brink of death." Death stood and approached Wolfe. "Do you recall what you were doing before you got here?"

Wolfe swallowed loudly and looked away from Death, apparently studying the large suitcase he'd been contained in. "We were doing our fraternity initiation. We took our pledges out to the pool and gave them an option. They could either endure a punishment or they could jump naked into the ice-cold water."

Roxy couldn't imagine why anyone would subject themselves or someone else to either option, but she reasoned that she couldn't be too critical of him considering how she'd gotten into her current predicament.

Death stood ready, looming like a bird of prey poised to strike. "Something went wrong. Do you remember that?" Wolfe shook his head. "You slipped while pushing one of your initiates into the pool and hit your head on the deck." Death laughed menacingly. "You're here because you're drowning right now."

The colour drained from Wolfe's face. "No! No, I can't be!"

Death interrupted, "Listen to me. If you do, a couple of your buddies will rescue you in time." He pointed at the suitcase. "You need to stop these kinds of shenanigans. You're making unnecessary work for me. If you see no issue with your behaviour, there is no point to letting you live."

"Okay, okay," Wolfe said, nodding emphatically. "I'll stop. You have my word. Just let me live!"

"Very well," Death replied with a shrug. He took a step back. "You're free to go. Don't forget your promise. There will be no second chances." Then he waved his bony fingers, and Wolfe and his suitcase vanished in a puff of smoke.

"At least he gets to live," Roxy muttered.

Death ignored her comment. Instead he hooked his fingers under his chin and pulled. The white face and pointed hood peeled away and fell to the ground. Roxy blinked as the gesture revealed a normal human face. The man had tawny skin and dark hair. He didn't look any older than thirty, but she wasn't sure at what rate Death aged. Or if he even aged at all.

The silent PA removed the mask as well, revealing the slender, pointed face of a young woman. Vibrant red hair cascaded around her shoulders. "Is that all for now?" the PA asked.

Roxy shook her head. Just when she thought this couldn't get any weirder, it did.

"Yes. You can get on with your next assignment. I'll let you know when I need you for your next training session," Death replied.

The woman nodded and promptly vanished.

Roxy pushed herself to her feet and pointed at the vacated spot. "I want to learn to do that."

"All in good time. Come with me. I'll show you where the break room is."

"This place has a break room?" Roxy asked as if this were, by far, the most remarkable fact presented to her today. Death gave her a funny look. Without the mask on, there was still something inhuman about the way his expressions worked. They were a good enough imitation of the real thing, but like the clouds, they were still slightly off somehow.

"Why wouldn't there be? Can you imagine the morale problems we'd have on our hands if there wasn't a place to take a break?" He waved his hand. The desert surrounding them transformed into a dull room with white walls and white floors. "Come with me."

She nodded and followed him into a corridor. "Does the break room have real coffee?"

"Of course. Being dead doesn't mean sacrificing all the joys of the living. We don't need food or drink to survive, but we can still partake."

"Excellent. That means I can still have a beer, right? All is not lost!" Death didn't dignify her observation with a response. "Where do we sleep?"

Death indicated a door to their left. They crossed the threshold into a break room that looked like any other she'd seen. There were long tables with hard chairs. A counter in the back came equipped with a modest coffee pot and a wicker basket containing a selection of creamers. Death could really do with a decorator, she thought.

"Sleep is one of the things we don't participate in, so we have no personal rooms. You can simply use the break room or roam the world in your spare time. There isn't a lot of spare time; this is a busy place, so choose wisely."

"Oh." She would miss sleep, but the travel sounded nice enough.

*

Roxy learned a lot in her first few days of work. She toured the Data Entry and Analysis Department that the redheaded PA was supposed to be managing soon. It looked like every other office she'd ever seen with grey cubicles encircling grey desks, manned by bored-looking workers staring at computer screens.

"Everyone who dies goes through an exit interview. The PAs who work in this department handle that," Death said. "The people here analyse those answers and data gathered about that person's good and bad deeds during their time on Earth. The results are sent on to the Judges, and they determine where that person spends eternity."

Roxy wanted to know more about these mysterious Judges, but Death wasn't much help. "I've never met them. I receive my orders, and everything I get is on a need-to-know basis."

Another thing she didn't learn was where this place existed, because no one would give her a coherent answer.

"This place inhabits the shadows cast by time and space," someone had told her.

"It doesn't exist so much as fail at non-existence," another offered.

It didn't take long for her to give up her questioning. She was either incapable of understanding, or everyone was teasing the new girl. Monty would have gotten a laugh out of her bewilderment. A pang of nostalgia struck her. Her old life hadn't been without its good times.

Learning the ropes of this afterlife was a bit more

complicated than her old job of stocking shelves, but it was similar in that she often found herself restraining the urge to wring the necks of stupid people. People had frustrating ways of meeting Death, from trying to bribe him, to outright denying they had died. She wanted to smack several of them. And Death, like most bosses, also seemed to have an eminently wringable neck. For starters, he had a way of sneaking up on Roxy that would have given her a heart attack were her heart still in working order. He also seemed to derive joy from saying no to what she considered to be perfectly reasonable requests.

"Can I scare some idiotic frat boys?" Roxy asked as they weaved around shelves filled with files.

"Not yet. You have to work your way up to that," Death replied. "Near Death Experiences are a big responsibility."

"Why? Is it that hard? Do I need to undergo some kind of training that'll help me warp their minds with fear?" She may have sounded too enthusiastic about that prospect.

Death paused as he snagged a file and tucked it under his arm. "Experience helps, but it's more than that. People love that job, so it's in high demand. You'll need to get some seniority under your belt before you get your chance."

Roxy snorted. "Is that likely to happen before the apocalypse runs us out of work?"

He shrugged. "It might."

"Do I at least get the inside scoop on how the apocalypse is going to happen?" she asked.

"I don't even have those details yet," Death said, and he definitely sounded a touch annoyed this time. "The Apocalyptic Planning Committee is working on a list of possibilities that will eventually go up for a vote. You'll get a vote when the time comes, but until then, we can only speculate." He handed her a stack of filing. "Put these away by death date, then by location after death, then alphabetically by last name. If you can't find the right space, ask for help." He started to walk away, but stopped. "Oh, and don't touch the blue shelves in the back. Those are where the Flora and Fauna people keep their files, and their Death is a prickly sort. You don't want to get on her bad side. One of my PAs knocked some files off a blue shelf once. Their Death responded by knocking over three of our shelves. That PA had a horrible time cleaning it up."

Roxy blinked. "There's more than one Death?"

Death shrugged. "Of course. There are a lot of species, and humans are troublesome enough that I can't oversee much beyond that."

*

Weeks passed before Roxy got to do an assignment on her own that didn't involve filing. Her task was to act as a recruiter. She didn't need to directly interact with anyone to fulfil this role, either. All she had to do was write ads like the one that brought her into the fold.

"I'm surprised you don't have an advertising department," she commented.

"We never needed one before, because we didn't start recruiting this much until recently. Having one would be useful, but I don't have enough people to make that happen yet. Now, for the ads, you can write whatever you want. Just make sure you include contact information," Death instructed her. "It's up to you where you do it, too. Anywhere people go is fair game. Use whatever materials you need. Be creative."

Roxy smiled with genuine delight. "I've never had a job where I was encouraged to be creative before."

"Most human occupations require a distinct lack of independent thought," Death mused. "This fact is one of the many reasons I am grateful I never had to endure that existence."

Roxy nodded. "I won't miss my old job. Or standing in long lines. Or paying bills. Or having my car break down at the worst possible time." A list of annoyances piled up in her mind, and it would have taken her ages to recite them all. Being dead had some benefits, she couldn't deny that. She thought back to Monty, who spent his days at a call centre, phoning strangers from all over Ohio and getting insults thrown at him without being able to return the abuse. Most anything had to be better than that. Monty would enjoy parts of her new job. She shook her head trying to dislodge the thought. Instead, she started drafting some ads.

The "flexible sense of morality" the ad called for guided Roxy steadily down the path Death needed her to travel for her duties. When she decided where to go to post an ad, that choice played a role in determining who saw the ads, which would in turn lead to people dying. She couldn't deny this. She could only justify it. They would all die sooner or later. It's only a matter of when and how, she reasoned. She wasn't the one making them call. She was only allowing them to see their career options.

It wasn't long before this evolution of thought had her using her supernatural skills to walk into the call centre Monty worked for in Trotwood, Ohio, at 3am. She remained aware that she might've been crossing some moral lines where friendship was concerned, but that awareness was no longer sufficient to stop her. The darkened interior was eerie. Rows of desks with unmanned computers and telephones stretched across the breadth of the room. So much space, so many potential uses, and yet this building had been designated as the home for irritating and unwanted calls made to peddle products and services no one needed. The people making those calls endured verbal abuse for dreadful pay. Death had once said that the living certainly made strange uses of their time on Earth. Roxy thought as much while still alive, but complacency prevented her from doing anything about it.

Stepping into the men's restroom, a remnant of her conscience lingered and kicked up a fuss. She scolded herself; this was selfishness at its worst. *If Monty responds, he might hate you for this and rightfully so.* The odds of Monty answering the ad were slim, though. He'd be seeing it in the sober light of day, if he even saw it at all. Someone would probably find the message first and clean it up. And if he never answers it, she reasoned, she wouldn't be hurting him. Logic. Crappy logic, but it would have to do, she thought. She pulled the purple glitter nail polish from her pocket and began to write out the ad she'd scripted.

Are you bored with your existence?

Do you like to scare the crap out of people?

Do you despise your current job with every fibre of your being?

Do you want to find a career that allows you to sneer down at the mortal plane while also getting to visit the

best of what it has to offer?

If you answered yes, you too could become a Servant of Death.

Call 1-800-DEATHPA if you're interested.

Anyone can apply. Death isn't a judgmental sort.

She leaned back and looked at her work with a sense of satisfaction. Monty would love the bit about scaring people. They always loved pulling terrifying pranks on people at Halloween. All that remained was to wait. And write other ads around the world, of course.

*

It didn't take long for Roxy to realize that her ill-conceived plan worked. She was having coffee and working on her next batch of recruitment ads when Monty slumped into the break room. She froze. His eyes were aimed downward, so he hadn't yet seen her. Death walked in behind him and shot her a meaningful look. Death was wilier than she thought. He always saw right through her.

"Hello, Monty," she said.

"Roxy?" Monty whipped his head up, his eyes wide. He dropped into the chair beside her and smacked her shoulder. "What are you doing here?"

"I died, so there's that," she said, trying to sound nonchalant.

"Yeah. When your mom called and told me they found you dead in a club bathroom, I could hardly believe it." He shook his head. "Now I've died in a bathroom too. What are the odds?"

She winced. "Pretty good, actually." She sighed, wondering how one was supposed to reveal to their best friend that they had tempted them to death. No one makes greeting cards for that kind of situation. "Well, let me start by saying that I missed you."

His eyes narrowed, the change in expression striking. "I missed you too," he said slowly.

She continued hedging. "And being dead, it wasn't like I was going to have a chance to visit you anytime soon.

Whatever the movies show you, hauntings don't happen that way." She was rambling now. "We don't get to choose who we scare, so I wasn't going to be rattling chains at the foot of your bed. We can only scare people while they're on the verge of dying."

Monty crossed his arms in front of his chest and started tapping his foot beneath the table. "You did this to me, didn't you?" He sounded less infuriated than he should have, all things considered.

"I wrote the ad with you in mind, yes." She scooted her chair away from him but failed to escape the kick to her kneecap delivered under the table. Death ignored both of them and made himself a cup of coffee.

"I should be furious with you. You understand that, right?" he demanded.

"Yeah, you probably should," Roxy conceded. "Remember, though, if you hate me, it'll make working here a lot less fun." Monty glared at her, and the strain of the moment made her uncomfortably aware that Death was watching them intently, a ghost of a smile on his face.

"That isn't fair," Monty said, though he sounded a tad calmer.

"I know. Death is simultaneously the most and least fair thing in the universe." Death smirked at her from the corner of the break room. She tried to ignore him. "I have to work around the person who wrote the ad that landed me here. It's part of the deal." Granted, she thought, I don't know for certain who wrote that particular ad, but it didn't matter. Not in the grand scope of things.

Monty huffed. "This is worse than the time you got us arrested for stealing that cactus."

"The cops overreacted," Roxy said defensively. "It was a harmless prank. We would have given it right back."

Monty deflated a little, the tension bleeding from his shoulders. "It's not like I had any prospects on Earth, I guess. I'm not missing out on much. Where are we, anyway?"

Roxy grinned. "Umm... a place that inhabits the shadows cast by time and space?"

"What?"

"Nevermind. You had a job on Earth. That's more than

some people have. Or had."

Monty rolled his eyes. "Oh, yeah. I'll miss being a telemarketer. That was going places, you know."

Roxy smiled. "I missed your sarcastic ass."

He grinned. Monty had always been resilient. "So, the ad said something about terrifying stupid jerks. When can I do that?"

She sighed. "You have to work your way up to that, I'm afraid. Maybe they'll let us team up for some of it." She cast a hopeful glance in Death's direction.

Death shrugged. "We'll see."

"That could be fun," Monty said, rubbing his hands together. "I'm guessing we can't just go after our childhood bullies, can we?"

"If only we could." Roxy slid her sheet of notes over so her friend could see them. "Want to help me come up with ad ideas?"

"Sure."

Death tapped her deftly on the shoulder causing her heart to stutter. "Start with the filing instead. Show him the ropes, and don't forget to warn him about the blue shelves."

∞

L.G.'s First Two Options

1. Fraternity brothers pull an elaborate prank on unsuspecting inductees.
2. First contact with aliens, and this is their weird idea of what will make humans comfortable.

The Last Protest

Joanna Michal Hoyt

Five minutes before the hour, in the fifteenth year of the Great Directorate and the third year of the drought, two hurrying figures converge on the same spot in the vast expanse of dust and dead stubble. The white-robed black-masked figure tucks away binoculars; the black-robed white-masked figure peers awkwardly at a GPS device, apparently struggling with poorly aligned eyeholes. The two stop dead, perhaps five yards apart, looking at each other, and at what someone else has thoughtfully(?) provided for them: the two high-backed swivel chairs; the battered, old and old-fashioned suitcase.

They turn, not quite simultaneously, to look around them. There is nothing to see but the mangy flatland stretching away in all directions and, away off eastward, a tumbleweed vanishing.

"It's early yet, I guess," the black-robed figure says. The voice is high and thin, slightly nasal, probably female. "Maybe they left this stuff last night. Well, have a seat while we wait for the organizers to show up." She—if it is she—strides up to the chair closer to her and perches on the seat, gripping the arms, ready to rise quickly if—

"Anyone who wanted to be here on the hour would be visible by now," the white-robed figure says in a deeper, softer voice. Male, probably.

"Anyone who *was going* to be here on the hour would be," Black Robe answers. "But *wanting*—it would be awfully easy for a car to overheat. And if they had trouble at one of the security checkpoints..."

"But of *course*," White Robe says, imitating Black Robe's volatile tones in a lower octave. "Many people must be *dying* to come out here."

"Is that your idea of a *joke*?" Black Robe asks waspishly. "This is supposed to be a *peaceful* protest. They said so."

"On whose side?"

"*Ours*, of course. The other—" Black Robe breaks off, resumes on a higher note in a more breathless voice. "Who *are* you, anyway?"

White Robe shrugs, and perhaps raises his eyebrows behind the mask. "This was also supposed to be an anonymous protest, for security reasons, wasn't it? They said so."

"All right. But what I really mean is, are you wearing gloves that make your skin look paler than it is? I hope you are—I can't tell at this distance, old age is supposed to make you farsighted but it hasn't done much for me yet. Because wearing blackface to a demonstration for liberty and equality would be *extremely* counterproductive."

"Do I detect tone policing?"

"No, you detect an objection to cultural appropriation," Black Robe huffs. "If, that is, you are... ah..."

"Not very postracial, are we? And would wearing whitehand be better?"

"Nobody's really postracial, and we're supposed to be acknowledging—Look, I know this is anonymous, but isn't there *something* I can call you? If we're going to be sharing a jail cell..."

"Then we're not going to be very anonymous anymore, are we? I hardly think they'll leave our masks on. I suppose you might be counting on us both being beaten beyond recognition, but I wouldn't be too sure of that either. At least, not at first." A pause in which both parties might have had reason to wish they could read the actual expressions on each other's faces. "But you can call me Ishmael, if you like. And you?"

Black Robe plucks at her sleeves. "Oh, Elphaba, I suppose, if that's how we're going about this. Though in that case I'm lacking a hat-brim and my mask's the wrong colour. But you're right, if only one of us gets arrested, the other one will be much happier and safer if there's no real name attached..."

Ishmael rises. "Lady Elphaba, possibly-not-so-wicked Witch of the West and definitely-not-so-ruthless eco-terrorist, what a pleasure to make your acquaintance." He makes a sweeping bow, bringing his hand very close to the suitcase between them. Elphaba rises in an awkward lunge, takes a giant step that puts the case within her arm's reach. As she bends and he begins to straighten their eyes meet, lock. Perhaps now they are both grateful for their masks.

"So you did hear the rumour about the suitcase," he says in a rather less amused voice.

"And about the spy."

"About the spy? I didn't hear that one."

"'Most sure and vulgar, everyone heard that which could distinguish sound'," Elphaba says. "Or however exactly that quote goes. I used to have Lear by heart, but now..."

"As my information came entirely from the Facebook group, sound has very little to do with it."

"Then you *must* have seen Offred's post about that! About Security agents and provocateurs..." She gives a little huff of startlement. Sits down gingerly on the suitcase, keeping some of her weight on her feet. "Oh, no. You are one, aren't you? You're *the* one. And you are most definitely wearing blackface. Look at your neck. How did I not see that right away?"

"Is my mask colour really relevant, in light of the fact..."

"... that you were planning to set a bomb off at the protestor gathering, and pretend it was something we'd brought along to lob in front of the motorcade? No, I—"

"So it is a bomb," he says very quietly, positioning himself in front of her. He doesn't quite touch her, but he'd be able to grab her quickly if she moved. She doesn't move, except to nod her head and smile a painful little smile.

"But it didn't work, did it? Most everybody else had the good sense to avoid this rendezvous point." She looks aside, bites her lip. "I do think Offred or *somebody* might have let *me* know we weren't supposed to show up here after all..." She shakes her head, glares at Ishmael again. "*One* dead protestor with a homemade bomb hardly makes a story worth pitching to the press, let alone a basis for another round of reprisals. You'll have to come up with another plan."

"You mean, you will," he says. "You do a very good imitation of righteous indignation, right down to the snorts and huffs, but you haven't fooled me. You're the one they told us to look out for. You're the spy."

She cocks her head in a birdlike gesture, regards him sidelong, shifting her weight a little.

"And if I were, don't you think I'd already be, so to speak, sitting pretty? Probably wearing a heel-mounted set of blasting caps?"

"Maybe, if you thought it was worthwhile to blow yourself up for one dead protestor and no good story. But do they use blasting caps anymore?"

She rests her elbows on her knees, her head on her hands. "I'm getting too old for this," she says. "Well, it beats dying young the way too many of them do these days. Or I guess it's better, anyway... I wouldn't know firsthand, would I, and neither would you, though I guess you might know soon if you're young now—it's possible, I suppose—and planning on exploding this thing. If it even is a bomb." She sighs. Gets up. "This position is killing my knees. Go on, blow it up if you want to." She settles back in her chair, making small unhappy sounds as she lowers herself into position. "I didn't know how to stop them anyway."

"Them?"

"The Directorate and the idiots who support them and the people dumb enough to try to fight them by shooting the idiots, who did you think I meant," she says irritably. "I'm not quite dumb enough to think blowing things up would help, and since I've spent most of my life trying to help people see reason, and people get dumber and angrier every year so you'd hardly think the government would have to squash them so hard... I think it's too late now. I think it's been too late for a long time."

He straightens up, hands on hips. "You're for real, aren't you?"

She shrugs. Pulls off mask and pointed cap, revealing bright black eyes in a beaky bronzed face under a wave of wild white hair. "I'm Spes. Really. Mum wanted to name me Hope, and Dad said that was common and old-fashioned, and yes, I know, Latin's even older, but... Nevermind me, I'm babbling again." Her voice is softer and more level now that she's unmasked.

He hesitates, then tugs his mask off as well. His face is round, pinkish, and, just now, extremely sweaty, his hair and eyes the same vague hazel colour.

"And I'm Bob," he says. "Okay. So you really don't know what's in the suitcase. And neither do I. So who left it here and what the hell did they hope we would do with it?"

"Only one way to find out," Spes observes, walking back to the suitcase. "I've gotten to the stage where I'll try anything. Has it occurred to you that maybe the others weren't too smart to stay away? That they might all be arrested now, or dead?"

"Plenty of things have occurred to me," he says, rubbing his chin. He seems to have lost his assurance along with his mask. "Most of them unpleasant."

"Well, here goes, then," she says. "Want to stand back, just in case?"

Bob shakes his head. Spes reaches gingerly for the clasps, opens them. Jerks back at the hissing sound, the slight shimmer in the air.

"Poison gas?" she says.

"With all this air to disperse in? We're okay, I expect. If—What are you looking at?" He looks where she's looking. "Oh, my god."

There's not enough breeze at ground level to stir their long robes or dry the cold sweat on their necks, but high above them there must be a wild wind. Clouds smear across the sky. Not blow, smear; it's eerie how their afterimages stick in the hot bright air.

The wind lowers. A tumbleweed blows back the way it came when they arrived—opposite to the path the clouds are taking across the sky.

"I suppose it might be your god," Spes says politely. "I wouldn't know. Have a seat."

Bob sits, shaking his head in bewilderment. Looks at Spes. Freezes. "My god," he says again. "Look at your hair."

She tugs an end of it round into her line of vision, squints. "Am I suffering from rapid-onset senile dementia, or has this turned black?"

"If you're demented, so am I," he says. "So we've done it! Gone back in time, undone the Directorate."

"No, somebody's sent us back so we can do something. Fix something. So it doesn't all happen again."

"How the hell are we supposed to do that?" Bob demands, scowling and fingering the acne patches that have appeared on his cheeks.

Spes lowers her head. "How should I know?" She runs her hand along the top of a clump of what had been dead grass. The blades are dull green now, not brown, and they bend at her touch instead of shattering.

She looks back up at Bob, smiles crookedly. "I don't know anything. But I think it's not too late anymore. Let's try again."

∞

Joanna's First Two Options

1. First I thought of them as enchanters and/or priests with different agendas, and pictured the suitcase containing the plagues of the Apocalypse (the protagonists don't quite see eye to eye about when and how to loose these). It seemed likely to me that this was the obvious idea that would have occurred to everybody.
2. Then I imagined them as actors in a much-anticipated (by the actors) play that no one turned up to watch. They're putting off the moment when they have to put their robes and masks back into the suitcase and be nothing but themselves (and they each have something rather serious to hide under the robes... something "litficcy", not "specficcy").

Brexit

Josephine Bruni

The coffee shop was very trendy. It looked like a warehouse with rough wooden planks as seats and tables, cardboard boxes filling the shelves that ran around the walls, big, professional coffee machines worth hundreds of pounds shining amongst stylish coffee cups and colourful mocha. It was said that this shop made the best coffee in North London and Marco was one of those who made it happen. It was a repetitive chore. Grind the beans, twist the percolator, press the hot water button, steam the milk, clean the steamer. Marco produced one drink after the other, immersed in Anya's musky perfume that blended perfectly with the bitter aroma of Arabic coffee. Sometimes Marco found himself looking at her, wondering what it would be like to kiss her, to untie her ponytail of full hair. She was tall, Anya, more than him and had a strong Polish accent that kept him company during the long hours at work.

Hot, not so hot, small, less water. More milk, thank you, no foam, more foam. Sometimes in the queue a friendly face said "*buongiorno*" and chatted a little. Marco acknowledged their kindness with an extra hole in their loyalty card. Not everyone was for Brexit, he told Anya.

An espresso with hot milk on the side and an Americano with cold milk on the side; a hot chocolate not too hot and a glass of water. Thank you. And Marco answered *prego* most of the time, because he thought in Italian. He wiped the counter, emptied the dishwasher, swept the floor.

Anya chatted to a woman with a little dog who licked Anya's fingers and wagged his short tail.

"I will vote against Brexit," said the woman who came to the coffee shop every morning.

"Do you think they will win?" asked Anya.

"Of course not," said an Englishman behind them. His perfectly white hair suited his face, his glasses, and his blue eyes. "You have nothing to worry about. England needs the Europeans. Besides, there are thousands of British people living in Europe. We've taken over entire villages. I live four months of the year in Italy. I love it, the food, the stylish people. And the Italians make great neighbours."

Marco thought of his village back home. It was beautiful, spilling over the cusp of a pointed hill, its rooftops the colour of wholesome cream. It was a very old village and some of the houses were ruins swarming with cats.

"Thank you," said Marco. "It's good to know someone is standing up for us."

"Nothing will change, don't worry," the woman told Anya.

At mid-morning Marco went outside to smoke. Across the street a homeless man lived his days lying on an old mattress, surrounded by tattered suitcases overflowing with clothes and other rags salvaged on the day of his eviction. Paper cups and old newspapers were scattered around him. The empty shop behind him had sheets of torn paper on the dusty windows making the corner bleak and unwelcoming.

Marco crossed the road with a self-confident sway. His cheap clothes hung on him neatly. A fine annoying rain wet his head, dripped along his gentle profile. He had nothing to offer the man but a cigarette. They lit up and the smoke surrounded them, softly rolling into the air to mix with the heavy pollution. Marco squatted beside the man. In front of him, the leftovers of a Thai takeaway spilt on the pavement. There was an open packet of crackers to keep it company and two apples looking lonely and forgotten in a clear plastic bag. Marco smelt the raw odour of wet, dirty clothes and cold runner beans.

"What is it that you are reading, Daniele?" Marco asked the man in Italian.

Daniele lifted his book and showed the cover, a nineteenth century portrait of the great Italian poet, Ugo Foscolo, whose dark eyes seemed to look at Marco, speaking of exile and the torturous pain of a rootless life.

"He died in London," said Daniele. "So poor that he had to

change his name to hide from his debtors. Poetry consoles me, you know, makes me think of home."

People came and went on the busy high street. It was summer but the sky was dark. A light constrained behind the clouds burst through with vivid strength. The trees, thick with green, rustled in the cool breeze.

"They are going to deport me," said Daniele.

"They can't do that! You're European."

Daniele looked at Marco without fear. He had an intelligent face with thick, dark eyebrows and a black beard. He wore a winter jacket and a black woolly hat. It was cold and damp down there on the ground.

"Oh yes they can," he said. "Me and my old mattress are like a punch in the eye on this high street. I'm on the brim of society and I'm falling off it. No one knows what to do with me. Did you read what they say of me in the paper? 'The sad and revolting spectacle of a man living on a heap of rubbish.' Revolting, Marco, that's what I am now. I feel like a worm trying to dig his way out of stone."

Marco threw his cigarette in the street. It was time to go back to work but he found it difficult to leave Daniele. "Maybe you'll be better off back home. Have you got any relatives there that can help?"

"No. I'm not going back to the hometown. I don't want them to see me with a bag full of nothing and a beard like a tramp. I'm going to Reggio Calabria. I might find a job there making cocktails on the beach. What do you think, Marco? One day I can have my own bar, with orange umbrellas to shade the good and beautiful from the North."

Marco thought of Reggio. People down there were warm and compassionate but the town was full of immigrants ready to work for nothing, happy to have survived killer journeys across the sea. If he were Jesus he would have told Daniele to get up and walk. But where to? Marco had to go. He left feeling that a part of him stayed with Daniele lying on a filthy mattress surrounded by damp, worn out books.

The time went by quickly that day as the shop slowly filled up. Saucers slid on the counter and drinks were made with perfect gestures, without losing a second of time in useless moves. There was a lot of talk of the Referendum and

Marco constrained himself more than once as Brexiteers brought forth their theories. The dishwasher steamed, the coffee machine steamed, and Marco steamed with them. He left the shop around seven, after cleaning, checking the till, noting how much coffee had been used.

Anya put on her red coat and untied her ponytail. Her long hair fell in ringlets on her shoulders. "You know, Marco, this Brexit thing is really disturbing me. That man on the TV barking about foreigners as if we were here to rob him of something. We are not Vikings. Are we? We work hard. I wish I could talk on TV too."

Marco closed the door with a heavy lock. "What would you say?"

"That if they want me to go they will have to drag me away. I am not going to do any residency form. I am here and I am going to stay until I have enough money for a deposit on a house. Then I will go back."

Marco thought of the house prices in Italy. There was no chance he could ever save that much money. He left Anya in front of the shop with a hug and a brotherly kiss on both cheeks.

Daniele was still in his place reading *The Last Letters Of Iacopo Ortis.* Marco lifted a hand to salute him then walked off, pulling up the hood of his jacket. He was never going to be English no matter how hard he tried. First of all, there was the accent that added vowels to the end of words that in English weren't there. Then there was his dark hair, his dark eyes, and a look of dreamy sensuality that lingered on his Mediterranean features. His fellow countrymen had been around London since Roman times, he thought. As a matter of fact, they had founded the place but he was still a foreigner and always would be. He realized suddenly that he could be deported. He stared into space with his fists buried deeply in the pockets of his worn out jeans.

The rain swished around the wheels of passing cars and hit the top of buses carrying people home from work. The polling stations would soon fill up. On his way to Camden Town, Marco passed the trendy pubs full of young professionals talking loudly and drinking beer and wine from shiny glasses. The area was quickly becoming gentrified. Soon the rooms would cost more. Some young men working in shops had to share a room.

In Camden, more of the homeless sat in doorways with mattresses and old blankets. A busker sang something melodic into a microphone. His voice reverberated along the walls, climbing up towards a purple sky. A man selling sugar coated nuts looked dejected as his merchandise got wet. He was a foreigner too, a Romanian, thought Marco, recognizing the Gypsy traits in his full cheeks and dark skin.

Marco took shelter in a supermarket. It was a huge thing, like a spaceship ready to leave the earth for another planet. The self-service machines gave orders and said goodbye. The aisles were full of white light and endless rows of goods. The rich West never ran out of food, nor out of water as a matter of fact. Marco wondered if people in Africa knew about people like him living in a box and working ten hours a day to buy ready meals and clothes made by children.

The queue at the till was long. It always was at that time of day. Marco bought his chicken korma and some fruit, sour grapes and rock hard peaches. He couldn't help thinking that at least in Italy the poor could still afford a decent peach. He lived on the second floor of a rundown maisonette just behind the famous Camden Lock. From his window he saw a small garden with overgrown ivy smothering an old oak like a lustful lover. A couple of chairs under the tree had lost their veneer, turning from green to a light blue. Marco too had changed colour since he had moved to London.

He lay on the bed with his hands behind his back. His clothes were damp and his feet hurt. He was young. Twenty-four years of age. He turned to look at the picture of his family on the wall. His father's face was deeply lined by years of working under the sun or against a fierce winter wind. His wife helped him tend to the olive trees and the tomatoes. She was a woman with large hips and her back was strong from generations of bending over the land. Marco's little sister, fourteen years of age, looked tanned and bursting with health but also a bit lost, as if something was happening to her that she didn't quite understand. She wanted to come to London.

"Will you help me?" she'd asked him last time he'd visited.

It was not going to happen. He didn't want her to have a

life like his. And there was Brexit. If Britain left the EU Marco would become an economic migrant. Would there be a sea to cross for him too? He poured himself a glass of Italian wine. It was his treat. The smell reminded him of the village bar where men shouted over card games that were a war of wills, where cheating was a question of pride and finding out was too. A stream cut the village in half and a slender Roman bridge joined the two parts. Children picked fights over which side was braver, older, less stupid. As men they took part in tournaments, competing with crossbows and heavy arrows that split the hard wood of the targets. Marco tried his best to go back to the village every year. His friends had never really forgiven him for going away.

"Still working in a coffee shop?" some asked him, with contempt. Those words stuck to his memory like the bite of a hornet and so did that underlining question: "Why did you really leave?"

Marco had left nepotism and bribes, the cocky self-assurance of a governing body full of contempt for the poor. Thousands of people killed themselves in Italy every year, many, owners of small businesses, compelled by taxes and bureaucracy. The bereaved wives of hundreds of men marched under the name of "White Widows". Their stories were harrowing, their courage immense. When Laura, his girlfriend, had walked away he had finally decided that only a plane could cure his malaise and he had landed in London.

Never again shall I touch the sacred home
Where once my small boyish body found repose...

Foscolo had died in London, impoverished and forgotten. Daniele's mattress would get wet, thought Marco. Daniele's feet were always sore because he never took off his shoes.

"They are good shoes," he'd told Marco. "If they steal them, I'm finished. They stole my food yesterday."

Marco had wondered who "they" were. He ate his meal and switched on the TV. The number one Brexiteer was spitting in the face of three million Europeans who called England their home. Many had children who were British. Marco asked himself if they were being bullied at school now that all that hatred had been stirred up. He switched off the TV and went back out.

He walked towards the canal. It could be dangerous at dark but he had nothing of value to be stolen and he was beyond worrying that day. He thought of another populist of the Brexit movement. He had a half smile always on his face and a contempt for everything left wing. "The poor are such because they are stupid," he'd said and Marco had thought of those words every time he counted the pennies in his pocket, every time he ate bread and butter for dinner. Did Laura leave him because he was stupid? He wasn't. He just didn't have it in him to walk on people's heads. He was a communist. An Italian communist who still believed in the old values of the Resistance: justice, freedom and truth.

He walked past the colourful boats and the small bridges cast over the dark water like arms around a friend. They spoke of times gone by when the canals were used as waterways for a country that still produced merchandise and not services. The great factories were now shut. The English poor didn't have much to look forward to as they grew up and fell into a system of economic torture, where benefits came with sanctions and destitution was the norm from father to son. They still paid for inspiring Marx.

A boat glided by with geraniums on its deck. Jazz music, coming from the lit-up interior, filled the air with expectations of quiet, friendly love. They were enjoying a wholesome meal there, thought Marco. He too had friends but that evening he wanted to be alone and think. A friend of his had gone back to Italy and was still waiting for a job after eleven months. Marco would have to go back to his father's house possibly with no money. He couldn't do that. The humiliation of failure would be unbearable.

Next morning he switched on the TV as soon as he woke up. England had left Europe. A heaviness fell on his shoulders and hunched them. He was filled with dread. He left his room in a hurry. He didn't want to be late, to leave Anya alone at the counter. She was always punctual, always efficient. He was one of the few friends she had in London. Anya from Poland, saving for a house.

As he walked towards the shop he thought he could

distinguish the Brexiteers by their demeanour, by an aura of anger that set them apart from other Londoners. A man with suit and tie, holding a case of documents, talking on the phone, a big smile on his face; a woman with heavy lips and a limp, holding onto her trolley; a drunk with no front teeth and dirty trousers, walking fast with the smug expression of someone who had been given power to hit back at poverty and powerlessness. Maybe Marco was imagining all these things, he told himself.

When he arrived at the shop Anya looked angry. She huffed while steaming the milk for yet another latte.

"I'm sick of this place," she whispered as Marco joined her behind the counter. Her hands shook. "I pay taxes. I do shopping and take buses. I wake up at six every morning and have never asked anything of anyone. But I am still a foreigner and always will be. It hurts, you know, here in my heart. I feel betrayed and used. I have never felt as European as I have today."

"What have we done to our grandchildren?" said the Englishman with the perfect white hair. His face was pale, his lip shook. "They have taken away our heart. I am so sorry."

"Who's going to make your coffees and clean your toilets?" asked Anya.

"Other people, poorer than us," said Marco. "With no rights at all."

Anya held onto the counter as if she was about to fall. Her head was low and she closed her eyes. "I can't take any more," she said.

That day Marco made his coffees with more energy than usual. He huffed often and he almost banged the cups on the wooden counter. He thought of the "White Widows" and their marches; he thought of his father and the calluses on his hands, the empty place at the table where his son should be sitting for Sunday meals. Marco wanted children but how was that going to happen? He couldn't even offer them the right passport. He had a break at mid-morning for his usual cigarette. He faced the old carpet shop with a sunken heart. The mattress and the bags were gone. Daniele had been removed.

Josephine's First Two Options

A well-kept secret!

The Lost and the Found

Amanda Marples

The Director let them keep their pennies.

She scooped the Lost from the filth of the Middle Cities with bronzed arms and offered them food, and shelter, and warmth. She had a wide face and an open smile but her forehead bore lines of determination and rage. Her hair was ornamented with Found silver and curled around her head unfastened, as though it, too, was angry.

Kettles had not been broken. Not like some—but he had certainly been Lost, certainly he had suffered. When she had come for him he had tried to scramble away, whimpering like an animal, clutching his suitcase against his thin body. It was lined and battered and fastened up with his father's belt. He had used that belt to hoist himself up to his father's laughing red-bearded face, just a boy then, and not so long ago. Before the fires started in the Middle Cities. The suitcase smelled of home and carried his pennies. Tourist pennies, old pennies, pennies his weeping mother had pressed onto him as he left—nothing more now than small circles of love, and otherwise worth little. Those he would never use, never exchange for crusts or clean water. Those pennies he kept and held, even while he capered and turned, even as new pennies showered down around him. They made his palms smell like blood. He knew how to tell those pennies apart. He studied them, finding new pathways with eyes that travelled along the copper curlicues and flourishes even while he slept.

He was small enough to fit in his suitcase if he opened it and flattened it with his street-blackened feet. He was invisible to most if he covered himself with rags and rubbish. He had journeyed east before the collapse, seeking his fortune. His father had been proud. There was a better life, or so the Rural people thought. It was a long walk to discover they were not welcome. The cities were already beginning to fold in on themselves, sagging under the pressure of increasing want. The wealthy were leaving, following an instinct in the pits of their well-fed bellies to flee. Or perhaps just the privilege of a warning. The Rural people as well as the City poor had no such forecast.

Kettles could lift and build and grow and dig: he was his father's son. He was sure he would soon find work. In the meantime, he mimed and clowned, as did they all. City children stood and watched with increasingly empty eyes, bellies rounded with hunger. Some could still smile, or clap. Pennies dwindled in volume and value. Then hysteria hit and everything started to burn and the continent split apart. Afterwards, he could do nothing else but play the fool and dance. Home was gone, people said. The Rurals turned to ash, the glory of the clustered cities conflated to a bland mess of cracked masonry known only collectively now. Civic pride blew away like smoke leaving behind what they knew now as the Middle Cities. Soon the Tourists from the Free Countries arrived, hiding their guilty curiosity from themselves under a cloak of philanthropy. The burned streets had a lustre, a romance of leaning billboards that creaked in the wind. But there were too many thieves and the Tourists did not like them. More and more Kettles found himself miming to empty streets and smashed windows just for something to do. Something other than waiting and sleeping and scrabbling for dirty food. Something other than losing hope.

*

It was during those feral days that he first crossed paths with Bella.

When, a few weeks after Kettles, she arrived at the Institute, ripped and raw and unable to speak, he remembered. Her hair looked paler, but it was her. He remembered her pirouettes and her high jumps. He had watched her from beneath damp cardboard, ignoring the musty wet on his cheeks. Her smile shrunk and faded as the weeks idled by. He watched her yellow dress grow dull and come apart. Around cobbled corners and reflected in broken shop windows, he watched her. And sometimes he thought she watched him too. Bella was the most broken he had ever seen come into the Institute and he worried about the bleeding cuts and scratches on her legs and arms. Some were old, yellow-bubbling, seething, when she arrived. She did not seem to notice or mind that her skin was tinged like rust or that her injuries took an age to heal. They had never spoken out there on the perishing streets of the Middle Cities, not with their mouths at least. They did not speak until they were under the green boughs of the Director's arms, pennies and suitcase intact.

In the Institute there were real green boughs too, the verdant kind. The earth beneath the boughs was warm, dry and clean, swept by unseen hands. Springy patches of bright moss covered the broad stones that served as seats in the gardens. The air smelled peaty, and of cooked food—real food. There were others. They were safe, the borders patrolled by the older ones—and they were together. Some had pieces of glinting jewellery, some clutched photographs as they moved about the grounds. Some had pennies like Kettles. Some had nothing, like Bella. The Director collected them and their things. She gave them new names to mark an end to their old life of suffering and to mark the beginning of a better life. But they kept their things. She was fair, and she loved them. The others said so.

She Found them, eventually. There was a healing room, a special room where she helped them after their bodies were mended. Kettles had seen a glimpse once when he was sifting through his pennies in the corridor. A skinny child was led in, much younger than Kettles, before one of the Helpers closed the door gently behind them. He saw delicate lemon walls, bright pictures in frames, and the corner of a colourful rug. He saw the open arms of the Director. He wondered when it would be his turn.

Eventually Bella could smile and speak a little. Kettles was her first friend and his rolling jester shoulders and new floppy hat gave her reasons to rise from her new soft bed and eat new soft bread in her new soft clothes in the sheltered green gardens. The Director had given her a skirt of tulle. It was blue like her eyes, like the sky, like the gentle sea that she remembered in her dancing. It gathered around her thin thighs and swept down to the floor in a tumbling frothing river. Above it, a fine grey woollen shirt was tucked in and bound in the middle with a soft leather belt. The Director saw the dancer in her more than in any of the others, and she acted accordingly. She thought of everything. She loved them all and they loved her back.

After they were nourished and plumped up, their brows stroked and the grime wiped away, fevers settled and the nightmares beaten back, after they had made friends with the others, they were given things to do. There were vegetables to pick. Hands were thrust deep into soft dirt, clean dirt, rich dark and crumbling dirt. It was not the thin dirt of the Middle Cities, fouled with shit and shared with rats. They marvelled at the sticky spikiness of courgettes, the deepening red of tomatoes, and the delicate filigree of carrot tops. It all smelled so good, like a dream.

Bella learned to make bread. To knead, pat, and shape it, and to smile as it rose and swelled first under a damp rag, then in the huge stone oven that roared and needed raking twice a day, and finally in bellies around the long wooden tables. The tables and chairs were also Found, rubbed down with wax that sat in the scars and deepened the colour, rescued from the burning and the guns and the fearful air of the Middle Cities. They ate at the table three times each day, still hardly daring to believe the food was real and would not disappear into dust at the first touch of the fork. Still fearing what the price of a full belly might be.

The Director sat with them, in a different seat each time, claiming no seat as her own, no special place, no special food. "You are the future," she could be heard to say. "One day the world will be new again." She listened and she heard, her eyes shining with what looked like love and sorrow. Sometimes she would hold a hand or wipe away a tear, and she would wait patiently for the day they would look at her freely without fear. They had all learned to look away on the City streets, to avoid connection, to avoid violence. They were all afraid to begin with that she would turn on them like an angry Tourist and all of this beauty and kindness would be ruined. The moment their heavy hooded eyes met her sparkling green ones was precious; it was the beginning of being Found.

Carder was smaller than Kettles but had been at the Institute longer. On the day after Kettles arrived, he lay freshly bandaged and tinctured and Carder had slipped into his room and pushed a tiny metal car into his limp hand. The paint was chipped and a wheel was missing but Kettles had wept, the kindness unbearable. Carder had held Kettles' hand for a moment with his dark lashes drawn down, a blush on his cheeks. He had smiled at the ground and scurried away. Kettles did not know the colour of his eyes until, one day soon after, he saw him look up from his meal of stew and bread into the expansive face of the Director. A soft sigh had run through the room. Carder's eyes were blue and alive. It was two days before Kettles saw him again. Over the weeks, he would often be missing at mealtimes for a day or two. The Helpers reassured Kettles that he was well and resting, being mended inside, being Found. One morning, Carder was eating oats at the table, bathed in a shaft of morning light. Kettles moved his bowl nearer. Carder had looked at him then, and smiled. Kettles had taken his tiny die cast car from his pocket and rolled it across the table, uneven because of its missing wheel.

Carder had smiled broadly and said, "I like that. Did the Director give it to you? She loves us all."

Kettles had opened his mouth to answer but Carder had already dropped his eyes back to his bowl, still smiling. He smiled through the rest of his oats and milk. Kettles, sharing the glow of the morning sun with his little friend, felt cold.

*

By then Bella had come, and Kettles played less with Carder and his new smiles. Bella did not look at anyone but Kettles. One day he asked her about this as they worked in the gardens.

"I know you," she said. "I saw you out there."

"The others were Lost too, Bella."

"How do you know?" she had answered, frowning as she picked blackberries, her skirt lapping about her ankles as she bent and turned.

"They told me. Pansy, and the others. The Middle Cities

are so big now, it's a wonder we met before."

She turned to him then, holding a shining berry to her lips, purple under her nails. "What was your name before, Kettles?"

He started. "We aren't supposed to..."

"Yes I know, I understand. This is for newness, for beginning again. She loves us all. I'm not ungrateful. But can you remember?" She dropped the berry in the basket and plopped onto the floor, cupping her chin in her hands. Her eyes glazed for a moment and she sagged in the shoulders like she had been held up all this time. "I had a baby sister." She frowned and shook her head. "No. I *have* a baby sister. She is called Callie. My mother is getting older and iller. I have to go back."

Kettles looked over his shoulders. He felt his pores open and his arm hairs stand. "But, Bella, everything is gone."

She nodded, her eyes still fixed somewhere in the past. "I don't know," she said. "Did you leave to make it better too, Kettles? Were your people hurting too?"

He dropped his gaze back to the earth where his fork was lifting potatoes. He nodded and poked at the ground thinking of his mother and father. He tried to still his racing heart, which had flooded his chest with nameless fear. Chopping onions on a wooden board, his mother would tell him always to listen to the small voice inside. To be kind. To follow the path of truth. Reading his book of first words to his father at night, he had pointed to *brave* with its picture of a boy fighting a dragon.

His father shook his head. "This is wrong. Brave is doing what is right even when you are afraid. Being afraid is part of life."

Kettles looked and looked now, his mind honing in on the words of his parents, but where their faces should be there was now only a blurred space. Kitchen flagstones and flannel shirts: the scent of peat smoke and their words remained, but their faces had gone. And so had his name.

*

At night they danced, wearing capes, shawls of feathers, and lengths of shining crispy silver from decorated fir trees of long ago. The elders remembered the trees as a ritual of the old world but the younger ones did not remember them at all. They performed for the Director. This was not something she could do herself, with her stick and her stiff back. She could work a little and joined them often in the gardens to pick strawberries and greengages. But the dancing she could only watch, smiling and clapping as they wheeled, mimed, and skipped; tamed lions and walked against wind; rode lifts and feigned surprise. Sometimes they danced together and sometimes each took the stage alone to shine with their individual talents across a courtyard lit by tiny flickering candles, Kettles with his white painted sad-happy face and Bella with her blue skirted pirouettes.

Every Tenth Day they would perform for richer Tourists who preferred the Institute safety to the wicked Middle City streets. They arrived waving their red tickets bought for the biggest pennies at the gates a mile away and rumbled their way across to the Institute in electric battery carts. They brought bags of pennies and held clicking cameras aloft. Tenth Day Acts were always full. It excited the Tourists to be in such proximity with those who had brushed close to death. They became hushed and poised when they saw the Found. The Director masked and gowned them in their City clothes even within the protective walls of the Institute. For protection and for status, she said. Anonymity was cheap. Regardless, the Tourists nodded at each other with puffed-up sympathy, releasing tears of condescension. Their cheeks anointed with redemption, they would throw their bags of pennies like so much rice and shake the Director's hand, murmuring of the grace of God. She would stand at the door and incline her head with modesty. The Tourists would leave in a state of grace, murmuring and shaking their heads, thanking the City and the Institute, feathers bobbing and heels clicking in time with their tongues. They would tell their friends and families to see the poor people, how well they have done, so brave, so brave. And then they would forget.

The Director always looked pained on Tenth Day dances; perhaps the voyeuristic pleasure of the Tourists made her uncomfortable. She endured her pain in silence, for the Institute needed oil and coal and bundles of rags and leathers. Kettles and Bella had heard from the others about the boats that weighed anchor in rusting Middle City harbours carrying goods and Tourists.

The cook, a big man with tattoos on his face and beads in his coarse hair, talked as he taught them to glaze bread and guided their hands to tie up straining muslin bags of curd. "Things we cannot grow or make, we must buy. If we are careful, we do more than survive—we live. They know of course, the Authorities. They could shut us down if they wished. But no. Because we do their job for them, see?" Kettles did not see, but Bella nodded. The cook gave them balls of elastic dough as he talked and took Kettles' hands in his own, kneading with him until he had the rhythm. "We clean up. We bring the Tourists. Without us, the streets would be too much, the Tourists would not come. Keep it all tidy, keep the Lost down. Those the Institute does not save, let them die. You understand?"

Kettles did not. The cook let go of his hands and mussed his hair. "Keep kneading."

*

Bella understood more. At night, she explained. "We dance for them and Tourists pay, the Institute stays alive, and the Middle Cities can put their fingers in their ears and close their eyes and sleep in warm beds while the people starve and the gangs run the streets and hurt people." She was panting and Kettles saw fear and anger shining in her eyes. He reached a hand for her and she recoiled from him. Wounded, he shrank back too. She put a hand to her ribs where she was still strapped up.

"It's all dirty," she whispered, looking away from him. "You know there are city people with guns at the borders? That no one can leave? I tried. For Callie." A tear squeezed out, fat and glossy. "I was dragged back, Kettles, and given over. Some Tourists come for other things."

"But we are here and safe now, Bella. You are safe now. The Director loves us all, we are the future. That's what she says. Doesn't she, Bella?" He heard the pleading in his own voice.

Bella reached for his hand and he took it. "She thinks she

is God," she said, and met his eyes, her cheeks wet. "Don't you ever wonder how there are always enough beds even when new Lost arrive? Something is wrong here. When was the last time you saw Flounce? Or Charm?" Kettles frowned, searching his own head. She nodded slowly, triumph drying her tears. "This place is dirty too."

*

He was taken to the healing room a few mornings after he'd withstood the green of the Director's eyes. She had welcomed him, wrapped him in her arms. She smelled of fresh wood; her hair brushed his cheek. The light was mellow, merging with the pale walls, and he was invited to sit on the couch, to relax. There were blankets should he feel a chill. She played music, which undulated around him, and gave him a warm drink flavoured with honey.

"Are you happy here, Kettles?" she asked.

He nodded and sipped his drink, allowing himself to sink into the couch.

"Good. I'm glad you came along with us. You are so welcome here in our little community. We can do such good together. Do you believe we can fix the future, Kettles?" He shrugged. She laughed. "An honest answer. I believe we can. You are the future. All the people who were Lost, who are still Lost. You went through so much; we owe you this. We owe it to the future. I will not rest until the damage is undone. And so we Find you a new life. Let me Find you, Kettles. Let the past slip away, let it be healed."

His head felt thick, like the time he had heatstroke from a day in the fields and his mother had cried with fear. Except now there was no fear or pain. He closed his eyes and his warm cup was taken gently from his hands. He shuddered with a sigh and there was a click. He heard the Director say from a great distance away, "Just listen to the voice, Kettles." A recording played just underneath the music. "Trust me and let it go. Nothing can hurt you now." He remembered nothing else when he awoke in his bed.

*

Lost people were brought to the Institute at least once a week. Sometimes in pairs, sometimes alone. One day there came a cartload of frightened and ragged girls and boys, older than he but no less vulnerable. He felt pleased for them. That was the morning Bella came running to him in the barn where he was sweeping. She was white and her eyes were too big for her head. Kettles felt that he was watching a ghost of the past. She was as wild as she had been on the day she arrived. She stood in front of him, her shoulders heaving up and down with her labouring breath. The back of his neck prickled. "What is it, Bella?"

"I know what it is," she had said, her voice quaking.

"You know what what is?"

"Stop eating the food, Kettles, it's..." She looked behind her at the motes of straw dust falling in the evening light. They were alone. "They're doing something to it," she whispered. Kettles screwed up his face. "Listen," she said, "I told you this place was dirty. I just needed to see for myself. And the healing room? A place of forgetting, Kettles, that's all. That woman is taking our memories. She is emptying us and sending us away."

"How do you know it?"

She stopped and sighed. "Because I've been looking and listening. I can show you. Tonight, after bed. Don't eat the food; pretend to be sick. Don't let her take any more than she already has. I've been eating garden things only for weeks and I know your old name has gone already, hasn't it, Kettles?" He had no answer for her. "That's what I thought," she said, and her eyes filled with tears. "My name was Lillian."

*

Later, hidden behind sacks of flour in the yard, the moon overhead and Bella's excited breath in his ear, Kettles saw the carriages whirr into the courtyard. He froze as the rear doors of the east wing of the Institute opened, casting yellow light into the yard.

"Look," she whispered. A Free Country man of course. There was no mistaking the fine cut of his jacket, the stones hanging from his ears stretching down to his chin. Helpers carried the smaller ones over shoulders, the larger ones on stretchers. Kettles' lips moved in silent counting. Six. The Director was there, casting a long shadow in the moonlight, her cane by her side. She shook the man's hand. Something was exchanged, but no words. The carriages slid away with an electric purr. Bella's eyes burned in the night. He hated her for a moment, two moments.

"See?" she said.

Kettles nodded. "What else did you hear?"

They had whispered to each other between their fingers, between the grey mossy stones of the outer courtyard, under shaded ferns and climbing roses. Bella's breathed words came in angry bursts like fumes of wasps, her brow creased and her blue eyes like chips of sapphire burning. She had relayed the conversation, overheard through a weak spot in the scullery wall: the Director's calm voice and the insistence of her visitor who was driving a hard bargain, but whose nerves belied his lower ranking. He was a go-between. More people were needed; the market was ripe. The Free Countries were poised on the brink of unity and expansion was delayed only by the size of the workforce. Surely she could work more quickly, if the price was right.

"You people have no regard for the equipoise of the human mind, of the complexities of the work," the Director had stated. "Do you want workers who have some modicum of reason? The ability to follow simple directions? Or do you want vegetables? Name a price as high as you wish. It will make no difference to my offer. Six is all I have tonight." The man had protested something that Bella could not catch. The Director had said she would discuss it further with the Minister, at the next Tenth Day.

"We can't stay, Kettles. We can't stay," Bella said, and he had nodded, his eyes lowered, his heart already swelling with grief in his chest. His soft bed. The crayons. The certainty of breakfast. He knew at that moment how trapped they all were, snared by comfort.

"The next Tenth Day, that's the day we should leave, while there is distraction with visitors," Bella said, worrying at a loose scrap of paper on the wall by her bed.

"We could just say we feel better now and want to leave?"

Kettles offered and saw her disdain even as he felt it himself.

"Why would we want to leave unless we knew the truth of this place? She would stop us and she would find a way to empty us all the way out. No. They cannot know we have gone. That woman. That woman."

She kept saying it. *That woman.* Through teeth clenched while tears trembled in the rims of her eyes. Her hate hissed out of her in those two words. Kettles thought she enjoyed the hating. But he had nothing to add; he just nodded again, thinking of the pennies and his mother. Looking at his feet, whispering in a voice so low that Bella had to turn her ear to him, he said, "Then we should dance away. Mime away. Show them the art of silence." His voice was hollow as he stared at his precious feet, wrapped in new soft leather slippers that clung to him with the certainty of a promise, or the steel jaws of a bribe.

They had finished planning their escape under the rose trellis at night while the Institute slept. All the while they had to keep a small compliant smile on their faces, like the others. They could not tell any of them, not breathe a word, not to Fellow or Pansy or any of the Found brothers and sisters they had come to love despite their vacant smiles. Not even to Carder. Kettles had tried to convince Bella that Carder at least should come with them.

"We can't take care of him," she said. "It is too late for most of them now. They are empty. They will tell. And think, Kettles. It will be hard enough to get out unnoticed as it is, even with the Tenth Day distraction. With others? We'd be stopped." Kettles chewed his pencil and ran his fingers over his pennies. Bella's brow softened a little. "We will come back for them. For all of them. But first we must tell the truth. There are places even beyond the Free Countries, I have heard. Someone will listen. We save ourselves to save them, see?"

"But the borders? The passage out? Guns, Bella!"

"The sea, Kettles," she whispered in the dark, her fingers combing through her long clean hair, bound at the top with deep pink velvet ribbons. A gift from the Director.

"The sea, yes, but we have no boat. We can't board a Free World boat. We don't have the papers. How can the sea work? Will we float on my suitcase?" He had not meant to be querulous. He waited to be admonished. But she half sat up suddenly, her eyes gleaming in the dark.

"Do you still have it?" Her breathing was loud and they both thought they could hear the hammer of her heart beneath the warm hum of the generators.

"Yes, I kept it. She said I could. We were allowed to keep our things."

Kettles wished his words back into his mouth because Bella had been found ripped and torn with nothing. He had felt her receding from him, her excitement ebbing. He reached across and touched her neck in the dark. At first she had turned from him, but then she squeezed his wrist tight and they had stayed like that for a while, Bella silently forgiving his unthinking. Then she spoke, and he was glad. "At the mime-play we leave. The Tenth Day. She will mask and gown us as usual in our outside silks. We can wear them until we are out of the city. The rest we can steal. No one will question us."

"But not if the Director gets word out that we are runaways. She has links in the City. What if they stop us? What if we are Lost again? I can't go back to the streets, I've forgotten how." His mouth had been dry and his arms had felt cold. He had begun to cry, and think of his mother weeping on the threshold as he left with her old pennies, off to seek a better life. How he had wished he had turned back to her broad arms and floured pinafore, to a place that understood him, where he did not have to be afraid.

"You never forget. The street will remember your feet, even if you won't." Her voice was soft but full of iron.

"It's not 'won't', Bella!" he half-cried out, tears cold now on his cheek. He had looked away from her and gazed at the wallflowers and yellow poppies in the gloom, easing their way out between the stones of the courtyard.

"Sometimes it is 'won't'," she had replied, and he had felt the weight of her eyes upon him, heavy and hard in the darkness. They had slept, eventually.

Their last performance had been perfect, a Tenth Day Act, but extra special. A very important visitor was here, a dignitary from one of the Free Countries, a Minister interested in the Director's cause. She had told them this before the performance, gathered around in their robes as the Tourists piled in, bearing their bright tickets. She would sadly not see their acts tonight, as she would be with the Minister throughout. She would watch a recording later, she had promised, but knew they would be as graceful and clever and funny as ever. Bella had danced that night with a fragility that took their breath. She was dancing out her resolve and her understanding of betrayal with a slow beauty that only Kettles saw.

*

But now Bella and Kettles have left the Institute under cover of daylight, hidden in plain view. Kettles sits in an old armchair, not yet a Found chair, its arms worn and probably containing a family of rats inside. He looks through the holes in his mask. It has slipped sideways a little, making him look pondering, curious, like a little bird. He is not any of those things. He presses his mask back on straight and adjusts the string tied behind his ears. Bella has been motionless for a while, seated opposite him in her own dirty chair. Bella is thinking and waiting. She is Kettles' Director now and he must follow her, but where? They have lost the path of the streets. They will have to learn again or discover a new way. He curses the thick soups, the custards, the breads and his own treacherous need, his want, his hunger. Kettles pushes the corner of his suitcase with the toe of his shoe. It shifts easily; he could kick it down the street if he wanted to. They are not wearing their old clothes or their first clothes, those rags and cloth bags have long ago been burned. But Bella still has her blue skirt. It is ripped down one side but it is still blue and will easily pass as Tourist-wear. For now, her rustling black silk is covering her against the wind that is rising, shuffling paper bags and dust around their ankles, and making the charred buildings creak and groan. Bella's smile had disappeared again after she'd learned the extent of the Director's work. Now she is wide-eyed behind her mask with knowledge and anger, but not fear. Kettles is full of fear. Full of it, full of it. He watches a tin can bounce and jounce down the street, blown by a gust of wind and wonders when Bella will move, when Bella will make the decision. They need to be off the streets. They need to be out of the Middle Cities. He wants to disappear in her skirts like a child and never come out again. His frantic breathing is trapped and condensing on his skin, making his fears double and triple until he thinks he will boil over.

"What happens now?" he says from his rotting chair, no longer able to wait.

Bella sighs behind her mask. "We wait. We wait for a space, Kettles, and then we walk into it." She watches his hands grinding against each other in his lap and she sighs again. "We wait until no one is watching and then you pick up your case and you follow me."

"What if someone knows we are runaways? That we are escaped?"

"We are not escaped. We are escaping," she says.

"But to what?" His hands are clammy, his face hot.

"To something better than she had waiting for us. That oblivion. To a life we will want to remember. To your parents. To my Callie. Or at least to avenge the memory of them."

"But what if we were wrong about her, Bella? What if we saw wrong?" He hears his own voice, feels the heat rising in his cheeks like a wellspring of shame that he cannot dam up. Bella hears it too.

She stands and crosses to his seat, the spray from the nearby ocean lifts her hair beneath her conical hat, her comical hat, her hat for laughter and diversion to better help the Tourists feel good about their sightseeing. The spray hits her cheeks and sinks into her breath so that when she sits next to him, perching on the arm of his chair and leaning into his face, he smells salt in her words.

"We saw the truth," she says and he stiffens, as if she might reach into his brain and pull out the wiring that has already begun to grow wrong. "It's just the Director speaking in you. If we go back—yes, yes, Kettles, I know that's what you are thinking—if we go back, yes, there is food, there are good beds, and friends, but listen to yourself. You still want to pretend her work is good? Collecting Lost people and calling them Found? Imagine how you would be if you stayed longer. Soon you would be collecting people yourself wearing an idiot smile and serving them poisoned soup, making them empty. And then you would be sold on, like the others, when you are empty and stupid enough. And when you have your own child

Kettles, what then? You'll have them stupid and empty too, and cleaning the boots of Free Country families." She stood then and turned to look at the ocean in the distance, just visible in the failing light, just audible above the rising wind. There were gulls.

"Sometimes I think I would like to be empty," he says, looking at his hands and remembering in pain his father's red beard, the powder scent of his mother's neck.

Bella laughs a thin laugh and smooths down her black silk robe, rustling bags of crusts and dried beans concealed inside, under pilfered layers of furs and satin and taffeta. "You think you are the only one who wants to forget?" she says, not taking her eyes from the sea. Kettles feels a coward, that his memories are nothing compared to hers, to what unspeakable acts she endured on the street. Bella shakes her head in the circling wind. "To forget is to die, Kettles, can't you see? To forget is to pardon."

The sea is calling them; Kettles knows in his heart this is the thing to do, senses his father in the interstices of his mind, nodding at him, pushing him on. There will be a boat soon. And then they can lose the silk buffoon robes of shame and step out as Tourists until they reach the Free World. They have pennies, old and new, big and small, found, earned, and stolen. Those shining discs of gold and their suitcase will encourage the boatpeople to absorb their story with no more than a blink. Bella will say their papers were taken by disgusting street people. After all the Tourists give them. What a pity! Bella knows how these things work. And they will make it to one of the Free Countries and perhaps beyond where the streets do not burn and the art of silence is not the only way. Bella cannot remember all of how it was; there is still much white noise before the pirouettes. But it is jewelled with intermittent memories shared with Kettles in secret. Her mother's palsied hands, her baby sister's breath against her neck. The Tourists at the Border who had shackled her, laughing. Her lips fold inward and become a thin line across her face. She shuts her eyes, her hand moving over the places on her body that still hurt, the changed bone-shapes, built up, calcified and concertinaed. They will never unfold. She opens her eyes and Kettles sees her head twitch in the direction of the horizon where the sea meets the sky. His heart strikes up a rhythm. A boat. There is no one around.

"It is time, Kettles," she says. His hand creeps into hers like a trembling mouse. He stoops to pick up his suitcase, hearing the jingle of his mother's old pennies inside. He feels Bella's hand squeeze his, once, twice, and they start walking.

∞

Amanda's First Two Options

1. A Game with God (the image reminded me strongly of *The Seventh Seal*, a classic Swedish film).
2. Satanists discussing a flight delay, a comedy.

Take Back Control

Clare Weze

When you finally see the fairy tale for what it is, there's nothing but relief. A great weight falls away and you're free to live life normally again. Free to eat, as nature intended. To munch through the hours, to stack up the days by weight of digested keratin instead of counting down to the afterlife. It's amusing, once you've woken up, to watch the rest of them still swilling in gullibility. Why would you need a brand new body? How would you acquire a totally new form? And this heaven they talk about, where you can defy gravity and fly—well, it's clearly a fantasy-land dreamed up by contortionists. Bait for the masses, a false promise to goad them away from the choicest woollen coat—the best silk shirt—and into the grave. Because that's what the cocoon is. Where's the evidence to the contrary? And they even concoct a new name for this new body: moth. *Moth!* It isn't even a beautiful name. There's no poetry to accompany the intellectual bankruptcy. No. I'm sorry, but when your time comes, you die, and that's all there is to it. One body, one life.

My best friend never shared my views.

"We *can* turn into those angelic forms," she insisted. "And moving reflections of the world will stream straight into our minds through tiny holes in our heads called eyes. It's true! We just have to live the right kind of life, then when the time comes, we're ready."

"When the time comes," I told her, "you and I will nestle together and remember how we used to sink deeper into the fields of the Woollen Plains than anyone before us. That was the meaning of our lives. Burrowing into undiscovered folds in the Valley of Silk, spinning twin feeding mats and bathing in celestial energy whenever the giants left the gateway open.

There's beauty in the life we've led. No need for fairy tales."

But my dearest one left this world believing those myths. There was no warning. Normally, the roar of the deadly tube precedes the nosing in of the terrible maw, but this time, the wind rushed in and my precious was on the outer reaches of our favourite cashmere, the tube at her back. Before we knew it, the great suction had begun. No time for goodbye.

So, don't you understand? If there was any truth in the tales I'd be the first to believe. But there isn't. She's lost.

∞

Clare's First Two Options

1. "Stripped Right Down", concerning a sixteen-year-old catfish called Peter, who is only ever seen when his tank is stripped right down.
2. "In the Moment", a story about a hairdresser with a client whose girlfriend is not from this place and she is not of this time.

Moirai

Molly McLellan

"*Sieg Heil! Sieg Heil! Sieg Heil!*"

The chorus of voices echoed in Colonel Stauffenberg's ears. He found it haunting that in the end, in the bitter end, the partial hearing loss he had sustained couldn't drown out the Reich. Not even in that instant when the final salvo took his life. With his one good eye shut tight, Stauffenberg prayed, muttering to himself. Waiting for the light of God to find him in this new darkness.

The faint sound of a gentle snore penetrated the dark. Stauffenberg quieted his breathing. Was it possible, he thought—had God slept through their coup?

The breathing and snores grew louder, almost to the point where each breath felt like shells tearing into the darkness around Stauffenberg. He pulled the stump of his one arm and other hand to his ears, trying desperately to drown out some of the noise.

A child's voice broke the snoring. "Lakhesis! Lakhesis, please wake up."

"What is it now, Klotho?" a woman's voice boomed down around Stauffenberg.

"We've made a grave mistake." The child's voice cracked and wavered on the final word.

A sliver of light came then, playing across Stauffenberg's eyelid, dancing, shimmering. *God has sent angels to guide me*; the thought caused a smile to break across the Colonel's face. The light snapped away, leaving him in darkness once more.

"What have we done?" The child's voice quivered with a fear Stauffenberg recognized. He had seen it amongst his officers as they pushed on through France and Poland. Seen their fears finally confirmed when so many fell around him as

Germany lost its grip on the African continent.

"Where's Atropos? Klotho! Where is Atropos?"

There was a sound of shuffling feet as no response came to the woman. A desk chair squeaked as it was pulled across what could only be sand and dirt. Stauffenberg's ears pricked up at the sound of the familiar crick and crack of ungreased metal pushing against the weight of whoever sat atop the chair.

"Klotho, do not make me—"

"She said she couldn't take one more." The child paused; the chair squeaked even louder. "She said she needed to rest."

"To rest? We do not rest!" The sound of a second chair squeaking reverberated above Stauffenberg's head as the woman barked out her words.

Stauffenberg tried to pronounce the names he was hearing in silence, rolling them over his tongue as best he could. They were not angels' names his father or mother had ever taught him. Perhaps they were saints, long since forgotten? Having heard his prayers, they had come to intercede with God on his behalf, to help him enter the heavens. He searched his mind, desperate for any memory of their names.

The child—Stauffenberg figured her name was Klotho—began to speak. "We could—"

"No, we can't; we do not wait. The Moirai do not wait." The woman Stauffenberg presumed was Lakhesis thumped her foot down, causing the darkness around Stauffenberg to shake. He reached out his hand, its three remaining fingers stretched. Blindly, he searched for a safe hold, anything to ground him in this darkness. What he felt was leather. The rough, creased edges made him recoil. Was it possible he could be in hell?

The sound of metal scraping and squeaking came again. "I'll go then, if I must." Lakhesis' voice softened as she continued, "Klotho, this is most important. You must keep the string tight as our mother taught you. Do not let it waver. And whatever you do, do not open the hold like before." There was a pause. "Klotho!"

"I know!"

A loud crack came from above, accompanied by the sound of a chair spinning uncontrollably. Stauffenberg could feel the pressure rising in his chest, a panic he couldn't swallow. The shaking returned to his fingers and his blackened eye began to ache; sharp pains would follow soon. He knew this feeling all too well. His lips and throat felt dry as he struggled to breathe. He reached out once more with his fingers, trying to find anything resembling the world he hoped he hadn't left. Was it possible the non-commissioned soldiers had taken pity on him? Could he just be unconscious, trapped in some dream world?

"Hilfe." The first time was hardest. His breathing had become laboured as he felt oxygen stretching and thinning in front of his very mouth. "Heilig mir helfen." He hit another wall of leather as the sentence spurted out of his mouth. His fingers scraped hopelessly against the edge. "Hilfe." The final word drifted out of him as if a last and final prayer. Stauffenberg collapsed against the wall, the pain in his blackened eye forcing him to kneel.

Μοίρες

The noise from the suitcase finally stopped. Klotho moved her chair closer, inching slowly, trying not to stretch the cord of string in her hand too tight. She leaned forward, quieting her breath. The suitcase remained silent. She looked across it to the empty office chair still spinning, slowing as time stretched forward. As the chair came to a stop, the suitcase wiggled, slowly at first and then more rapidly from side to side. Klotho's eyes widened.

"Please stop," she muttered under her breath. "Please."

"Hilfe!" The man's voice grated against her ears, like metal scraping across glass. It made her bite down on her lip. She decided to turn her back to the suitcase, slowly wheeling her chair around. She stared down at the cord of string in her hand. She had started to pull it tighter.

The man's voice came again. She clenched her fists around the cord, trying desperately to hold it in place. Lakhesis would be back soon. Atropos would be with her. This would all be over then. She tried to focus on her breathing. In and out, pulling the string closer. Examining its many fibres that crisscrossed each other, weaving and braiding. Simple lines that told such a complex story, holding for an instant the whole history of one being. Klotho knew this string well. It had been her constant companion since birth. Although she could not read it as well as her sisters, she still managed to pull pieces, fragments of life from its secret scriptures.

"Hilfe!" The voice made her skin begin to crawl. Her fingernails dug into the fleshy underside of her hands. Biting harder down on her lip, she pulled the string closer to her face. She hunched over in her chair so that her white robe enveloped nearly all of her tiny frame.

"Hilfe!"

"That's it! Stop it!" Klotho exclaimed as she stood up and stomped over to the suitcase. "Stop it, stop it, stop it!" She gave the suitcase a swift kick with her foot, knocking it on its side.

Silence reigned once more around her. A warm liquid seeped into her mouth. Licking at it, she tasted the bitter tang of iron and salt that was her own blood. As she swore under her breath, the latch to the suitcase silently clicked open.

άνδρας

When the mortar bomb hit and so much of him had been taken at once, Stauffenberg remembered thinking of his family. His children especially: how much they made him laugh. As he felt the ground underneath his feet peel away from him, felt his body thrown through the air once more, he wondered what else would be taken from him this time. He tried to relax his body, to brace in some way for an impact. But in this darkness he could barely tell up from down as he flew for what felt like days. When the rough leather hit his face he wondered if it was the same wall he had been crouched next to before.

His limbs stiffened and ached as he tried to peel himself away from the leather. He had managed to struggle to his knees when somewhere in front of his face there came the quietest click he had ever heard. The sound was so faint he wondered if he had imagined it, until a fracture of light crept towards him.

He wanted to get to his feet and run but his better judgment warned him to stay still. The light had come before and been snatched away just as quickly. Instead he crouched, hunched over his missing limb, and waited to see if the light would stay. The child was still close, he figured, as he had yet to hear her return to her chair. No footsteps had come since the darkness had spun him into the air.

Dust drifted softly through the light into the space around him. The breeze it rode made the hair on his good arm stand on end. Then footsteps came; Stauffenberg fumbled behind him, searching for anything to brace himself against. Nothing but darkness greeted him. He crouched lower. The footsteps passed by the light, briefly blacking it out. As they shuffled past, more dirt rose up, and a glare of white followed them. The familiar sound of an office chair squeaked as it once more gave way to the weight of the child.

Stauffenberg crawled to the edge of the light, the dust playing before his eye, twisting and beckoning him forwards. With a deep breath he pushed past the edge and into the light.

The sun beat down with a heat that made the ground feel as though it could melt the very leather off his boots. The breeze he had felt was completely gone, replaced by air that stood stiffly, as if stunned by the heat. The brightness made Stauffenberg grimace, his good eye blacking in and out from overexposure. He waved his three fingers ahead of him, trying to block out the light even if just for a moment.

Slowly his eye adjusted. At first it only saw darker blurs against the blinding white, then gradually a desert formed in front of him. Dirt and large monstrous thorn-covered trees as far as he could see, the only hellish plants capable of surviving such a heat. He had seen trees and shrubs similar to this from his time in Africa. Felt this heat, this stinging air burning his lungs from the inside out.

He coughed as dust seemed to fill every nook of his lungs. He pulled at his collar, hoping to use some of the cloth of his jacket as a filter. Slowly he moved forward, glancing to his left and right, searching for the office chair he had heard so clearly before. As he inched forward he realized he must be on a cliff of some sort. The leathery ground appeared to stretch before him, only to come to a rolled edge. Steadily, Stauffenberg moved closer to the edge, maintaining an ever-safe distance should it become unstable.

As he did so, the familiar sound of the office chair came from the right just as a shadow fell on the land. Stauffenberg rubbed at his one eye as the shadow fell. This was certainly no child.

Μοίρες

Klotho clung to the cord in her hands, twisting it slightly, trying to get the light to hit certain threads. As she moved the string she pushed her chair backwards. An old song her mother Nyx had once lovingly sung played in her ears. Nyx used to sing it as she taught Klotho how to carefully wind the string in her hands so that Lakhesis and Atropos could examine its many fibres. The chair continued to move backwards as Klotho sang the song of darkness and the night meeting one celestial eve.

Sitting under the boiling sun alone now, Klotho couldn't help but find her situation ironic—that being the daughter of darkness and night had sentenced her to a life of brutal light. As she sung she pulled the hood of her robes over her long black hair, tucking it back carefully with one hand, while the other held fast to the string. That was when one of the legs of her chair grazed the suitcase lying behind her. She turned, startled by the feeling of hitting something other than dirt.

"Stupid suitcase, stupid sisters." Klotho turned back to her string. She placed it gently across the folds of her robe, wondering if the heat of this never fading sun was powerful enough that day to melt the string into her robes. As she waited patiently, she heard the unmistakable scratching noise of a human cough.

Sighing she turned to look down at the suitcase. "Would you please—"

There standing as still as he could was Stauffenberg, his few fingers shielding his one good eye as he stared up at Klotho. She had only seen a human this closely once before. Often it was from afar, or only when her sisters allowed her a glimpse of what they saw in the string's fibres. Their tiny frames always startled her. As of late her sisters had especially been shielding her from the sight of any of them, claiming they had turned into monsters even the Titans might fear. As she looked down at his disfigured arm, missing fingers, and eye, she understood now what they meant. This man had barely any human parts left to distinguish him from beast. As her eyes flitted over his wounds, Klotho slowly let the string slip to her feet.

η συνάντηση

The two stood staring in fear at one another for several moments. Stauffenberg could barely believe his eyes at this massive white robed figure sitting before him, taller than any building or beast he had ever seen. Yet it had a child's voice much like his own son's had been as a tiny boy. How could something so large sound so small?

Klotho stared down at this half-human, wondering what horrors had taken so much of him. In his eyes she recognized something she had only seen once before, in a similar man.

He had been a Greek soldier fighting at the battle of Corinth. It had been days of spinning and cutting string. When night fell on the second day, Klotho and her sisters finally had a break. As Atropos and Lakhesis drifted to sleep, Klotho attempted once more to stretch and read the fibres of her string. As she pulled at it, coiling it through her hands meticulously, a man arrived in their suitcase. He had pleaded over and over for the Fates to make a decision. The pain from his wounds was driving him to screams that sent the same shivers down Klotho's spine as Stauffenberg's pleas for help. Somehow the soldier's guttural sounds of torment had not raised her sisters from their slumber. Desperate for it to end, Klotho had peered sheepishly into the suitcase to try and explain to this man it would only be a matter of time before her sisters would wake. When she opened it, the smell of blood, guts, and rot was so strong she could barely open her mouth without vomit rising to the back of her throat, making her eyes burn.

Now as she stared down at Stauffenberg, she remembered the blow that had come to the back of her head for her previous mistake. "Go back, no, please, she will—they will be back any minute."

The child's voice crashed around Stauffenberg, making the ground beneath his feet tremble. He moved his hand to shield the light of the sun, hoping for a better look at this giant. What stood before him appeared to be a female figure cloaked in a white robe. The robes glistened in the bright sun, almost blinding Stauffenberg.

"Where am I?" He managed to fumble over the words with what little English he knew.

"You need to go back." The robed child rose from the chair, towering over Stauffenberg. Klotho tried her best to quiet her voice, to stop it from shaking this poor man to his core. "Now. Please, I beg of you."

As she bent forward, Stauffenberg tried to shield his eye one last time to glimpse this monstrosity's face. The folds of the robe and hood, however, kept her shielded from sight.

"I refuse, not until you tell me where I am. Where is the Lord?" Stauffenberg's legs trembled beneath him. He looked down at the unfamiliar leathered land beneath his feet, realizing they were shaking because of fear and not because the ground moved from Klotho's words.

"There are no lords here. Now, please." Klotho brought her hand forward, slowly bending down towards Stauffenberg. Her robe slipped back, revealing some of her black hair as she readied herself to push him as gently as possible back into the suitcase. As she stretched out her fingers, Klotho looked down at them. She stared at their bareness, snapping them back. Her string was gone.

"No, it can't be!" The child's shouting created a gust of wind that blew Stauffenberg right over. He crumpled back into the opening he had crawled out of, falling backwards once more into darkness. As he felt his body crash against the leathered walls once more he felt for the first time in his life like giving up. How can there be hope without any Lord and Saviour?

Klotho picked up her robe and scrambled around her chair; dirt clung to her, kicked up by her frenzied movements, turning her white robe into a faded reddish pink mess. She glanced from her sister's chair to her own, bending down to claw on hands and knees for the string. How could she have dropped it?

Stauffenberg sat up slowly and stared at the fading light as it crept through the darkness. What was the point in fighting now? Clearly his beloved God, his one true hope in all this darkness, had never been listening. Had never been watching over him. How could he have been if he was willing to send Stauffenberg to this hellish place? Swirls of reddened dust began to form at the edge of the light. The ground moved left, then right, as Stauffenberg heard the child sweeping her hands across the dirt.

A glint came from under Klotho's chair. At first she suspected it was simply the hot sun playing a trick on her eyes, refracting light off the metal bottom of her chair. As she crawled closer, she held her breath, praying silently to the gods that she had found the string. There at the base of her chair was the serrated edge and rusted handles of Atropos' shear.

"Damn it!" Klotho pushed her chair over in a rage.

The metal and leather spun in the dirt, colliding with the suitcase. Once more Stauffenberg was sent flying, colliding this time with the edge of the leathered surface where it met the light. As he stumbled for a grip, he lifted his head in time to see the sun sharply fading as darkness encroached on the land. A great wind picked up, sucking dust off the ground, twisting it into clouds that rushed by.

Klotho bent down again; panic-stricken, she scrambled across the dust and shrubs searching for her string. The small shrubs and grasses cut at her fingers. She was so consumed she barely noticed the light fading nor the wind picking up. As a crack of thunder hit her ears, Klotho's fingers finally wrapped around something pulled tight, fibrous, and familiar.

"Sister, what are you doing on the ground?" Lakhesis' voice broke across Klotho's back, making her stiffen as she clasped the string to her chest.

"Lakhesis." Klotho looked down at her dirt-covered robe. "Back so soon?"

Μοίρες

Lakhesis stood before her chair, her black robe rustling back and forth in the breeze that followed her return. Over her face she still wore her black mask. Calmly she stared down at Klotho, who was rising from her knees. Klotho's white robe was now so stained from the red ground that she practically blended into her surroundings. As she stood, she worried at the glint in Lakhesis' eye, matching her dark mask.

"What are you doing?" Lakhesis spat the words at Klotho.

"I was just trying to study the string, see if I had finally gotten the hang of—"

"You know that's my job." Lakhesis snatched the string from Klotho's hands as she snapped once more at her sister. She pulled at it, stretching it this way and that. "I think I know how we can solve this." Lakhesis shoved the string back into Klotho's hands and rifled around the ground herself.

Klotho watched her sister moving quickly across the dirt and shrubs. Lakhesis paused only briefly once to adjust the hood of her robe, trying to get a better look at a shrub. As Lakhesis moved, Klotho tried inching herself closer to the suitcase that was still tipped over, open slightly.

"Have you seen them?" Lakhesis' voice was still sharp, piercing Klotho's ears.

"Sorry, seen who?" Klotho mumbled as she stepped closer to the suitcase, keeping her eyes fixed on her sister.

"Not who, you fool, them. The shears, Atropos' shears!"

"Um, I think they were somewhere..." Klotho realized she couldn't remember now where her chair sat before. The ground suddenly looked all the same. "Sister, I... where is Atropos?"

"Never mind, where are her shears!" Lakhesis spun around to face Klotho, her face still hidden behind her black mask. Her voice sounded more strained than usual.

"Why don't you try removing your—"

"I can see just fine." Lakhesis paused. "Oh fine." As she reached to remove her mask, her hand froze at the rim of her hood. "Klotho, what have you done?"

Before Klotho could answer, Lakhesis pushed past her. She shoved Klotho so hard that Klotho could barely hold on to the string. As Klotho regained her balance, she saw out of the corner of her eye what Lakhesis had seen.

"Again? You fool! What have you done?" Lakhesis' voice boomed, causing the darkening sky to turn to a deep blackish purple.

άνδρας

Stauffenberg felt the ground shake under him as the woman named Lakhesis charged towards him. Her voice ricocheted off the leather surface, sending shivers up Stauffenberg's spine. Would he never escape this hell?

"I ought to—"

"Please, sister, it was a mistake, I didn't open it on purpose this time."

"*Genug*!" Stauffenberg's voice surprised himself.

"What was that?" Lakhesis said.

"He speaks sometimes—"

"Enough with you, Klotho!"

Stauffenberg heard the child scream out as something struck her. His guess was the hand of her sister. As he tried to think of something to say, something to protect this strange beast-child, the light in front of him snapped away with a click. Plunged into darkness once more, Stauffenberg felt in his gut this was the end.

"So this is *mein Schicksal*! *Gottes Schicksal für mich?*" He felt his feet shiver as the words escaped his lips. Had all his devoutness ended in this?

"Your *Schicksal* still waits for you," Lakhesis spat the words down at Stauffenberg. They surrounded him in the darkness as if they were sent to scold him for his foolish outburst. Stauffenberg began shaking again. As his legs wavered he clenched his remaining fingers into a fist.

Lakhesis tried to keep her tone even. "Find me the shears, and this may be forgiven, Klotho."

Μοίρες

Klotho got to her knees and rubbed at her reddened cheek. Lakhesis sighed as she folded herself into her chair, exhaustion showing in the way she shifted her body. Klotho searched the ground quietly, the sting of the shrubs brushing against her hands once more.

"Where is Atropos?"

Lakhesis sighed. "I couldn't find her."

Klotho lifted her hand to her burning cheek. "What do you

mean you couldn't—"

"You will not concern yourself with this. Find her shears." The tension in Lakhesis voice had returned.

Klotho kept crawling on her hands and knees, searching for some sign in the dust of where her chair sat before. The wind brought up from Lakhesis' return seemed to erase all trace of her spot. Desperate, she closed her eyes and mouthed a prayer her mother had taught her many moons ago. Her lips formed each word carefully as she silently prayed for Zeus, Hera, or any god who would hear her plea to find dear Atropos and bring her back. If not for Klotho's sake, then for this man who had clearly suffered enough.

As she prayed silently, her fingers grazed across a sharper blade, then that of the needles protruding from the shrubs. The feeling startled her. Klotho stared down at Atropos' shears. Cradling her hands to her chest, Klotho continued her prayer, begging for the gods to intervene, knowing full well they held no real power over her or her sisters, but perhaps they could urge Atropos home.

Footsteps, slow and steady, came from behind Klotho as Lakhesis stood from her chair and moved towards where Klotho kneeled.

"I knew of the two of us, you could find them. Your eyes have always been better than mine. For this, be thankful you cannot read your precious string; it takes far more than it gives." Lakhesis bent down. Smiling, she picked the shears up delicately, holding them up to the ever-darkening sky. "It's time, little sister."

"But how do you know where to cut; how do you know it will be his fate?" Klotho stared up at her sister's mask, wishing she would remove it. Hoping she could see into Lakhesis' eyes and understand the focus that now coated Lakhesis' words.

"I have read this man's lifeline. I know."

"But do you know his—"

"Enough, or I will teach you a more painful lesson. Mother was wrong in thinking you would ever be helpful to this family."

Klotho felt a knot form in her stomach. It bent and twisted with Lakhesis' words, threatening to make her sick.

"Hand me your precious string."

Klotho stared at the red ground in front of her, still clutching her hands to her chest.

"Klotho, the string." Lakhesis was getting impatient.

Klotho felt for the string at her side, twisting its fibres in her fingers. Looping it around her wrists and arms, allowing it to embrace her. As she did so the memory of the soldier covered in his own blood, crying out for his gods, flooded her eyes, his voice ringing out. She could not hold in the sick rising up her throat.

"Klotho, enough!" Lakhesis' voice broke the image floating before Klotho's eyes, shattering it as if it were little more than an eggshell.

Then it came: the blow to the back of her head, the dirt pressing itself against her cheek as she hit the ground, the imprints of sharp shrub needles piercing her soft skin. Atropos had made Lakhesis swear to never raise a hand to their sister again. She had made her swear it on their mother's life.

Klotho's voice was quiet but steady. "You are not the keeper of the string. It was allotted to me, not you. I alone spin it, not you. You cannot do this, Lakhesis, you cannot."

"How dare you, you think you can—"

"I think you should put those down."

Klotho turned at the sound of her eldest sister's familiar voice.

"We do not touch what is not ours." Atropos stood over Klotho, cloaked in a purple robe, hood pulled back to expose pale skin that was nearly transparent. Her red hair was pulled back into a long, tight braid. Klotho smiled up at her, but Atropos stared straight ahead, keeping her eyes fixed on Lakhesis until she dropped the shears into the red dirt.

άνδρας

Stauffenberg watched as a warm glow started to form at the edge of the darkness. Lakhesis and Klotho's arguing seemed to be coming to a peak, and yet before him stood a warmth. A light he was not familiar with. The rumblings around him quieted as the glow grew until it felt like a warm lamp was bobbing towards him. It gradually filled the space until it completely surrounded him. The leather surface disappeared, replaced by the light. Stauffenberg felt his legs steady, his trembling cease. As the light filled every inch around him he felt a smile grow. *Finally* was the only word filling his mind when a woman cloaked in purple walked from the edge of the glow towards him.

Her hair was a red he had never seen before, so dark it seemed dyed with blood. Her skin glowed, nearly blending into the light that now surrounded them both. As she approached he called out, "Angel, what is your name?"

"Angel?" The woman paused. "I suppose I am, in a way."

Stauffenberg frowned. "You are not an angel?"

"I am the allotter of fate. Beholder of destiny, angel to some, I suppose... And you, you're Colonel Stauffenberg."

"That's correct." Stauffenberg stood up straighter, felt his pride come back to him.

"Yes, soldier, hero to some, definitely your children. Your wife. Your men."

Stauffenberg felt his chest puffing up: finally, justice.

"Villain to some."

Stauffenberg twitched. "You've clearly not heard of my attempts at ending this war, then. My God would have seen that; he would not send an angel who hadn't."

"Oh, I have seen. I have seen you try three times, even sacrificing your own life for it. I saw the way you shook in outrage at the slaughtering of the Jews. But I also saw how you helped to destroy Poland. How you agreed Poles should be slaves and Poland colonized." The woman paused, a smile breaking slowly across her face. "No one is truly innocent to their core, are they?"

Stauffenberg stared defiantly back at the woman. "Poland was rightfully ours. It belonged to the German Empire. We didn't know it would—"

"Go so far? So many lives ended, for what?" The woman waved her robed hand at Stauffenberg, stopping his response from leaving his lips. "When will it be, you just let yourselves live in peace for once... I wonder... I pray." The woman sighed, closing her eyes.

Stauffenberg watched her closely, waiting for her to speak again. When she opened her eyes once more, they had changed. What were before a crystal blue, a Führer blue, were now dark as the blackest of skies. No stars, no light—and yet there was still life behind them. A power. Stauffenberg wondered if his deadened eye now looked this black.

"Your fate has been decided, Colonel. It is time you claimed it."

"And my God, will I see him? Has he seen the good I've done?"

"He's seen what he needed to."

The light began to fade until all that was left in the darkness was Atropos, her eyes faded from black to ice blue. The life in them waned ever so slightly, so only the most keen might observe the way they turned a shade lighter, the way her body slumped to the left with a hint of exhaustion. Her power drained in such an infinitesimal way that perhaps only the kindest of eyes might notice. Before she left the darkness, Atropos adjusted her robe and pulled at her braid, making sure of its tightness.

"Atropos?" Klotho's sweet voice rang out in the darkness, putting a smile on Atropos' face.

"Coming, sister."

το τέλος

∞

Molly's First Two Options

1. Wizard conference: the two hooded figures are the first to arrive and are mortal enemies.
2. Ku Klux Klan meeting. Started researching hoods and cultural references, discovered at one point the Greek Fates or Moirai supposedly wore hoods.

The Judges and the Suitcase

Josh Dygert

The desert was barren. A hot wind rattled the sparse greenery. In the distance, I saw them. The two giants. The black-robed and the white-robed aliens sat as silent statues. The black-robed one had skin as white as the surface of the moon; the other had skin like cobalt. The robes of each rose above their heads and formed sharp points. The people who looked on them thought first of the KKK except that there was nothing about these beings that indicated any human concept of race. The next thought might be a wizard's hat, except there was no magic to those faces. The third thought was that of a judge's robes. This seemed somehow more accurate.

They sat on identical plush lounge chairs. Every so often, the movement of wind or perhaps of the slow accumulation of small movements that must be happening somewhere within those robe-covered bodies would cause the chairs to rock softly. Between the two alien judges, a rope-bound suitcase waited in expectant silence on their decision.

The world never knew when they first appeared. But appear they did, and since then people came from all over the globe to watch these strange silent aliens that are clearly alive. One could never get too close to them, nor does one ever want to. There was a fear that came from looking upon them, a fever that crawled along the base of the neck and wormed its way into the base of the brain.

It's not just the fear that kept people away though. When one got too close, one found an invisible wall barring the way. It did a person no harm. It was merely solid.

Everyone who watched knew that there was a conversation at play there even as they acknowledged that these seemingly unmoving faces and bodies gave no sense of what we understand as communication.

And so many watched. The moment that the news broke, the deserts outside Discomber swarmed with people from all over the world. They came bearing flowers, and they came bearing candles. They came bearing Welcome signs, and they come bearing great beaming smiles. Like some sort of army of peace, they descended on my judges. The incessant sounds of a thousand voices speaking two dozen languages went silent as they reached them. As they came to that invisible line in the sand.

All those smiles waned for a moment.

And then someone started playing an exuberant tune upon a trumpet. And in combat with the fear that now crawled through their brains, they resumed talking and laughing and singing and smiling.

The judges did not move.

And so the vigil began.

The governments of the world did not take long in pushing back the masses. They came in helicopters and Jeeps, their guns and weapons hidden from sight but present. Armed with loudspeakers, they created a perimeter around the judges and began their own work.

Not much is known about their attempts. According to the official releases, a team was assembled with representatives from all the world's major nations. The appearance of aliens in an American desert was a world event, not only an American one. For long months, I watched from my hiding place as they attempted to cross that border. I caught vague wafts of words in every language of the Earth, and I saw them hold up enormous boards at a level with the eyes of the judges, boards filled with words in language after language, in alphabet after alphabet.

Although they endeavoured to hide their efforts from prying eyes, I saw enough to know that they worked day and night for weeks. That every day, they forced themselves to attempt ever more creative and ever more bizarre methods of communication. When once I saw an assembly of people all waving their arms in strange patterns and dancing around in circles, my feelings washed down between those two judges of condescending amusement. Of mocking laughter that could not quite be heard.

After that, efforts declined.

After that, people started to get impatient.

There are those that do not appreciate the presence of these judges. Once the governments felt that all their efforts had achieved was the aliens' scorn, power shifted to those who desired a less amicable response.

The night of the first bomb, sirens echoed across the desolate sands of the desert. Planes, helicopters, and Jeeps once more appeared. This time, they did not hide their guns. Once more, they drove back that army of peace with their candles and their flowers and their posters.

I was there to see it all that night. No one understood what was about to happen. I didn't understand what was about to happen. Even after the first bomb dropped and the fire lit the night and the earth shook, I did not understand. After the second bomb and the second flash and the second quake, I began to get the idea. And when the third bomb came up from down below, and rocks fell from the ceiling of my hiding place, only then did I understand.

When it was over, the aliens sat on as they always sat. Still and silent.

Over the next few weeks, this continued.

Governments tried to end them with bombs from above and below, but the giants never showed any sign that they noticed. If one stood there just after such a bombing had taken place, there was the tremendous sense of a wrong done. There was the sense that one of the two was smirking while the other seethed with shame and anger. In those moments, one felt certain that one of the two was *for* us and that one of the two was *against* us. I was never sure which was which.

And yet, for all the bombs and for all the fear, the vigil of the army of peace did not end. Their numbers shrunken and their line pushed far back, still they kept up their quiet welcome. Their candles burned on even as their flowers drooped and the colours of their posters faded. They remained.

The little town of Discomber, Nevada was the closest little

piece of civilization to the giants in the desert, and I was a reporter at *The Discomber Gazette.* I was the first to break the story because I was the one who saw them first. Outside the town, the desert stretches inexhaustible but for the occasional exclamation mark of great brown mesas. Amid some of these mesas, time has hollowed out caverns and tunnels, some of which are well-known and well-walked. Others, though, keep their secret from all but a few, even today.

When my father was a boy, he found one such cave. It became his secret place. And when I was a boy, he shared that secret place with me. It became my secret place, and it has continued to be mine long after my father left. I filled it with the secrets of my teenage years, as my father did before me, in the form of old notebooks with yellowed pages and the posters of banned movies and forbidden music. The books came and went, but I was never without reading material. I went there to feel close to a father who couldn't be bound to his family, and in the going, I became bound to the place.

In my little cave, a slit in the rock looks out upon the empty desert. Since I was a child, I've loved to watch the sun emerge above the horizon line of sand.

Any day I can, I go there to watch the sun rise or set.

One day, as the sunlight fell across the sand and sparse vegetation, the light brought them. I thought I was seeing things for a moment. Or that I was dreaming. One moment they had not been there, and the next, there they were.

And thus, the biggest scoop in history fell from the sky into my lap as I drank my morning coffee.

When the big news networks came sweeping in, I didn't move from my little place in the mesa's cave. I found that it gave me the perfect view of both of their faces. I wanted to be the only one who could take the pictures, who could look at them this way. Miraculously, no one ever appeared in my little hiding place. They busied themselves with getting as close as possible on the ground or in the air, and they wondered how my shots always turned out quietly superior to their own.

It turned out that there was little to report on after a few months. When two giant aliens appear, it's very big news, but when they proceed to do absolutely nothing, there isn't too much that the news can say. After the initial weeks of fearmongering about planetary invasion and right or left wing conspiracies, everyone was appropriately terrified. Certain that one motion of one alien's right hand ring finger would be the strike that blows open the confetti-filled piñata of the planet, the press moved on to the next item on their agenda most likely to stir fear, anger, or preferably, both.

I should have moved on with the others.

But I remained, and I watched. And I waited.

Discomber is a quiet town. Much like our visitors. Yet even in Discomber, life moves on. And it moved on without me. Texts went unanswered. Phone calls went unreturned. Voicemails went unheard. I didn't go to work. I didn't see friends. The texts, the calls, the emails, the voicemails all stopped. And just like that, the strings that bound me to life snapped. And still, my judges sat and waited and watched. And so did I.

Some part of me still equates my actions with self-destruction, but how could I give way to normalcy when the great fantastic sat waiting in the desert? The moments not spent in my mesa cave had all the reality of a dream. My real life stopped being real. The only real thing was my aliens. And while the world turned its eyes elsewhere or brooded upon a crueller, more powerful type of bomb, I was patient.

I had read my science fiction with its hasty bugger wars, its bloodthirsty pioneers on Mars, too quick to turn to violence, and its unfaithful Frankensteins with their ever more vengeful monsters. And I had observed life. I knew that not all things happened in the blink of an eye. I knew that there was more than one way to hold a conversation and more than one tempo at which to wage a life. I spent a childhood watching a loving father and husband become a phantom. There were never fights. There were never words. It was always in the silence. And then he left. And it was over. And so, too, my alien judges would come to a decision in their own timeline and I wanted to be present when they did.

It happened long after the rest of the world had left. It was a few minutes past 2pm on a Tuesday afternoon in the middle of August. I'd arrived around noon and eaten a turkey sandwich on rye bread. There was a feeling in the air, but there was always a feeling in the air. When I settled myself to watch, though, I got the sense that today was different. There was nothing different to be seen and nothing different to be heard. The difference was only in the feeling. For some time, I thought I must be mistaken. I thought I was imagining things.

Then, in perfect synchronization, both giants turned in their chairs to stare directly at me and lifted one hand each. They motioned for me to come forward.

The moment remains in my memory, but it tastes like a scene from a movie, not like something that really happened to me. I remember that I felt no surprise. Like I had expected to be summoned all along. The movements were only a confirmation of a role that I already knew I was to play. I barely remember the passage from my place in the mesa to the border that no one crossed. Dying flowers, wilted posters, burnt down candles, and candy wrappers edged this border, along with the discarded detritus of soldiers and scientists. The line of the barrier was sharp as a razor, but I stepped through, my foot displacing the litter. How many times had I watched people trying to force their way through fruitlessly?

I walked through as if there was no wall at all. I remember the hot wind through my hair. I remember the way those two statues looked at me without looking. The two giants each pointed a long index finger at the suitcase. As they did, the two ropes that bound it came undone. I took a step toward the suitcase, towering above me as large as a house. I looked up at it and the two sides came unstuck, and opened. Each half fell flat against the earth, sending a wave of sand and air over me.

The suitcase that had looked so full that its seams strained turned out to be completely empty. The two aliens looked down at me and then at the suitcase. They pointed at it. I understood. I will never be able to explain fully why I did what they asked and never hesitated. It could have been that the hours I'd spent watching them had somehow made me theirs. It could have been that the strange telepathic communication that passed between them could somehow find its way into a human skull and compel it to do as they directed. Whatever the reason, I stepped over the side of the suitcase. I stood with one foot on each side of the open case, the two sides sprawling out to graze the robes of both giants.

Then I turned my gaze back up at the aliens.

As one, they stood. Their shadows fell upon me as I stared up at them, their monochromatic forms making of the afternoon an artificial night. Each head tilted in my direction. And their eyes met mine. Eyes like darkness and shadows and pits and voids. Eyes that bored down into me. Eyes like mine.

They threw off their robes of white and black, each with only one simple gesture that stirred a rush of wind. The sand and the sky, their hard faces and their empty eyes, vanished behind the curtains of those cloaks. The robes came off, falling gently into the right side of the suitcase, folding themselves neatly as they went. I jumped wholly into the suitcase's other side, narrowly missing burial beneath the fabric.

When the robes settled, my giants no longer loomed above me. On either side of me, two men stood. Gone was moon skin and stone skin. The shadows of their former eyes now hid behind human irises.

The two men looked very familiar.

The two men looked like me.

"For many days now, we have debated the merits of your people and whether they were worthy of our aid," said the one on my right who had once worn a white robe.

"For many days now, we have been tempted to end you all," said the other, the one who once wore robes of black.

"For many days now, we have been interested."

"For many days now, we have debated."

"Interest and annihilation."

"Help or harm."

"And did you choose between the two?" I asked.

"No," they said at once. I saw carnage and mushroom clouds sprawl outward from that moment. The sands of the desert would turn to glass before the nearest cities fell. The oceans would consume the continents, and finally, the globe would explode from the inside out. I saw no other future.

My breath caught in my throat. In my fridge, the leftover pizza from last night and the brand new six-pack of beer would go untasted and untouched.

"When first you came with the flowers and the candles and the trumpets, we felt amused but inclined toward you. We thought we might help you. When the bombs came, we felt certain we would kill you all. Such strange extremities in you and in our reactions. And then, all throughout the bombs and the peace sign holders, there was you. You always stayed and watched. And all the while, we did not know why."

"It was you watching," began the other, "that made us realize we were wrong. We did not understand, and the lack of understanding drove us mad."

"The lack of understanding showed us that we cannot preside in judgment over a people we have never been," he said.

"But we could help," said one.

"And we could hurt," said the other.

"We decided to try on your skin," said one.

"We decided to live as men," they said.

"But how did..." I began. I shook my head, feverish words and questions sticking in my throat. "Thank you for choosing to live with us."

"Your lot will be our lot," they said.

"Your soul will be our soul," they said.

"But why tell me this?" I asked.

"Because you are the reason for our choice," said the one.

"And you are the model for our humanity," said the other.

"When you stepped into our suitcase," said the one, "you became our undecided model."

"When you stepped into our suitcase," said the other, "you became our template."

"When you stepped into our suitcase," they said, "we became you."

They were me but they wore my flesh differently. They wore it in ways that I didn't think anyone would ever confuse them for me.

I stared at my judges, my aliens, my clones. Within the last few minutes, they'd threatened to kill us all. Now, here they were wearing my face. And what exactly would they do with my face? With my hands? What would the help they mentioned mean should they deign to give it? Would my hands run red with the blood of the world? If so, everyone had to know. More important, I had to know.

"What will you do in the world?" I asked.

"Who knows?" asked the one.

"Maybe we'll help."

"Maybe we'll hurt."

"Maybe we'll do both."

"Maybe we will simply watch," they said.

Then they both smiled with lips that looked like mine, but these were smiles I would never smile. And then, the two of them turned their backs to me and left the suitcase. I stood in stunned silence and watched as they walked away. My eyes remained focused on their fading forms until they had walked so far I could not see them.

It was then I realized that the suitcase was gone, and so were the chairs. The desert looked now as it had through all the other days of my life. There was nothing to suggest they had ever been here at all.

When I got back to civilization, I found that all the pictures of them disappeared from the newspapers and the Internet. The world got amnesia. Only one picture remains. The first one I ever took on that first day. It was in my pocket the day they used me as a template. I often wonder if they carry the same picture with them.

Only I seem to remember. When I show my picture to anyone else, they become confused and angry until I put the picture away and they can forget once more. I carry the image with me through the long desert of my years. Every so often, I meet someone I don't know who says they've seen me.

"Maybe you just have one of those faces," they'll say.

But their eyes will be troubled. I can always tell in that moment whether they helped, whether they hurt, or, more often than not, whether they did both.

∞

Josh's First Two Options

1. A dark wizard and a white wizard sit down to debate the ultimate magic contained in a suitcase, trying to negotiate for control over ultimate power.

2. Two alien kings meet on a barren planet to debate the meaning of the suitcase that is full of the body parts of both their races.

Good Night, Travel Well

Emma Venables

After the third group of men left, Hannelore went from room to room, tearing the blackout curtains from their poles, the sheets from the beds. Silke watched from the hallway, her heels turning white against the skirting boards. Hannelore shook her head. Don't cower, my child. She rested her chin on top of the ball of material she held, and smiled at her granddaughter. Silke had smiled back. A gap-toothed smile, a smile pulled down at the corners: the type of smile that comes out of wartime. Hannelore watched Silke's fingertips worrying at a crack in the wall. She tutted. We don't want to bring this place tumbling down around our ears, do we? Silke dug her nails in, as if embedding herself in the fabric of the building would keep it upright.

Hannelore turned away. One more room: her own. The room she lost her virginity in; the room she birthed babies into; the room she trembled in when the air raids came; the room she sobbed in when the letter arrived with the bad news; the room she shared with her daughter-in-law when her apartment caved in at the whims of a bomb blast; the room in which she wiped the bloodstains from her daughter-in-law's face and pulled the plaster shards from her hair when a daytime attack caught her in the grocery queue; the room in which she tried to console her fifteen-year-old granddaughter on the nights the Bolsheviks barged in and pinned them both, facedown, against the mattress. As she listened to the threads on Silke's petticoats snapping for the third time, Hannelore's resolve to stay put, to face the enemy with a steely eye and a straight back, unravelled. After the men had gone, she announced they would go to the city: to Tanta Ada, to Onkel Fritz, to safety in numbers. The journey, by foot, would prove dangerous, of course, for the Bolsheviks filter into Germany like ants through a crack in the wall, but she would figure something out; she would get them there.

And so, down came the curtains, off came the sheets, into a pail of water with them. Then Hannelore threw them over the low branches of the trees at the bottom of the garden, so they drip-dried in the afternoon sun. As Hannelore planned and packed, poring over maps, calculating distances and rest times, folding their meagre possessions into a suitcase—a spare dress between them, the bedsheets and blackout curtains, scissors, some precious needles and thread—Silke watched without saying a word.

As the night drew in, and Silke napped, Hannelore opened the suitcase, unpicked a corner of the lining and slipped in a small brown paper bag containing her most prized possession.

*

They walk. For miles. Parched earth beneath their feet. Hannelore trips on a clump of grass, but rights herself. The suitcase bangs against her shin. She bites her lip, distracting herself from throbbing in her leg with a sharper pain. Hannelore pushes her free hand to her face, pulls it away, and looks for blood. None. One cannot afford to lose anything these days. That's why she holds the suitcase. The girl offers to help, but she walks like a wisp of smoke in a breeze, and Hannelore cannot risk losing any more of her.

Silke looks straight ahead. Her eyes never leave the horizon: the snapped cathedral spire, the chewed outlines of the apartment blocks, the skeletal figures leading the way. Hannelore wonders what Silke thinks of the women and children ahead, of their tattered outfits, dirty knees, the merciless way they bicker over any scraps of food they find. She wants to ask Silke her thoughts on this animalistic humanity they suddenly find themselves a part of, but Silke stopped talking the first night the Bolsheviks kicked down the door. Hannelore tried to probe, navigating the awkward space a grandmother should never reside in with her granddaughter—asked if Silke was sore between her legs, if there was blood, asked when she usually expected her monthly, tried to work out the timings of

Silke's uterine functions from the silence.

Hannelore takes her Silke's hand, squeezes it tightly, tighter than perhaps necessary. Silke does not flinch, does not look at her grandmother, but does look down at the suitcase. She even reaches out her free hand and runs her thumb against its battered corners.

*

They find a spot for the night, away from the droves already lying out in the open air, a spot somewhat sheltered, somewhat invisible, between a large tree and a hedge. Cattle low on the other side. Hannelore crouches, listens to the crack of her bones, before sliding onto her stomach and peering through the undergrowth. She wants to see potatoes within reaching distance, but no such luck.

She stands up and shakes her head.

"Sorry, Silke."

She apologises almost hourly—sorry for holding her right arm up at every portrait of the Führer she passed; sorry for the bomb that extinguished her mother; sorry for the lack of food; sorry for the splintered door that was supposed to hold steady; sorry for the soldiers who yelled in a language neither of them understood as they forced themselves into her; sorry for throwing everything into a battered suitcase; sorry for the ceiling of stars.

Sorry. Sorry. Sorry.

Silke shrugs. She sits down, rests her back against the tree's trunk. Her stomach roars. Hannelore's replies. At moments like this she wishes to catch a smile on Silke's face, a shared understanding, a hint of humour during these soulless days, but her granddaughter simply closes her eyes, rests her head against the mottled bark.

The dusk nestles in. Hannelore crouches, flicks open the locks of the suitcase, and waits until Silke's breathing steadies into the rhythm of sleep. Only then does she pull forth the sheets, her needle and thread. She closes the case, clicks the locks shut, and perches on it; the damp floor does not provide any comfort for her aging bones. With the material wrapped around her knees, she begins. Needle in, needle out.

Hannelore pricks her finger, frowns at the bead of blood in the dusk and wipes it onto the grass. She admires her handiwork by running a hand across it. Silke's outfit is nearly complete. Made from the very sheets Hannelore tore from her bed before they left, before they joined the crowds heading for the city. She has pinned and tweaked the material all from imagination, all for her granddaughter's protection. A few more rows of stitches here and there, and it will be finished.

Silke twitches in her sleep—a trait she developed after the first group of men barged into their home, until after they ploughed her face into the mattress and ripped her clothes from her. Hannelore longs to reach out her hand, to steady the tremble in her granddaughter's limbs, but cannot risk tearing her from such a fickle friend as rest. Needle in, needle out. She predicts the costumes will be ready for when the landscape flattens, for when the trees become sparse, the pause between where scorched bark becomes scorched brick; when they become most vulnerable she will hide herself and her granddaughter beneath layers of material with stitches so tight no man can tear through, creating a spectacle, boggling the minds of the soldiers, striking fear into their red hearts.

Needle in, needle out, the moonlight her only guide. She listens to the sounds around her: to babies sniffling; to mothers serenading; to grinding teeth; to night terrors; to the crunch of grass as the soldiers wander amongst them, picking the women off one by one. The sounds change then, from slumber to resistance—nails against faces, fists against flesh, profanities against eardrums. She grimaces, recalling the body of the woman they walked past that morning. She lay on her side as if sleeping on the dewy grass, but when they looked at her face, it was obvious she would never get up: eyes wide open, a cobweb weaved across her forehead, her lips bloodied by someone's unwanted kiss. Silke had looked away, continued walking a few paces ahead, but Hannelore had looked down at the remains of the woman's skirt, at the rust-coloured stains smeared down her legs.

Hannelore shakes her head, dislodges the image of the corpse, carries on sewing. An eye on the fabric. An eye on her sleeping granddaughter's outline. If the men come near them again she'll sew their mouths and eyelids shut, sew their cocks shut, too. She creates ten stitches, in a neat row, and then stops with her needle poised. She has the hearing of a hound, or at least, that is what her father used to say in the days long before World Wars, Great Depressions, and National Socialism, before old age, fear, and hunger occupied her thoughts. A dog barks somewhere in the distance. Hannelore's muscles tense, but she carries on sewing in the dark, feeling her way around the material. Needle in, needle out. Again and again, until her eyelids droop and she stumbles past caring, into sleep.

*

The forest curls around them, dangerous when tree trunks are thick enough to conceal skinny soldiers. Silke watches the sky overhead disappear. Hannelore mutters a prayer under her breath—gratitude for the shade, for the potatoes they found earlier, and a wish for an unhindered path ahead. She longs to reach out and touch the back of Silke's neck, just to test if the girl's voice still remains, but that would be a foolish move. She wonders if her granddaughter can still speak in full sentences, and whether if she does not use words herself, can she understand the words of others? She wonders how it would feel to hold her own words in, to save her own breath, when she has so much to say. For now, her needle and thread communicate with her. She pours her rage, her disappointment, her guilt into their costumes. She must finish them before the city comes into the view. She finished Silke's last night, the dress at least, decided against unpicking the suitcase's lining, opening the brown paper bag and adding its contents. Silke has worn enough costumes over the past ten years. Hannelore remembers how she cooed over the blue skirt and white blouse of her granddaughter's Hitler Maiden's uniform; how her granddaughter reported those not giving money to the Winter Hilfe; how she encouraged such actions; how they noticed Frau and Herr Meister's front door ajar and after a few weeks Herr and Frau Müller moved in, newlywed and ready drop any coins necessary into Silke's tin. Perhaps such embellishments on this costume might help her hold her head higher, might provoke her to mutter her first "thank you" in a month. No,

Hannelore will save them for her own. The child has enough guilt, enough confusion, to bear, to comprehend; she does not need to take on more.

Silke bends, touches a lone flower. She holds her fingers around the stem as if tempted to pluck, but lets go. Hannelore watches her digging her fingers into her palm, punishing herself for her instincts. She considers grabbing Silke by her shoulders, and shaking her until the words tumble off her tongue. *Halt. Bitte. Oma.* She nudges Silke out of the way and bends down. The stem snaps apart with little effort, and she hands the red flower to Silke.

They walk on. Twigs snap beneath their feet. The suitcase handle creaks at intervals. Birds chirp overhead. They are never alone. Women flank them. A few dozen of them. Mostly family groups. Their collarbones and hipbones visible through their clothes. Eyes down. Mouths fixed. She has listened to their dresses tear, their pleas for release, as the soldiers raped them. Sometimes she considers rushing out of her own hiding place, stabbing their assailants and allowing them all to escape together, but she cannot stop sewing until her head droops and her hands fall.

Hannelore pauses, waits for the other groups of women to choose their spots for the night before she chooses their own. She ushers Silke away, towards the edge of the forest where she can sit and observe, poised like a bird of prey. She opens the suitcase, rummages around until she feels rough skin of the potatoes. She hands one to Silke, and watches her bite into it as if it were an apple. Silke winces.

"Toothache?" Hannelore asks.

She watches her granddaughter move her lower jaw from side to side. Once. Twice. Three times. She continues to eat the potato.

"If it's a rotten tooth, it might be best to pull it out," Hannelore says.

Silke pushes the last bit of potato into her mouth, and lies on the ground. She keeps her back to her grandmother, more and more these days.

Hannelore pulls the black-out material from the suitcase: time to start her own costume. Black material across her lap, she leans over the open suitcase and slips a finger beneath its lining, and feels for the scrunched-up paper bag. She withdraws her hand, and threads her needle. Perhaps she can do this in the future—victorious men will want well-dressed wives—and make a steady living in the city.

The moon hangs low over the trees, like a lamp lit just for her. A woman cries out somewhere nearby, although Hannelore cannot be sure. The forest distorts. Her skin prickles, but she continues with her task. She reaches for the scissors and begins to snip, throwing the offcuts into the open case. A rust-coloured streak still stains the scissors, but she refuses to lick her finger and rub it off. After all, it has clung on throughout the creation of Silke's costume, why remove all traces now?

She stitches quick as she can, and somewhat haphazardly now; hunger blurs her instincts with a needle and thread. The strength of the stitches on her costume does not matter so much, she tells herself. She has had her life, her loves. She recalls the first time she made love to her husband: clumsy, her hair caught beneath his elbows, trying to catch her breath beneath his weight, but safe. Perhaps time still exists for Silke: time to heal; time to have a lover, a husband, an awkward first encounter.

*

Silke paddles in the lake with an almost-smile on her face. Her mud-stained dress clings to her thighs. Hannelore calls, suggests she take it off and bathe. She does not know when they will have such a supply of water again. She can see the cathedral's spire, small but definitely there, between the trees. Soon the land will flatten. Soon army vehicles will replace the trees. Soon groups of Bolsheviks will replace the stragglers they have encountered thus far.

"Wash your dress, too," Hannelore says.

Silke stops, considers for a moment. She looks around.

"No one here, my child, except your old Oma," Hannelore says.

Her back to Hannelore, Silke pulls the dress over her head, revealing the ladder of her spine, the sharp point of her shoulder blades. Blue, black, and purple bouquets, which refuse to fade, adorn her back. Hannelore rubs her eyes and looks away. She hears the slap of Silke's dress against the water's surface, and carries the suitcase over to a tree stump.

She sits down, looks over at her granddaughter. Only Silke's head and shoulders are visible, and the dress, floating around her like a parachute. Hannelore opens the case and resumes her work. Her own costume completed, except for the small pouch she begins to fashion out of an offcut of material. Wings flap overheard. Insects thrum in the long grass around her. A grasshopper lands next to her foot, big enough for a snack, she thinks, but he does not stick around long enough for her to scoop him up and stuff him into her mouth. Hannelore sighs. She looks back at the lake, at Silke splashing, rubbing water into her face and neck as if it were soap.

When the material resembles a pouch, Hannelore retrieves the paper bag from the suitcase, opens it, and peers in. Six yellow fingernails. Yellow index fingernails, to be precise. As Silke slept, blood-soaked and sweat-stained for the third time, Hannelore followed the men from her home, into the night. Scissors in hand, she ran. She knew they could turn around at any time, knew they could kill her, but she stormed after them nonetheless. And then she waited, waited until they had drunk themselves into a stupor, until they keeled over in a stolen house with no windowpanes and an open door. She let herself in, and removed nails from fingers that had pointed them into corners. Yes, she yanked out the nails that had torn her last pair of stockings, had snagged Silke's last stitch of sanity. Some of the men had cried out in their sleep, too drunk to fully comprehend the pain, but sober enough to notice a change. Some had not even flinched. One had woken, clutching his hand to his chest, tears streaming down his face; he called for his mother. Hannelore had held the scissors to his neck. He nodded. She fled, her left palm clenched around her tiny revenge, bloody and sharp.

She holds the rancid nails in her hand now, drops them into the pouch, and stitches it shut, before attaching it to the waistline of her costume. A talisman of sorts, she thinks, or a secret power. If they come near her, tear at her dress, the nails will fall out. Perhaps they will embed themselves into their flesh, find their way home. She smiles, snaps the thread with her teeth, and shakes the costume like a freshly laundered sheet.

*

Silke holds the costume, rubbing the material between her thumb and forefinger. Hannelore wonders how she will react, feels her heart pounding its way up her throat. Silke's soaked, tattered dress clings to her frame, and Hannelore finds herself overwhelmed with the urge to use the costume she has worked so hard on to dry the girl off, to wrap it around her like a towel, to pull Silke to her chest like a child. But then Silke's almost-smile returns, and Hannelore's heart returns to its usual place.

"For me?"

The words crackle. Hannelore wants to ask all the questions she has thought of, longed to ask, on this journey, but simply nods. She watches as Silke puts the costume over her head, as her hands appear through the sleeves.

"No one will touch you in this, my child," Hannelore says.

Silke wiggles her fingers as if she has never seen them before, as if they too are part of the costume, and then frowns at her grandmother.

"Seriously, we will scare them all away," Hannelore says.

The lines between Silke's eyebrows deepen. Hannelore stares at her granddaughter, awaiting a protest, but she does not say a word. Hannelore considers asking a question, just to see if the words are still there, still forthcoming. Silke stares at her grandmother, as if awaiting further instruction. Hannelore pulls her own costume on then. Silke giggles, a sound both familiar and unfamiliar to Hannelore. She considers reaching out, touching her granddaughter, wiping the damp strands of hair away from her heart-shaped face, but resists the urge.

"We need masks, hats," Silke says.

Her voice does not crackle this time; a certain excitement crinkles the skin about her eyes. Hannelore nods. Her own voice, her own verbs and adjectives, shocked into silence. Silke bends, opens the suitcase, and holds up the various off-cuts of material. Hannelore watches; beads of sweat form on the back of her neck. She had often thought, as grandmothers do, of her granddaughter in white, in her old wedding dress, with the lace neckline and the long skirt, snipped here and hemmed there into something more modern, more befitting of the time. But Hannelore had dabbled, sold the dress on the black market, got a reasonable amount of cash in return, bought a loaf and two potatoes.

Silke holds a white piece of material to her grandmother's face. Hannelore feels her trace her cheekbones, chin, lips, eyebrows, and, even gentler, meander a finger around her eye sockets. She pulls the material away from her grandmother's face.

"My mask should be black," Hannelore says.

Silke shakes her head.

"It should be, Silke."

Silke holds a finger to her lip. A branch cracks behind them. Silke's pressure on Hannelore's lip increases. They both look in the direction of the trees, but no one comes forward.

"I reckon we're only a few hours away from Tante Ada and Onkel Fritz," Hannelore says.

Silke nods. She sits on the tree stump, begins cutting holes with the scissors.

"Bathe," she says, pointing at the water.

Hannelore nods. "Good idea, but I'll be quick."

"Take your time. The men won't find us here, will they?"

Hannelore shakes her head.

*

Silke places the hat on top of her grandmother's head, and steps back. Hannelore reaches up, touches the marvel, fashioned out of twigs and the remains of the black-out material. She reaches all the way up to the hat's point. Silke hands over the mask she has made her from the bedsheets.

"I didn't know you had such a gift, my child," Hannelore says.

Silke shrugs. A moment existed, when Hannelore stepped onto the lake's bank and called out to her granddaughter, in which she had feared a regression, a new layer of silence, but Silke had answered, had even curled her fingers in a wave.

"We should move along. We might get to the city tonight,

if we're lucky," Hannelore says.

Silke nods, puts on her own black mask and white pointed hat.

"If the men come near us, we can poke their eyes out," Silke says.

Hannelore grabs the child by the shoulders, and pulls her into an embrace. Silke does not resist, but Hannelore can feel the girl's heartbeat raging against her own. She lets her go, and Silke bends to close the suitcase

"Let me carry that," Hannelore says.

"No, Oma. Let me."

*

They walk onwards through the forest, across uneven ground, flat ground, grass, branches, dust, until they find themselves out in the open. The costume weighs heavy on Hannelore's shoulders. Her armpits dampen. Her leg gets tangled in the skirt but she shakes it free, continues, eyes fixed ahead.

"The city," Silke says, pointing.

"Yes, the city."

Hannelore can smell the remnants of the bombs; her nostrils sting and her eyes begin to water beneath the mask. She looks at the buildings, jagged as teeth. To their left and right, droves of people walk towards this hallowed place where there might be food hidden in attics and cellars. A few look at Hannelore and Silke in their costumes, but most keep their heads down, their eyes on the patches of grass beneath their feet. A few women stumble. Their co-travellers bend to retrieve them, but realise it's a hopeless task and leave them where they fell. The stench of unwashed bodies soon covers the stench of the burnt city.

Hannelore's stomach rumbles; she cannot remember the last time she ate. She gave the potatoes to Silke, topped herself up with water from the lake in the hope of fooling her vital organs. As she bathed, a fish swam against her leg, but by the time she got her hand down it had swum off with an energy she could no longer muster. Hunger shakes her entire frame, and she stops. Inhales. Exhales. Silke walks a few steps ahead; the suitcase bangs rhythmically against her shins. Hannelore tries to call the girl back, tries to suggest a rest, but nothing comes out of her mouth.

A child stares at her—a boy in torn shorts, wearing a flat cap that must have belonged to a grandfather or father—Hannelore waves. He buries his head in his mother's skirts. His mother laughs. Hannelore hears the word "crazy" and holds a hand to her ear.

She looks in the opposite direction, sees two chairs, black and wing-backed, a few steps away. She walks towards them, despite her shaking legs. She needs to sit down, needs to feel the comfort of a static support beneath her buttocks. She bends her knees, lower and lower, until the chair takes her weight; she rests her head back, grips onto its arms for safety.

"Silke."

Hannelore closes her eyes. Sweat forms on her upper lip. Her skin turns clammy beneath the heavy black-out material. When she opens her eyes, Silke sits on the chair across from her. The suitcase rests on the ground between them.

"Just a quick stop, Silke," Hannelore says. "We must keep going. Before night falls. Before the men."

"Oma. Oma. Oma," Silke calls.

Hannelore jolts in her chair. She opens her eyes and closes them against the low-hanging sun.

"Sit down, Silke. Rest a moment. Sit on the chair."

"There aren't any chairs."

"And your father will be here soon, in the car. Although I'm not sure how I'll get into the car with this hat on, Silke."

"My father's dead. We never had a car."

Hannelore laughs.

"Please be quiet, Oma. You need to get up."

Hannelore feels Silke's hand under her arm, feels the gentle yank as she helps her up.

"I was quite happy on that chair, Silke."

"You were lying on the floor, Oma."

Hannelore rests her head on Silke's shoulder and allows her to lead her onwards. She stumbles several times; Silke grips her tighter. Her head droops forwards. She feels the hat slip from her head, tap against her arm, thigh, foot on its way down.

"I dropped my hat."

"Leave it."

Hannelore scrunches her eyes shut, opens them again. Him. He walks towards her, reaches out a hand. She feels her lips stretch into a smile. She knew he would return, all in one piece. He twirls his wedding band as he has always done—a man unaccustomed to jewellery. She had told him he would get used to it, and then resorted to slapping his hand whenever she caught him fiddling with the gold ring. She reaches out a hand, feels the bristle of his stubble against her palm. Her nose wrinkles; he smells unwashed, unfamiliar. She feels his hand around her wrist, a grip so tight she almost hears her bones protest.

"I'm so sorry. Please if you'd just let us carry on, we won't be any trouble," Silke says.

Hannelore looks at her granddaughter. Her hat and mask lie on the floor. Her wrists are encircled by the hands of another man.

"He won't snap your stitches. I made sure of that," Hannelore says.

The man laughs, his belly stretching the material of his uniform. He tugs at Silke's dress, tugs so hard she falls to her knees. A piece of material comes off in his hand; he waves it in the air like a flag. A scar points, arrow-straight, down his chin.

"Let her go," Hannelore says.

He laughs, beckons with his hand. Another man appears. He grabs at the material of Hannelore's costume, pulling tighter and tighter until her thighs crush together, until she can feel the fingernails digging into her waist through the pouch.

Silke screams. A hand grips Hannelore's throat. She tries to speak, tries to beg for Silke's freedom, for her own, but she cannot get any air into her lungs. She remembers how women have escaped moments like this by rolling their eyes back into their heads and drooling, by dressing as men. She wants to tell her granddaughter to play dumb, diseased, dead, but the hand around her throat moves to the mask, tearing it from her face. She stares at him, stares right into his brown eyes, as she listens to the shredding of material, unsure whether it belongs to her costume or to Silke's. He stares back. She notices his right eyelashes clump together and focus on those, imagines separating them, pulling harder than necessary, until he looks away. His grip slackens, and she lands on the ground. She listens to the sound of footsteps flattening blades of grass. She reaches out, feels for Silke's hand.

"My dress didn't tear, Oma," Silke says. "But we must carry on. We're nearly there."

Hannelore smiles at the lie. She must teach the girl to tell the truth, no more costumes, but not until they arrive in the city, find Ada and Fritz, find a decent piece of bread.

∞

Emma's First Two Options

1. Something vague about a Nazi war criminal on trial, and the two figures visit him in a dream to discuss his life, his crimes, etc.
2. A woman attempts to escape East Berlin but is killed at the border. The two figures, representing East and West, debate who owns her soul.

One Way Out

Dean Knight

A suitcase lay open on a table. Miles stood over it, beads of sweat forming on his brow. It is hard to think straight in these times, especially in this heat. He remembers when the sirens used to regularly make jagged cuts through the air. That doesn't happen anymore, which is worse; now the air is still and full of silent threat. He no longer goes near the window.

The best time is mid-afternoon, between three and four o'clock. The mornings are always filled with fresh lurches toward further chaos and the nights are horrendous, unspeakable. But the hottest hour usually contains a lull, at which time it is safest to venture out if necessary. Miles still tries to behave, at least at these times, as though things are somewhere near normal. Making a 4:00 walk to his regular store, he shuts out the new unexplained sounds, the distant whines and creaks. The store itself seems shaken, as though the foundations had trembled. The battered shelves are half-stocked with cheap foodstuffs of obscure origin. The clerk at the counter is near the edge: his eyes dart around, constantly on watch.

The suitcase now stood next to the door. Nervously, Miles bounced his fingers on the now-empty table. It was too late to leave now; tomorrow would have to do, as early in the afternoon as felt safe. To the fields of the North Country, where it wasn't so hot, and where the sirens still played, and where the walls that were supposed to be stable wouldn't groan.

In bed, he thought for a while about what this life had become. He tried to tell himself that a better world was just around the corner; he only had to make the leap and get out to get there. He wasn't sure if he believed it. It was, indeed, possible that all the world was like this now. He eventually fell asleep and dreamed semi-lucidly:

Standing on an unending plain. The earth has flattened out to one long dusty trail leading into the infinite. Patches of dead grass litter the field. I walk a long time and although it looks like nothing changes I can sense that everything is changing but I can't see it. The sky swirls; it's a sickly vivid ochre and I feel as though I should be nauseous but I am not. I sense something enormous passing by in the sick-sky, an air-leviathan, but something does not allow me to turn my head to see it.

The sky peels off for a moment and slaps back on. But the fit is slightly off and everything seems tilted. The clouds start to slide slowly downwards. In the moment that the sky was gone I saw something so vastly dismal that my throat sunk into itself and I wouldn't have screamed even if I could have because I knew that such a puny act would be meaningless.

The horizon somehow shifted and I finally saw two human-shaped things in the distance. Closer in they looked less human, as they both had elongated cones atop what would be their heads, and their bodies were encompassed by octopi. Closer still the octopi writhed, ink spraying out and blurring my vision.

Between the two figures there stood on the dirt-plain an old-fashioned suitcase that looked exactly like my own. Straps congealed around its body and its prominent bulge pulsated to the beat of my own heart, which I was suddenly very aware of.

The beating grew quicker as I approached closer to the figures. Ink lashed my body; my gaping mouth filled with ink and then everything faded.

Miles awoke at dawn, coated in sweat.

The day threatened to be dangerously hot, but in the early morning Miles could still think. This time of day was when he thought he could see behind the scenes of things. Trucks slowly passed by him on the street. He did not look at their insignia—many familiar ones from the past had been erased, replaced with cold generic runes. Some trucks had no signature at all, and these were the ones to beware of, as they could be anything.

His eyes seemed to be still coated with something of the ink-dream, and thus it was as through a veil that he moved through the streets, and into one of the now-ubiquitous massive gaming halls. Everyone's face seemed shaded, but Miles couldn't tell if that was a result of the residue of his dream on his eyes.

Arriving and staring at an interface he remembers a time, not so long ago although it seems it, that he wanted to be a hero. Not a world-saving one; he didn't have the ambition or imagination for that. Not even something big at all but just something very localized like rescuing a friend in distress or stopping a fight in a bar. He used to fantasize about such things with some regularity. Those ideas seem obsolete now, relics from an ancient past dimly recalled.

The screen in front of him filled up with a cold fluorescent glow. The game played itself out in front of him, and not for the first time Miles had the sensation that he was not needed, the game could play without him. His hands gripped the controls only loosely, moving them in short jerks from side to side at various times. Around him the hum and whine of the gaming hall closed in on him, vibrating in his ears. Miles risked a direct look at the face of the player closest to him and he quickly recoiled in horror. The man's face was a mask of frozen agony drained of other life. As though he sought in the machine any way out of the mask, he repeatedly hit a button on the console, to no apparent effect.

Miles stepped away from the screen. He felt something was about to happen. As he swiftly moved away from the machine one of the other players, a man with an owlishly contorted face, strode up to the mask-man, opened his mouth wide and spilled noise into the air, surrounding the man's head. Mask-man clutched his head, then his heart. He staggered away from his screen, and the noise-man stepped into him and wrapped him in his noise, blaring yet contained. A burst of the noise slipped out and flew by Miles. The noise-man enveloped the mask-man entirely and then abruptly abandoned him to the floor. Miles could not see the mask-man anymore. The noise-man lurched away, eyes blank. Miles exited the hall quickly.

Down six city blocks in succession he moved as quickly as he could without attracting undue attention. He jettisoned his previous plan to leave in the afternoon—he was going to go now, as soon as he could reach the portal. It was still early enough in the morning that the day had not fully revealed itself. He realized he had left his suitcase at the apartment, but abandoned any thought of retrieving it. There was nothing back there for him.

The portal, he had been told, was difficult to find and constantly changing. The information he had gave the location as between two nearby streets, but he had been warned that that could change quickly, and may have already done so. Portals could slip away as quietly and quickly as they had appeared.

His right hand wrapped around the metal token in his pocket that it had taken weeks of searching to locate and obtain. He had pried it out of a dead man's hand. He hadn't killed the man, or had anything to do with his death, but the thought of it still chilled him. The token was painted half white and half black, an oddly warm artisanal touch to such a cold object. The texture of the paint was thick and vibrant, alive, as though it was trying to speak to Miles. The white and black paint piled up at the convergence of the two, as though both had tried to meet—or overtake—the other, but were prevented by some overseeing presence or an invisible border, made tangible by the collision.

A jagged slab of metal stuck out from a building at the corner of the street: he went in, feeling this to be the sign. In the lobby a group of men sat around a folding table; there was money on the table and at first Miles thought they were playing cards, but as he passed them by he saw no evidence of any game. Grim-faced and weary, one of them stared at Miles as he went by them, the others waiting motionless for him to go. After he turned the corner he heard something that sounded like a muffled pistol shot. He gritted his teeth and kept walking.

At the rear of the building sat a teenaged boy, dirty and rumpled, wearing a newsboy's cap; he looked as though he could have emerged from a century ago. The boy gave Miles a questioning look. Miles pulled out the token and showed it to the boy, who stepped aside to reveal a narrow tunnel. Miles grimaced and slipped into the tunnel; he heard something closing irrevocably behind him. He did not look back.

He landed at the bottom of what might have been a drained sewer. Ahead he saw a faint glimmer; he went toward it. A shrunken old man wearing opaque glasses sat next to a bucket of oily rags. Next to the man a rectangular outline shone on the wall. Miles showed the token. The man made no motion but the rectangular outline started to glow brighter the closer he brought the token towards it. He pressed the token against it and the rectangle fizzled with white light and became a door, while the token itself dissolved. Miles stepped through the door; it closed and everything disappeared behind him.

He stood on a blasted plain that seemed to stretch out to infinity. Sparse patches of dead grass served only to heighten the barrenness of the field, to show that life was attempted here but failed. *This is what the end of the world looks like,* he thought. *But I must keep on, that is the thing. I cannot surrender; I must try to live in some way.*

After walking some ways, he saw something in the distance and his dream of the previous night flooded his head. Closer in he saw that the scene in front of him resembled the one in his dream, although the dream painted the sky a sickly yellow and the air in front of him was dull grey. Two figures sat before him, each wearing a tall conical hat. The one on the right was cloaked in black, the other in white, and both were masked, but in their opposite colours so that a gleaming blank-white face shone out from black swaddling clothes and a pitch-black mask resonated dully within a gleaming white coating.

The black-cloaked one seemed on the verge of motion—it leaned forward and its head was slightly thrust forward and inclined to one side, as though it was waiting to move out of the chair and into action. But it remained completely still and when Miles tried to look into its eyes he saw nothing at all and had the eerie feeling that it was looking completely through him.

Miles thought, *They've traded masks and now they're even more the same, more intertwined.* He did not know where this thought came from or what it related to, except that in a child's fantasy-tale he now remembered lore about suited figures who controlled the world and turned the ball of Earth at its axis. But if these two are here, on this plain, who is turning the world? Is the world still there? Why does everything look so flat?

A suitcase stood between the two figures, one very like

the one Miles left behind in his apartment. It seemed to be meant for him. "Is this mine?" he asked. The scratching in his hesitant voice reminded him of how long it had been since he had spoken to anyone. There was no answer. A knife-like wind cut suddenly through the sky, across the plain. The figures shimmered in the slashed air; they rippled like paper and then they disappeared.

The suitcase remained. After an uncertain moment, Miles seized it and opened it. It was empty. He crouched in front of it for a minute, thinking. Then he closed the suitcase and stood. Taking his bearings, such as they were on the blasted plain, he resolved to move forward. If the end came while he was on the road at least he'd be in motion, moving against the darkness.

∞

Dean's First Two Options

1. A comedy with wizards arguing over where to go on vacation.
2. Sci-fi/fantasy story about a telepathic duel between good and evil, with good winning since the suitcase is further toward the white side, and white is traditionally associated with good magic.

To the After

Lyle Skains

THIS USED TO BE SUCH A LOVELY STATION.

Really? What was it like?

LAST TIME I WAS HERE, IT WAS A BROAD BLUE SEA, BRIMMING WITH LIFE. IT'S A SHAME THE OCEAN-DWELLING CIVILIZATION HERE GAVE WAY TO THE LAND-BASED LIFE FORMS.

I wish I could have seen it.

HMM.

So...how many times have you done this?

TWIDDLED MY THUMBS ON A COLLAPSING WORLD?

No, I mean, you know. Cycled.

I STOPPED COUNTING A FEW THOUSAND CYCLES AGO.

*

"Don't sit on that."

Kelly lifts one butt cheek. "What, this? You don't even know what this is."

"It's a suitcase." At his blank expression I roll my eyes. "You use it to carry stuff from place to place. In the Before, I mean."

He twists around and flips the handle up. "Seems like a stupid way to carry things to me. Can't strap it on, can't squish it up, can't roll it."

"Well, they didn't need to do that before, did they? Just carried it from their 'ship to car to aero to back again, eh?" I know it's just a stupid old suitcase—a space sucker, even—but once he's off it I squirrel around him and shove it under my cot. It's a chunky box encased in leather, two straps circumnavigating its belly and biting their own tails in locked ouroboros. The leather-wrapped handle is thick and cosy in the hand, hefty but manageable.

Without the suitcase, Kelly doesn't have anywhere to sit in my cramped quarters, so he thumps on the cot next to me. Its joints whine, and I wonder why guys have to be so damn loud in everything they do. He's so close I can smell him: he's been out foraging today, and the arid scent of desert marries the sage soap that Lola trades out only for special occasions. I can't imagine what special item or favour Kelly's traded for it, or why he'd want to.

"What's in it?"

"Huh?" I jerk my head up, still thinking about soap.

He leans in, whispering, the scar on his cheek pulling as he quirks a smile. "What's in your special box, Hetty May?"

I smack him on the backside of the head. "For real, you trying to play?"

He rubs his head, laughing, and falls back against the wall. "What else have we got to do today?"

I shrug. "Fair enough," I say, and toss my shirt into the corner. "Play on."

*

"Aunt Ida, d'you have keys for that old suitcase?" I poke some thread through a needle, darning my favourite pair of jeans again. It's not like we can make or get more.

"That old one in your room?" She slaps a new dough around on the breadboard, waking up them yeast. "Why would I have keys to that?"

"'Cause it was my dad's."

She pauses. Talking about my parents bothers her more than it does me, since she knew them better. "I didn't keep everything they ever owned, you know. Commun—"

"Community property, back into the commons, I know, I know." I weave the needle back and forth, making a little pattern over the top of several other little patterns I've made before. "Still, you took the suitcase from their 'ship before Charlie and Soyuz took it over. Thought you might have the keys, too."

She shrugs. "Never seen keys to it."

Jeans mended, I slip over to my cot and sit on the floor, protected from the earth by a rag rug I made with Aunt Ida when I was eight or so. It used to be all kinds of bright colours, but now it mostly looks like it's trying to become one with the floor beneath it.

I don't know why I've never opened the suitcase. I used to fantasize about it when I was a kid. That I would open it and it would be full of books. Nothing but books. Especially once I'd read everything in the colony at least twice. Something new would have felt like the richest find in the world. The locks aren't heavy-duty; I've broken tougher ones on scrounging runs, no problem. But here's the thing: this isn't just some hunk of junk I found while sifting through the remains of a burned out car. This was mine, and it was my dad's before me, and I didn't want to destroy something that was wholly mine, wholly his, something that wasn't communal, something that no one would ever see the worth in fixing afterward. So I got used to it just being the outside of a suitcase, and once I got a little older I knew whatever I might find inside wouldn't be near as interesting as all the things I *imagined* could be inside.

Only I'm not eight years old anymore, and I don't have to break it. And I'm running out of imagining. The world has shrunk to these mud-brick walls dotted with glass bottles to let in a trickle of light, and the corpse of a desert outside under that ash-grey sky. A new book might as well be a dinosaur for all that I thought it could possibly happen.

I drag it over to our little communal area, where Aunt Ida is sliding her dough back into its basket to rise some more. She lifts an eyebrow. "You know it's probably just some old undies in there, right?" But her eyes narrow in interest, her crows' feet gathering.

"Every little bit helps," I say with false cheer.

"I'm not wearing anything made out of your dad's old undies."

"Machine-made cotton. Just think of how soft it would be on your skin." I grin. "I'm gonna make you a pillowcase out of 'em."

"Hmph." Aunt Ida actually says "hmph". I've seen it spelled out in a couple of those old novels she keeps wrapped up in her hidey hole, but she's the only person I've ever heard actually say it out loud. "So open it, already," she says.

Taking that for collusion, I poke a twig of wire at the flimsy locks for a few moments until each springs open. "Voila."

I always let Aunt Ida open anything mysterious I find. Gives her a little of the thrill she misses out on by not getting to scrounge, what with the bum leg and all. She houses me, clothes me, and heals me when needed; it's the least I can do. Out of habit, I let her open this one, too.

She pushes open the top, and we hold our breath, half-expecting a cloud of irradiated dust to waft out. Instead, there's a soft sucking sound as a seal is broken, and the interior of the suitcase is as pristine as if it had just been packed yesterday.

I say "packed". Like it might actually hold what a suitcase is supposed to hold: a few changes of clothes, pyjamas, some toiletries. If I'd scavenged it, I'd maybe imagine some keepsakes, small heirlooms or jewellery that its owner just couldn't bear to leave behind for looters—or, more likely, to just rot away into the dust of our once-great(?) civilization. It's my dad's, though, and those sorts of trinkets were never accepted in the colony, and my dad was as gung-ho about the code of the colony as anyone, so it's more likely Aunt Ida's right: that it's full of ordinary things, and he used the suitcase for storage.

No underpants. No socks or toothbrush or grandmother's pearls. The suitcase, mundane, almost relic-like from the outside, is a different world on its inside. It's like staring into the night sky, so much bigger and more expansive than the mind is capable of handling. Except it's not a sky. It's the desert.

My desert. I've never seen it like this before. There's desert, and then there's desert. There's the desert of romantic imagery, Lawrence's Arabia, adventurers trudging through sand like waves, hot, desolate, and murderous. Then there's the desert of the (former) American West, painted in words by Zane Grey and Louis L'Amour: a screen of death and desolation over a teeming bed of life, each organism battling for survival against the sun, the climate, and every other plant and creature slithering along the desert floor. Sit still, and watch this desert for longer than ten minutes, and you'll see them:

the cacti siphoning every molecule of H_2O from the soil, the reptiles flitting from sunlight to shade and back again, the hummingbird wavering over a lone prickly pear bloom. You'll hear the drone of the insects through mesquite and juniper, smell the pollen drifting on the dry wind in search of its mate. This desert is harsh, but she's alive.

My head spins, upending the room, and I latch on to the tabletop to keep from falling off the floor. I don't even know if anything I just saw was real, like some kind of memory embedded in my genes, or just a fantasy stitched together from stories and fairy tales.

I'm staring into the suitcase, but I am also staring at the desert. My desert, but not my desert. My desert before they killed her, before I even knew her. She's so beautiful I want to weep. I can almost reach out and touch the hot soil at the base of the scrub, pluck the horned toad from its shade. I reach into the suitcase, my fingers outstretched, my eyes straining to reconcile its outside with its innards.

The lid snaps shut as Ida lets go, catching the tip of my middle finger in a fireburst of pain. "Shit!" I yelp, clutching my hand to my chest and examining the digit.

"Well, that was a bust," Ida comments, wandering over to her favourite chair.

"What do you mean?" I say, suckling at my bruised fingertip.

"What do you mean, what do I mean?" She groans as she settles into the chair and puts her leg up. "Nothing in there but old papers in gibberish. I don't even know what language that is. Navajo?"

"Nava… what?"

Aunt Ida shakes her head. "You want, you can take it over to Doc tomorrow. She might can make some sense out of it."

Confused, looking between Ida and the suitcase, I manage, "What's Doc going to know about it? She's a medic, not a… a…"

"Linguist? Anthropologist? Accountant?"

I blink. "I don't know what any of those are."

Aunt Ida waves a hand at me. "She's not called 'Doc' because she's a medic. She was a researcher in the Before. She was pretty tight with your folks, too."

I pry the lid up an inch. Not papers, not even a little. "It's really just papers in there?"

"Just kindling. Told you there wasn't anything interesting in there. Now you know." And she drops her head back on the chair, drifting into her late afternoon nap.

Tucking the suitcase under my arm, I silently disagree. The inside of this suitcase is the most interesting thing I've ever even heard of.

*

I did some research on our options. I have all the data right here in the bag—I'm pretty good with numbers and things. I cross-referenced all the sentient forms with longevity, cultural personalities, fertility, length of life cycle, parental roles, sociological structures, political profiles, geographical characteristics—

WHY?

Why?

YES. WHY? WHY BOTHER WITH ALL THAT?

Well... I thought... We have to make a decision somehow. We can't sit at this transfer station forever.

IT WON'T BE HERE MUCH LONGER ANYWAY, IF THESE IDIOT NATIVES KEEP SHOOTING AT EACH OTHER.

I know you have a lot more experience. How have you decided in the past?

WHIMSY.

Sorry, what?

YOU HEARD ME.

How is "whimsy" a process of decision-making?

LOOK, KID, YOU'RE TAKING THIS TOO SERIOUSLY. YOU'RE GOING TO DO THIS HUNDREDS, MAYBE THOUSANDS OF TIMES IN YOUR LIFETIME. JUST PICK SOMEWHERE THAT LOOKS INTERESTING AND GO WITH IT.

But...

BUT WHAT?

It's just...it's my first time. I want—

YOU WANT IT TO BE *SPECIAL*. HOO BOY. OF COURSE YOU FUCKING DO.

...

...

Do you even want to look at the report?

FINE. GIVE IT HERE.

Just a sec. It's right here. I put it on top, but now it's somewhere else. Here—oh, no. That's not it. Where...?

LOOK.

It's got to be here. I know I put it in.

LOOK. STOP FOR A SECOND. WHERE WERE YOU BORN?

With the Caerleckai.

YEAH, I'VE BEEN A CAERLECK. PREHENSILE ANTENNAE AND NO CONCEPT OF PERSONAL SPACE.

That's them, all right.

YOU WANT TO BE A CAERLECK AGAIN?

Well, no. I want to try something different. New.

YEP. YOU WANT TO BE HUMAN?

Have you been Human?

NO, I CHOSE A SPECIES OF WHALE WHEN I WAS HERE.

Oh.... Well, I don't think Human is an optimal choice. I'm not sure they'll still be here for a full generation.

DON'T WANT TO COMMIT SUICIDE, HEY?

Of course not.

*

It's the largest 'ship in the colony, but it still struggles to hold everyone after the evening meal. It's also one of the safest spots in camp, completely underground, its only connection to the upper desert an old bomb shelter hatch scrounged from the ruins of nearby Taos, and a flue for the fire that can be sealed off against radiation and acid rain. No natural light, just the fire in the middle. Doc says they used to call these things *kivas*, that civilizations thousands of years ago created them as some kind of sacred space. I asked her what was so damn special about a big-ass hole in the ground, and she said it wasn't broke, so no idiot tried to fix it.

She's right. I mean, I never got to be in one of those city theatres in the Before, but I've been through a couple on big scavenges. Cavernous, everybody in rows, regimented, separated. Seems like it'd be stiff and cold and boring. In the communal 'ship, the older folks get the benches and cushions around the outside wall of the circular space, while the rest of us pack in on the ground on blankets and pillows and each other. We get too warm and sometimes the kids get in half-hearted wrestling fights, but in the jostling and the snuggling we know we're all here, and we're all still alive.

Charlie gets us started. He was my favourite storyteller when I was little. He always acts out the parts, and his stories are usually fairy tales. They're good for the little kids, before they go to bed. I still like them even now, though I know them so well I could just about tell them myself. They let me remember being a kid, laughing, or jumping during a scary bit, snuggled into Aunt Ida's side.

There are stories that are made up. There are stories that are so old it seems like they not only existed in the Before, they existed before that, before humans, before the animals and the oceans and the sky. There are stories that are just about people's days—Rosario tells us about her first week, this week, training as a cook, and how she baked a bread so hard they had to give it to the scouts to use as weapons against rovers. Tariq tells us about his latest scrounge: finding a trove of collared bottles we can use in more of our 'ships, to let in the greylight. The way he tells it, it's an epic journey of trials and terrors and loss and joy. Tariq is good at making his stories so memorable—even if they're not entirely true—that there's no way anyone ever forgets how to get back to a spot he's been, or how to find something he's spotted.

I haven't told many stories. I used to read some out loud from books, but most people like stories about themselves rather than some long lost people in a dead world. The ones I do tell come from adventures I get into with Luna, my scavenging companion, an old sow who's so amazing at sniffing out caches of food she's more valuable as a scrounger than as bacon.

This time, though, my story isn't about scrounging, or food, or a bit of history from the colony library I've read time and time again. I don't even really mean to tell the story. It just comes out in one of those quiet times, those pauses between stories, when everyone takes a deep breath and the night wavers on the edge, where someone could toss out an "I ever tell you about..." or a "Remember that time...", or else the moment goes on too long and everyone just slips back home to bed.

"This wasn't the only world," I say, and the room's restlessness stills. "There were others. There was a world where the people were small, smaller than our children, and they lived three times as long as we do, and they never developed music. And there was a world where the people communicated through scent instead of language, and they had no literature or stories, only memories. There are so many different worlds that even people who live forever can never experience them all. And there are people who basically live forever. What else would you do if you lived forever, other than explore the universe? You wouldn't want to stay just in one place. How boring would that be?"

I hear a chuckle from Babo, who's so old he doesn't even have colony duties, and who always sits so close to the fires Aunt Ida fusses about him catching alight.

"If you lived forever you'd visit a world where there's not just one intelligent species, but three who evolved separately, yet live together in peace, if not total harmony. You'd see people who harvest energy from neighbouring stars, who mine asteroid fields for water, who reshape new planets to suit their needs. You'd spend time with civilizations so ancient they're built on layers and layers of remnants as new intelligent species evolve, build, destroy themselves, and a new one evolves to take their place. You'd keep an eye on people who can't help but bring disaster to everything they touch. You might avoid them.

"It seems like heaven, doesn't it? But there are downsides. A species that can live forever gets itself into a lot of tangles and relationships and rules, and it doesn't even remember how these things came to be. So when the ones who are even older than your millions of years tell you it's time to cycle, time to partner up and find a new sentient species whose form you can take long enough to have some offspring and keep them alive to adulthood so the whole fam can ghost the planet and rejoin your immaterial race, well, you do it. Otherwise, it's ostracization: no more mates, no more cycling. Just the cold, unending boredom of space.

"And even though there are so many thousands of worlds to see and experience and get to know, you live forever, so even you will get bored. Tired. You'll develop a terminal case of ennui. You will stop looking forward to new people and new worlds because they're all just a rehash of all those you've seen before. You'll stop avoiding the destructive ones, and instead you'll land amongst them. You'll play in their wars, and you'll set yourself in their sights. You'll let yourself become them, be destroyed by them, because what else do you have to do? Live forever?"

I stop. It's not an ending, but it's all I've got. The fire has dwindled to embers, only occasionally popping. This is not a story that anyone has ever told before, and it's not from the books we all know. They don't know what to make of me.

"Whoa," Kelly says. "How you feeling lately, Hetty?"

A burst of laughter. Camp delirium is a real danger; humans aren't that great at living under earth most of the time, especially the ones who can remember when our world was large and they could go anywhere they wanted, any time. The ones who remember the sun. But no one really thinks I'm sick and so it's a little funny, a little break in the tension my weird ass story wrought.

I don't laugh, though. I smile a bit, rolling it off as everyone shifts and stands and drifts off to bed.

Aunt Ida doesn't say much as we head back to our 'ship. She's not limping much this evening—the fire always makes her leg feel better. She takes my arm anyway, and when we get home she sits in her chair instead of going to bed.

"Quite a tale," she says. It's dark in here, and neither one of us lights anything, so I can't see her face. "I don't recognize it."

"No," I say softly. "It's just... thoughts."

"You harping on a storytelling gig instead of scrounging?"

"Can't scrounge forever," I say, even though that's not at all what I'm doing.

Those stories came from what I've seen in my father's suitcase, in the scant minutes of free time available between eating, scrounging, general colony duties, and sleeping—which is taking the biggest hit. I look into it, and I feel words forming in my mind, incoherent thoughts and noises. If I try to hold on to them, they squish and squirt like I'm trying to hold fast to running water. If I can lie back and let them wash over me, though, they become tangible, like memories of dreams that only come back to you at quiet moments in the day.

Then it will all fade, slipping away from me, a dream dissolved by the first light of dawn. I struggle to hold on to the details, to the shapes of the words, to their inflections and tones; I usually manage to hold on to an outline of the conversation, but much of the flavour is lost as my conscience slips away from the desert within the suitcase. It's gotten to where I can't think of anything else but what those voices whisper to me.

"Are there things you haven't told me about them?" When I ask Aunt Ida my question, she's not surprised. At least she doesn't sound surprised.

"Course there are things I haven't told you." I sense a hmph coming, but she sighs instead. "You go on over and reach behind the *horno*. Got it? Bring it here."

It's a cool jug that I sense has something stronger than water in it. Soyuz has been known to distil a rotgut from the odd potato crop, but I've never had firsthand experience of it.

Aunt Ida takes a swig and actually passes the jug to me. It dissolves my throat on the way down, and she laughs her raspy gutlaugh. "Har har," I tell her grumpily.

"You get used to it," she says, and downs another gulp. "What do you want to know?"

"Were they happy?"

"Hard to be happy in a post-nuclear wasteland."

"You know what I mean."

She taps the jug, and it hums hollowly. "Nobody ever knows what the inside of anybody else's relationship is like. For all I know, Charlie and Soyuz go home and beat each other silly every night. For all I know, you and Kelly just like to talk." I hear the raised eyebrow in her voice, and I grin. "From what I saw, though... your daddy tried. He tried real hard. I don't think this was ever what he expected out of life, but whatever he got, he gave it everything he could. Man could make sunshine in a grave."

"And Mom?"

She doesn't answer straightaway. I shift, wondering if maybe she fell asleep, warm and dark and lubricated. Then—"She was funny. Oh, damn, she was funny. Not funny like Kelly's funny. Dark. Dry, witty humour. She'd pull the rug right out from under you and you didn't know how scorched you was until your subconscious told you about it in a dream.

"She wasn't older than him. She wasn't sick, or weak, or injured. She always pulled her weight, never gave nobody trouble. But I always felt like there was a hole in her, something nobody could fill up, not even you. Your daddy was the one who was desperate to join the colony, just before the... just before. We used to joke it's like he knew what was coming, and he found the most likely place to survive, seeing as how we'd already been here decades. Never felt like he was really happy here. Your mom, though, I always knew she *wanted* to be here. Needed to be here. And he just made the best of it."

I want another pull from her jug, but she's not passing it to me and I'm not sure I could handle it anyway. "I don't understand," I say.

"Neither did I, honey." She reaches out, finds my arm, and squeezes it. Then she shuffles off to bed, her jug hanging from one finger.

I sit in the dark for a long time, wondering about holes and choices and places people are meant to be.

*

In the morning, Luna and I go out on a scrounge. I lug the suitcase out with me. I tell Aunt Ida it'll help me carry back what I found, but I'm pretty sure she knows I'm bullshitting her. I have no intention of ever putting anything in it.

Instead, I wander. I have a dozen destinations in my head, some from firsthand experience, some from scouter stories, of where I might go to find something of use to the colony. But I don't head toward any of them. Instead, I walk straight into the dead heart of the desert. Luna snorts along behind me in confusion, and I try to ignore her. I walk until the colony drops behind the horizon, until the desert swallows us up. Until it's just me, a pig, and an old suitcase.

Then I sit, and I open the case.

This time, the whispered words come clear almost right away, as though the thick walls of our Earthships have been blocking them, and I can glean their meanings almost as easily as listening to Aunt Ida singing in the next room.

*

I'VE SEEN HUMANS COME THIS WAY BEFORE, YOU KNOW.

What, here to the waystation?

DON'T BE SO LITERAL. I MEANT TOWARD WORLD DESTRUCTION. THEY CAME PRETTY DARN CLOSE ABOUT 100 YEARS AGO.

They're a whole lot closer now.

SURE, BUT IT'S PRETTY HARD TO KILL A PLANET.

It just seems so...futile. Wasteful.

YOU EVER WORRY ABOUT DYING?

I'm afraid I don't understand.

DIDN'T THINK YOU WOULD. FINE. WHAT ARE YOUR TOP THREE CHOICES FOR YOUR VERY FIRST OH-SO-EXCITING CYCLE?

Oh! I don't know that I've ranked them so much, but my key suggestions were Kantail, Norkatio, and Deorkiztart.

WITH PROCREATION CYCLES OF 350, 290, AND A WHOPPING 1500 YEARS, RESPECTIVELY.

Let me see... I think the Norkati enlh species is closer to 500, but the arlh are around 290, yes.

AND ALL OF THEM FAT AND HAPPY MIDDLE-AGED CIVILIZATIONS.

Advanced, non-spacefaring, peaceful global civilizations. I thought they sounded like nice peoples to raise a family amongst.

AND WHERE DO HUMANS, TADORTHI, AND JALS FALL ON YOUR LIST?

Are you joking?

DO I LOOK AS THOUGH I'M JOKING?

Those three rank so high on intraspecies—and interspecies—upheaval I hadn't even considered them. Humans might not even be here by the time we finish this conversation!

*

"You gotta be shitting me."

I blink, and then I blink some more. I've got nothing but blur and grey in front of my eyes, but I can hear okay.

"What the hell are you doing way out here, holding a séance?"

"Kel'?"

Kelly sits on his heels in front of me, his palm flat on the suitcase. He must have snapped it shut. He waves a hand in my face. "You awake? Don't tell me you found a glow pocket and got yourself fried." He holds a hand out, lifting me off the ground.

I brush sand from my thick oversuit. "What are you doing out here?"

His face is covered by goggles and breathing filter, but since he insists on sticking every feather he's ever found in the hood of his oversuit, you can always recognize a scrounger as Kelly. "I was on my way back from a water scout, and saw Luna oinking around with nothing to do. Came this way and saw you having a little love fest with your... what is it, again, a sockbrace?"

"Suitcase." He probably can't see me roll my eyes behind my dirty goggles, so I make sure to roll my neck as well.

"Sure. What'd you drag it all the way out here for, anyway?"

"To help me carry stuff back." The lie had worked with Aunt Ida, but I kinda forgot Kelly knows what scrounging is like.

"I know I'm pretty, but I'm not dumb." He waggles a finger at me and crosses his arms, a pretty decent imitation of Cate, one of his mothers.

I cross my arms back at him, but the effect is ruined by Luna nudging the back of my legs and nearly knocking me over.

"Come on, Hetty," he says, and the goofy laughter is gone from his voice. It's almost hard to tell it's still him talking to me. "I know something's up with you. You've been mopey and cooped up. And that story you told the other night... I mean, have you talked to Doc?"

"I don't have camp delirium," I protest.

"So then what?"

"It's... weird."

He waves an arm around. "We live in hell."

"Hey," I say.

"I mean, don't get me wrong," and the jocularity is back, "it's *our* hell, and I wouldn't give it up for all the sockbraces on the Moon, but it's not exactly like your fantasy booklands, is it?"

"Fair enough."

He folds himself down until he's sitting in the dirt. Luna nuzzles him; little traitor has always loved him more than me. "One time, a couple years ago," he says, "I was scrounging in this old ranch house. You know, middle of nowhere. Thought whatever family was there probably went into town when the bombs started, to one of the public shelters. Or just to be with people, you know? Anyway, I'm rummaging around, and I hear a noise behind me. I'm about shit my oversuit, you know? I'd have had to get all the way back to camp with that mushing around in there—"

"I got it, I got it."

"Yeah, anyway, I turn around and there's this *kid* there. No fib, a kid, no taller than my belly button. Wearing a pair of jeans and a T-shirt, only no holes or patches—brand new, like. She doesn't say a freaking word, just stares at me, and then I see next to her is a dog. A goddamned dog! And they're both just staring at me like I was some kind of alien."

"You probably looked like one in that oversuit." I drop back down to the dirt with him. Luna gives up and flops to her belly between us.

He nods. "Prolly. But what was this kid doing out there? How did she get there? How long had she been there? I tried to talk to her, but nothing. Didn't move, didn't say anything. How was she surviving without radiation protection? What the hell was she *eating*, much less the dog!

"I left, figuring anything I found there ought to by rights belong to her—either her family was there, somewhere, or she'd found it before me anyway. I've tried to get back there, tried to find it again, to see if there's a family, a group. I mean, they'd be neighbours, right? But nothing. I've never even found the house again, let alone some little kid and her fracking dog."

I poke at Luna through my gloves. I know what he's doing. Still, though, seeing some weird kid who has strangely survived the apocalypse unscathed isn't quite the same as getting a conversation in an unknown language downloaded into your brain by a suitcase.

He waits, though. He waits me out, and I'm dying to tell someone, anyone, so I blurt it all out in a rush, never taking my eyes off the dusty sow.

"Whoa," he says, and unlike when he said it the other night he's not trying to get a laugh. "Can I see?"

"I don't know. Aunt Ida couldn't see it."

"Lemme see." He pulls at the suitcase, and I let him open it. I watch his face, or as much as I can see of it through all the protective gear. Confusion, disappointment, but no awe. He doesn't see what I see. "Papers," he confirms. "Like, a lot of really nice, valuable paper. But I can't read any of it."

"I know," I sigh, and pull the case back, closing it. "That's what Aunt Ida said."

"Hetty, hey." He waves a hand in front of my face. "I don't think you're nuts, okay?"

"I kinda do."

He sits back, his palms on the ground, and looks up at the sky. "It's like a vision quest."

"Oh god," I moan, and flop back in the dirt. "Not this again." When he was fifteen, Kelly had decided to take his Mama Trinity's old stories about her ancestors and their rites of passage seriously, and had walked himself out in the desert (in thorough protective gear, of course—his mothers would never have let him out of their 'ship otherwise) with nothing but a canteen of clean water. He'd been out there five days. He told everyone he'd been on a vision quest, but I knew he'd just gone out, tripped on some mushrooms that Rita cultivates, and lay there laughing at talking rocks for a few days.

He kicks my foot. "Shut up. I'm not playing."

I sit up. "Why is it only me? How come I'm the only one who can see this?"

"Good question."

"Thanks for that."

"No, really." He stands up and offers me his hand again, but I get up on my own. Luna shakes herself off. "It's a question worth answering."

He walks back to the colony with me and Luna, chitter-chattering the whole way about his day, his week, his life. He's a fool's story in human form, but he's the best anything I've ever had.

*

MY FIRST CYCLE WAS WITH THE O'RELADEAI. IT'S NOT REALLY PRONOUNCEABLE, OR SPELLABLE, IN A HUMAN LANGUAGE, WHICH MAKES IT REALLY IRRITATING, I KNOW, BUT WHAT CAN I SAY. HUMANS AREN'T THE CENTRE OF THE UNIVERSE. YOU'RE MORE LIKE THE... BACK SIDE OF THE MOON OF THE UNIVERSE. YOU'RE KIND OF A FLASH IN THE PAN, REALLY. YOU HAVEN'T BEEN AROUND LONG ENOUGH FOR MOST OF US TO TAKE NOTICE. YOU'RE MOSTLY IMBECILES, AND I FIND THAT AMUSING.

MY FIRST CYCLE WAS LONG BEFORE HUMANS. LONG BEFORE ANY LIFE ON EARTH, REALLY, LATECOMER THAT IT IS. THE O'RELADEAI WERE A GOOD STARTER SPECIES. PEACEFUL, GENDERLESS, WITH RELATIVELY SHORT PROCREATION CYCLES—ONLY TEN YEARS AS YOU UNDERSTAND THEM, FROM BIRTH TO MATURITY. I THINK I ENJOYED IT, WHEN I WASN'T TERRIFIED.

IT'S HARD TO BE IN A FIXED, PHYSICAL FORM. YOU GET USED TO IT AFTER A WHILE. YOU LEARN TO USE LIMBS, ANTENNAE, EYES, EARS, MOUTHS, TONGUES, GENITALS. YOU SOAK UP LANGUAGES AND MOVEMENT. WE'RE PRETTY GOOD MIMICS, AS IT TURNS OUT. WE HAD TO BE; SHITTY MIMICS DON'T PROCREATE.

I USED TO LOVE STARTING A NEW CYCLE. I REMEMBER THAT. I THINK, AT ONE TIME, I WAS MUCH LIKE MY YOUNG PARTNER: EAGER, ENTHUSIASTIC, OVERLY PREPARED, IMMERSED. THE LONGER I COULD STAY WITH A SPECIES, THE BETTER. BUT SOLAR SYSTEMS HAVE BEEN BORN, LIVED, AND BURNED OUT SINCE THEN.

It's easy for me now to drop into the suitcase, to feel the words. I'm learning to differentiate voices in the notes. In one, I hear the hole that Aunt Ida talked about. In the other, I feel wonder, and it feels so much like me I even hear it in my own voice.

My partner calls our nature a curse. It makes me weep for them, for the joy and wonder they have lost. I don't know how they could have seen what they have seen, lived the lives they have lived, and come to feel this way.

Even now, even in this least of all possible options for my first cycle, the hardship of this world, the sorrows of this species, I cannot but marvel at them. This small patch of the desert we huddle in should be a desolate graveyard, and yet they have burrowed into the Earth, protected themselves. They have made their home in the body of their planet, wrapped it around themselves.

These aren't written, as I have written them here, in the spaces of a book no one but me has read in years. Their words are not words, not really. That's just the only way I know to translate them. It's more like... like I am sifting through their memories.

THE CHILD I DIDN'T WANT IS HERE. I TRIED BUT I COULD NOT RESIST THE BODY CHEMISTRY OF THIS SPECIES: WHEN I LOOK AT IT—HER, THEY CALL IT, FOR THEY HAVE TWO GENDERS HERE, AND THE CHILD AND I ARE BOTH FEMALES, WHICH BEAR THE YOUNG—WHEN I LOOK AT HER, I AM ALIVE AGAIN. I AM WHOLE. I WOULD DO ANYTHING TO SAVE HER FROM SUFFERING. I HATE THAT I AM THE ULTIMATE CAUSE OF HER SUFFERING.

Almost there. I am reaching so deeply into this case it feels as though I am going to fall into it, to slip inside, to drift until my body is no more, until I am nothing but a cascade of the feelings and thoughts and memories that these two people poured into it, a receptacle of themselves. I am dizzy, and my chest feels heavy, but I cannot pull back now.

THE END I HOPED FOR WHEN I PUSHED FOR THIS

IDIOTIC DESTINATION IS HERE. I'M NOT SURE HOW I COULD HAVE BEEN MORE STUPID. I LIVED FOR MILLIONS OF YEARS, AND I THOUGHT I KNEW ABSOLUTELY FUCKING EVERYTHING. WHAT A DICK, AS THIS SPECIES LIKES TO EXPRESS IT. I SHOULD SAY I'M SORRY. I AM SORRY. WHAT A DICK.

WE BOTH GOT CAUGHT OUT IN A RADIATION STORM TODAY. WE COULD NOT RETURN IN TIME FOR TREATMENT, AND THERE IS LITTLE THAT COULD HAVE BEEN DONE ANYWAY. IDA HAS AGREED TO TAKE THE CHILD. WE CAN DO NO MORE. SHE IS NOT OLD ENOUGH TO END THIS CYCLE; WERE WE TO TRY, WE ALL THREE WILL DIE. AND WE CANNOT GO WITHOUT HER. THE GIFT AND THE CURSE.

CHILD. HETTY. YOUR PARENTS SNEERED AT THE HUMAN SPECIES AS BENEATH US, AS TODDLERS THROWING THEIR TOYS AT ONE ANOTHER. IT IS TRUE, BUT IT DOESN'T MEAN THAT WE ARE ANY LESS STUPID, DESPITE OUR MILLIONS OF YEARS AND EXPERIENCES. WE HAVE STILL FUCKED THIS UP BEYOND ANY RECOURSE. FUBARED, I THINK DOC LIKES TO CALL IT.

THIS IS ALL I CAN DO FOR YOU NOW: I CAN GIVE YOU A SMALL PIECE OF MY KNOWLEDGE. THE MOST IMPORTANT PIECE OF MY KNOWLEDGE. THE PIECE THAT MAKES ME, YOUR HUMAN MOTHER, AND HIM, YOUR HUMAN FATHER, NOT HUMAN AT ALL. THE GIFT AND THE CURSE.

WHEN YOU HAVE PROGRESSED THROUGH THE NIGHTMARE I AM TOLD IS HUMAN ADOLESCENCE, YOU WILL HAVE THE CHOICE. YOU MAY STAY HERE, ON EARTH, AS HUMAN. WITH THE FAMILY THAT YOU KNOW, AND THE WORLD AS IT IS. OR YOU MAY TAKE THIS SMALL PIECE OF KNOWLEDGE, AND JOIN YOUR TRUE KIND, YOUR ANCESTORS. YOU MUST CYCLE TO LIVE, BECOMING ANOTHER ENTIRELY, WEAK AND VULNERABLE, FOR AS LONG AS IT TAKES TO PROCREATE AND PROTECT THE OFFSPRING TO ADULTHOOD, WHEN YOU ALL CAN RETURN TO YOUR NATURAL STATE. IN DOING SO, YOU WILL BE THOUSANDS OF PEOPLE, IN THOUSANDS OF WORLDS.

IN DOING SO, YOU MAY FIND JOY. IN DOING SO,

YOU MAY LOSE YOUR SOUL. I LEAVE THIS TO YOU. I DID BOTH; I DENIED THE PERSON YOU KNOW AS YOUR FATHER ANY OF IT.

And there it was. A gentle ping tolled through my body. The knowledge. The way.

I shut the suitcase. I locked it, and I slipped it under my cot. I slept.

*

"Here, Aunt Ida, let me do that."

Aunt Ida eyes me sideways, but she gets up and out of the way. I kneel in the soft earth we've cultivated under rows and rows of heat lamps—one of the few dedicated uses of electricity we need—and poke the soy seeds in. The dirt is soft and cool around my fingers.

"Not that I'm complaining," Aunt Ida says between long chugs from my water bottle, "but since when does a scrounger dig in the dirt?"

I shrug. "I just realized I haven't spent much time with you lately. Thought I could help."

"Mm-hmm." She doesn't believe me. That's okay. I plant her seedbed for her anyway.

"I'm going out with Luna this afternoon. Need anything in particular?"

"Wire." Always wire. Many uses, but we can't manufacture it.

I poke, poke, poke the seeds in. Once she's had a rest, rubbing her bad leg, Aunt Ida gets back in the dirt with me, next row over.

"Aunt Ida," I venture, "are we still going to be doing this in fifty years?"

She snorts. "I ain't. I'm gonna be feeding these here plants more direct-like by then."

I laugh. She's right. We don't bury anyone here—in a way, we do eat them. Eventually.

"You, though," she muses. "Hell, girl, I hope not. This isn't supposed to be forever, is it? Living like moles."

I wasn't quite sure what a mole was, but suspected it lived

a dark and damp life.

"How, though? The radiation... that's not going away for a long time." I think of the girl Kelly saw in the ranch house. Was she real? Was she immune? "What else is there?"

"These ain't questions for me to answer, Het. Life goes on. It isn't always an easy life. Shoot, it *usually* isn't an easy life. But it's what we've got. Are you gonna see big cities like we had in the before? I doubt it. Are you gonna see other people, other places? Maybe. Maybe not. But we keep going. Because maybe one day, your grandkids, or their grandkids, they walk out of here in just the skin they're in. They see the sun. They walk and they grow and they come together with others, and they build it back up again. But they can't do that unless we do this. So we do this." She punctuates each point with a jab: one seed in. Another. Another. Another. And move and plant and on and on.

I plant and move and jab along with her.

*

It isn't just Luna who comes out with me on the scrounge. Kelly hitches along too. I haven't seen much of him lately, though I have a feeling he's been around. The scent of that soap he must have traded dearly for occasionally lingered in my room, in my memory, and I know he must have been checking in, making sure I wasn't so deep into my "vision quest" that I couldn't come back out.

"You ever wonder what ol' Luna's insides look like?"

"Huh?" I ask. We've walked for twenty minutes, him regaling me with some story or another, and I haven't been paying much attention.

"She's been coming out with us for years. Nobody ever puts an oversuit on her. She's still alive. Either that pig has a hide made of lead, or her insides are just competing cancers."

"Maybe she's not even Luna anymore," I say, glancing at the perfectly ordinary, perfectly content specimen of a pig. "Maybe she's just a Luna skin with an entirely new civilization of intelligent pig organs scheming inside her."

"Poor things. Awfully dark and smelly in there."

Luna snorts at him, showering him with snout-mud made

of mucus and dirt. Good girl.

We've been walking for two hours, heading toward a spot we think used to be a small landfill, before I manage to tell him.

"Holy sheep on a cactus," he says, whatever that means. "My best friend, my mate, my lover, my *life paaahhhtner—*" I shove him to reset him "—is actually an *alien*?"

"I hadn't really thought of it that way."

"What other way can you think of it?"

Luna snuffles around in a circle, and I scrub at the ground with my boot to see if there's anything of interest. She rolls her eyes at me and moves on.

I say, "I think of it as my parents became human, and had me, and I'm human, and then they fucked up and died."

"All true. But we've always known that."

"Then nothing's really changed."

"Oh sure." He pauses, and when he starts back up it's through a barely contained giggle. "Hey, later on, when we get back home, do you wanna probe me?"

"Oh Jesus Christ."

He chortles. No one loves Kelly's jokes more than Kelly.

"For real, though," he says, finally. "I still like you."

"I'm so glad."

"I know."

*

Kelly's always been able to wake up before me. If he stays over, by the time I wake up all I have left of him is his scent, and maybe an errant sock. He claims it's because he likes to get to breakfast early, but I think it's because I mostly want to maim and/or kill anyone in my vicinity for the first hour after I wake up, and he doesn't want it to be him.

I do wake up, and he is gone, but he hasn't left any socks behind. That's all right.

I tidy the cot, stack my few sets of clean clothes. I pull out a piece of paper—not a new one, not even an unused one, but one with at least a little space for what I need to say. To Aunt Ida. To Kelly. Even a little note on Luna's favourite spots. I lay it out on the middle of my cot.

Then I pull the suitcase out. I have to jimmy the locks again, but they come open pretty easily. I half thought that when I opened it, it would all have been a dream, that it would be empty inside, nothing but leather and lining and dust. But there it is, that desert, the shadows of my parents, the whispers of their memories. The weight of the knowledge. The gift and the curse.

I hold it in my mind. I let it draw me. I feel the pull, falling, flowing, sucking me into that world. And then I am gone. And then I am new.

And then I am forever.

*

I just don't see why you're pushing this so hard.

YOU WOULDN'T.

What's the draw? What do you think you'll learn by becoming Human?

I DON'T THINK I'LL LEARN ANYTHING.

Then what's the point?

EXACTLY.

...

LOOK. I KNOW YOU DIDN'T ASK TO BE PARTNERED WITH ME. I SURE AS HELL DIDN'T ASK TO BE PARTNERED WITH YOU. I'VE DONE IT YOUR WAY, THOUSANDS OF TIMES. IT'S FINE. IT'S DANDY.

You make it sound so pedestrian.

YOU'RE NOT GETTING IT. IT *IS* PEDESTRIAN. TO ME. EVERY DOSSIER YOU HAVE IN THERE—I'VE SEEN IT. I'VE WRITTEN IT. HELL, I'VE *BEEN* IT. ALL YOUR RESEARCH AND PLANNING, IT'S NO BETTER OR WORSE THAN CLOSING YOUR EYES AND POINTING TO A RANDOM SPOT ON A STAR CHART.

What?

IT'S A THING. YOU'LL DO IT SOMEDAY.

I don't have the experience to negotiate a species in as complex a political upheaval as this one is.

BUT I DO.

I might fail.

PROBABLY NOT.

It's my first cycle.

OF THOUSANDS. HUNDREDS OF THOUSANDS. MILLIONS. LET'S START OFF WITH A BANG, EH?

It's like you have a death wish.

...

Okay, okay. Just...let me do some research first, okay? Put us in a good situation, one that will bear out.

SURE, WHATEVER YOU WANT.

There must be Humans who survive this.

THERE ALMOST ALWAYS ARE.

Almost.

∞

Lyle's First Two Options

1. Ingmar Bergman-type god and devil playing chess. *Good Omens* keeps coming to mind.
2. A trade or transfer of documents or goods.

Afterword

Lyle Skains & DeAnn Bell

It all started with a weird picture and a throwaway tweet:

> @lskains: *I want to do a fiction anthology where everyone writes a story just based on a weird ass picture. And then use that pic as the cover.*

As creative writers and researchers, we are both attracted to writing that challenges borders, whether these are artistic, political or social. Would a short story collection built around a single image by authors with no previous association with one another end up as just several people trying to explain the picture? Was there a way to get a creative deviation from the normal narrative line inspired by the picture without prescribing or disallowing an approach?

In order to get the strange and unusual stories we wanted, we introduced a concept in our call for submissions called "Third Option Thinking". In the first instance that a writer encounters a creative writing prompt, particularly one that requires a writer to make causation connections, the first ideas they have are typically ones they remember from another story they have encountered. This creative recall leads to both clichés and genre tropes. To get around this, we asked writers—established, new, young, old, white, black, human, lizard, and breadbox—to respond to one weird-ass pic. While choosing which response they would develop, we asked them to think of three possible story ideas, to discard the first two and develop the third. In the name of research, we also asked writers to include their first two discarded ideas with their submission.

The next step was getting the right cover image. Choosing

images from the crowd that did not immediately have a logical explanation, we learned quickly what *not* to Google when looking for possible weird pics. We picked five and then asked the public to vote on the one they wanted the anthology based around. Neither of us correctly predicted the results. The poll closed on June 1st 2017 with a landslide of votes for our cover image "Suitcase" by Valery Sidelnykov.

On June 3rd 2017, we posted our picture poll results and put out our call for submissions. Like the final image selection, the similarities between the stories that emerged *because* we asked for Third Option Thinking were nothing like what we had predicted. Some similarities such as duality, power play, and good & evil were clearly suggested by the image, but others such as time travel, alternate realities, and aliens were harder to trace back to a source. Writers writing in complete isolation from one another managed to produce works that seemed to respond to each other. It was fantastic. We collected the best of these into the full-length anthology that you, reader and lover of weird and fantastic stories, have just finished. The transmography from Tweet to anthology is now complete and we hope that you've enjoyed reading our works and following us on our journey.

Acknowledgements

Lyle

Massive thanks to DeAnn for jumping aboard this crazy train with me; I definitely wouldn't have attempted it without you.

My spousal unit Paul deserves thanks for feeding me and making sure I occasionally go to bed at what the rest of the world deems a reasonable hour. I'd also like to shout out to Eben Muse, who taught me most of what I know about publishing a book (if I've stumbled along the way, it's entirely my slackage, and not his tutorage). Thanks also to the School of Creative Studies & Media at Bangor University for supporting all my various publishing adventures, and to each and every weird-ass author who has contributed to this volume. I couldn't be prouder of the thing we made, y'all.

DeAnn

I would like to thank my husband, Rob, for being supportive and for making dinner when it was clearly my turn and I said that I would only be another minute. A big thank you is also owed to Dr Emma Ransom-Jones who has nursed me as my critique partner through a PhD, a novel, and two short story collections. And finally, I would like to thank Mai Thai cat, who even at eighteen years old unfailingly disturbs any hope of my writing in peace. I couldn't do this without you.

30517836R00137

Printed in Great
Britain
by Amazon